LISA K FRIEDMAN

HELLO WIFE

sfwp.com

Library of Congress Cataloging-in-Publication Data

Names: Friedman, Lisa K. author
Title: Hello wife / Lisa K Friedman.
Description: Santa Fe : Santa Fe Writers Project, 2025. | Summary: "Single, unfulfilled and well into middle age, long-troubled Charlotte Lansing desperately reaches for love and acceptance. When she announces her engagement to an unemployed morphine addict, her family falls into a tailspin. Her mother is determined to prevent disaster, her father seeks to mend the growing chasm, and her sister stubbornly hopes that their sibling bonds can keep Charlotte safe. But Charlotte resists all this because she thinks she is finally happy. Ultimately, all her loved ones can do is watch as Charlotte disappears, slowly and inevitably, into her new husband' s illness."—Provided by publisher.
Identifiers: LCCN 2025010002 (print) | LCCN 2025010003 (ebook) | ISBN 9781951631536 trade paperback | ISBN 9781951631543 epub
Subjects: BISAC: FICTION / Women | LCGFT: Novels
Classification: LCC PS3606.R5656 H45 2025 (print) | LCC PS3606.R5656 (ebook) | DDC 813/.6—dc23/eng/20250331
LC record available at https://lccn.loc.gov/2025010002
LC ebook record available at https://lccn.loc.gov/2025010003

Published by SFWP
369 Montezuma Ave. #350
Santa Fe, NM 87501
www.sfwp.com

To Debra

ONE

My wedding dress was made by a costume designer I met while buying weed at the 7-Eleven one February, which is also where I met Jimbo, my husband to be. I went to 7-Eleven every day. I liked standing around the counter, drinking coffee and talking to Plots, the franchise owner. The nicest people come into the 7-Eleven. Real people. People who don't look down if you're shopping in your pajamas with no bra underneath. Heavy girls like me have to wear a bra. Otherwise, we look like a walking pickle barrel with a massive movable girth.

Plots was semi-single, a phrase he used to explain that his wife refused to emigrate to the States with him. She stayed behind in Bangalore—which is now called Bangaluru—with her mother. Plots thinks she may have a lover there, but he isn't sure.

Plots is over six feet tall and he looks more Maasai than Indian. He has the highest cheekbones I have ever seen on a man and his lips are eggplant purple. Once when we went driving around in my car, we kissed, but then we abruptly stopped as if some far away referee had blown a whistle. I was lonely; my human interactions depleted to an ancient cashier at the diner and the guy who used to deliver dirt to my driveway back when I was still thinking about becoming an organic gardener. He still came around sometimes for a smoke, and a hand job if I was feeling generous.

There were no sparks between Plots and me, and between my antidepressants and his methadone, neither one of us felt any tugs of sexual interest. We were friends. I'd buy coffee and cigarettes and a cruller or two, and Plots and I would greet the regulars like Norm on Cheers. "Hey there," I'd say. "How's it hanging?" The men liked me because I shared my cigarettes and also I was good for a ride. A guy needed a lift to the train station: I took him. Someone wanted to run over to the OTB and I'd point to my car and say, "Sure, get in." The women, the few who came into the store rarely, spoke to me. Their glances said it all. Fat lady at the counter.

It's funny to think about it now, but when Jimbo came in through the glass door of the 7-Eleven, I didn't even notice him. He was a slow-moving blur, nothing to hijack the imagination. His only notable feature was a lollipop stick protruding from his tiny, pursed mouth. I remember thinking that I might like a lollipop too. A Charms cherry lollipop. Of course I didn't see the actual candy in his mouth at that time. I had no inkling that morphine came in lollipop form. The point is, I had no idea that this person, this small and ghostly stranger, would alter the course of my future. No surge of attraction excited the neurons in my brain. No weak knees as described in novels. No indication whatsoever that he would be the groom in my wedding photographs. I once read that physical attraction was not based so much on chemistry, but on rhythm. Each heart has its own individual pattern, its own unique rhythm. When two compatible rhythms are in proximity, they meld into a single beat. Symbiotic. Like music. As a former bassoonist, I liked the analogy. But nothing like that happened between Jimbo and me. Nothing at all like that.

Other than the wedding pictures, there are only a few images of me as an adult. I did not like to have my picture taken. I'd skirt out of the room when my parents pulled out the old Nikon they kept handy in the living room. Later, I'd spin away from pesky cell phone cameras and claim to be Amish. I'd read somewhere that the stricter

Amish sects consider the photographic image a sin against the second commandment which, if I remember right, is about not creating graven images. I don't know what graven means. But it seems appropriate now, given what transpired eventually.

"Look at you crying!" Jimbo said, looking over my shoulder at a picture from the wedding. My father and me, walking arm in arm toward the camera, his square face a slab of gray granite with a thin vein line for a mouth.

I did not wear a veil that day and the tears on my face were obvious as a neon sign. I wasn't crying, I told him. I was weeping!

"Weeping at the prospect of marrying me?" He twisted his face into surprised horror. "Little old me?" He tickled me, and we giggled for a while.

In the upper right corner of the photo, a fleshy smear obscures a portion of my father's head: the photographer's index finger had fallen into the frame as she snapped the picture. She wasn't a real photographer. She was the wife of one of Jimbo's childhood friends, and she'd offered to take the pictures free of charge. Well, not entirely free. But it was still much less money than if we'd hired the photographer my mother wanted.

The musical entertainment at the wedding was provided by a distant cousin of Jimbo's who played the bicycle pumps. Really. He's a bonafide musician—he did the music for the wedding of Jimbo's no-good nephew. I saw the video: He had all these different bicycle pumps lined up in a row, and he pressed the levers down in a certain order, at a certain speed, and music came out! It reminded me of running a wet finger along the rim of a wide champagne glass. People make music on that, too. He'd given us one of the pumps as a wedding gift and sometimes Jimbo would try and play it, which was virtually impossible, but it made me laugh. He was always making me laugh.

We were silly together. We challenged each other in *Jeopardy!* and *Wheel of Fortune*. We laughed at the same jokes. I was happy then.

Jimbo was the right man for me. His real name was James but his mother called him Jimbo, and the name stuck. It suited him. He was small and round and mostly bald, his head shone as if polished. He looked very much like J. Wellington Wimpy from Popeye. *I'll gladly pay you Tuesday for a hamburger today.* Once our hearts touched, there was no pulling us apart.

TWO

I was remembered as a gorgeous child. Wisps of breezy hair, light as morning, swept across my forehead. "The color of tea with milk," my mother described my hair color in the padded pink baby book, given to her as a gift. My eyes were a stunning centerpiece in my face, large and green in tone, fringed with dense black lashes that looked stained with ink. The rest of my features were dwarfed in comparison, little buttons of mouth and nose, hardly noticeable. My skin was a dewy pale pink. My eyes were magnets, pulling strangers in for a closer look.

"What a beautiful little girl." Strangers stopped my mother as she pushed the stroller along the sidewalk. "Such a gorgeous face."

Beauty is a difficulty. It inspires too much appreciation, too much attention. Beauty in a child suggests an easier life ahead. *What fortune*! *That face is certain to open a lot of doors.*

My mother described me as joyous. She said I had a ready smile. My father called me Sunshine because, as he liked to say, my face lit up the room whenever he walked in. My grandmother remembered that when she pushed me in the stroller, strangers would comment on my sparkling personality. But that was not to last.

When I was ten, my elementary school hosted a fifth-grade graduation party at the end of June. We were to gather in the gym after school for music, food, and ceremony. All day, my belly was full of twitching rabbit whiskers. I wasn't nervous. I was excited.

Someone's older brother volunteered to be the party photographer and he wandered along the perimeter of the gym in his all-black Ninja outfit, a camera strap secured behind his neck.

We posed together, we danced to the disco music flooding from a borrowed set of crotchety stereo speakers, we ate cupcakes and cookies baked by the PTA. We drank fizzy punch with blueberries bobbing amid the bubbles. Bliss. Until I hopped up onto the radiator where my friends perched like pigeons, and I felt my jeans tear in the back.

Of course, the students noticed. A white-hot flash of embarrassment bled across my face as boys and girls raced at me, pointing and shrieking. I didn't see the boy with the camera, kneeling beside the bleacher.

Ratty Fatty!

I ran for the hall.

Hey, Fatso where're you going?

Even my friends were laughing.

The photos followed me for years. In middle school, someone taped the black and white picture to my locker where everyone could see it, causing a dreadful first-day uproar. An enlargement found its way to the high school, where it was found glued to the wall above the sinks in the boy's bathroom. An image of fat me, from the back with an apple-sized wad of white cotton bulging from between the seams of my too-tight jeans.

My mother was always careful about my weight. She deemphasized the superficial simplicity of physical beauty and held her praise for true achievements. Her compliments were not frequent, but they held a significance that I cannot explain. More than filling the library reading list chart with shiny stick-on stars. "Anyone can be beautiful," my mother often said. "Not everyone can be clever."

"Charlotte's a good girl," she'd brag. "She's smart as a whip."

I wasn't smart. She simply assumed I was smart because she didn't yet know otherwise.

By the time of my puberty, I had become an ordinary-looking girl. Moppish hair in a moody brown. Freckles like smudges darkened my once light skin. Worse, I'd inherited my father's physique: dense layers of adipose tissue padded my short frame, thickening my limbs and banding under my chin. My shoulders sloped forward as if under constant duress from my excess weight. My eyes remained sprightly, shining green and festive with lashes like flags.

During high school, I had a summer job in my father's office, opening mail and filing papers into folders while making cheery conversation with the secretaries. They liked me. They told me I was smart and funny and generous and kind. They told me how much fun I was to have around, and that they were sure to miss my smiling face when high school started in fall. They remarked on everything but my appearance, an absence loud as a gong.

THREE

"I'll take five lucky sevens and the racing papers," Jimbo said, pointing to the lottery spools. Plots and I were playing tic-tac-toe on the counter. I had already lost the game. Plots counted out the lottery tickets and handed them to Jimbo who opened a canvas wallet that had Mickey Mouse emblazoned across the front. The sound of Velcro made me smile.

"I love Velcro," I said.

"Me too." A connection! He moved the stem of the lollipop from one side of his mouth to the other.

He went outside through the glass door and stood under the eaves, away from the snow. He looked like a garden gnome out there, small and hunched and capped in a pointed red hat. An interesting comparison, I thought, given I was just telling Plots about my new business plan to start an organic garden. I love gardening. It's my favorite year-round hobby. In the winter, I select seeds to plant in my grow kits. In spring, I transplant the saplings into the planter beds in the yard, and by September I'm harvesting and canning and making compotes and soups to stock in my freezer. What I can't preserve I give away. My giant gourds were once featured in the local paper, *The Sound*, and that's where I came up with the idea of growing for profit. I always had new business plans in mind. I'm a born entrepreneur.

Plots and I watched Jimbo for a moment. "What does he do with the racing papers?" I asked.

"Why don't you go out there and ask him?" Plots reached under the counter and withdrew the spiral notebook marked 'Inventory.' He nodded his head to the front window. "He seems like a nice enough guy," he said. "Go introduce yourself."

Just then a jacked-up pick-up truck screeched into the parking lot and skidded to a stop a few feet from where Jimbo stood. I watched a Paul Bunyan look-alike descend from the cab. Huge hiking boots, canvas pants with pockets loaded, three shirts with a bulky vest hanging open. A white construction hard-hat added unnecessary inches to his height. He was a wall of a man.

Jimbo didn't so much as flinch as the giant marched past him.

I tucked the tic-tac-toe sheet under a box of Slim Jims and stepped aside. The big man was thirsty. Two Dr Peppers and a case of Budweiser. He threw a rumpled bill on the counter and awaited his change without speaking.

Plots and I watched him leave. I thought I saw his boots cracking through the floor like jackhammers on pond ice.

Jimbo turned his head just slightly at the approach of this behemoth. He twisted his narrow shoulders to make more room. The rest of him remained in place, as if planted on the sidewalk.

"Move!" The big man's voice quivered the glass panes on either side of the entry.

Jimbo was a bird on alert. A bird in a knee-length parka and a fuzzy red hat.

"Outta my way," the man bellowed.

I could see Jimbo's profile. His head seemed nearly translucent, fading into the grayish snow accumulated on the dumpster. The short stick of his lollipop caught my eye, weirdly white.

Silently, I urged, *Move. Move away.*

The big man swung the carton of beer and, not accidentally, it connected with Jimbo's shoulder; I watched Jimbo's white hand flurry up in defense, the newspaper floated to the ground, the lollipop arced through the air in cartoon-style slow motion. Jimbo fell backwards, collapsing against a pyramid of firewood stacked against the building.

I hurried outside as the truck pulled away. Jimbo was on the sidewalk, curled like an embryo. "Are you hurt?" I asked.

"Yes." The voice wobbled.

I put out my hand and pulled on his jacket. He was light. I was surprised to feel his weight lift off the ground with little effort from me and none from him. I settled him onto his feet and tugged at his parka until it hung straight.

A spasm of pain twitched his face. "I think he broke my collar bone," he said. "I need to go to the hospital." His eyes spun; his pupils were miniscule, like poppy seeds.

I held his arm and guided him toward my car. "I'll take you."

The emergency room was quiet. It wasn't long before an orderly retrieved Jimbo and wheeled him away. Jimbo was mobile; he had walked comfortably to my car. But he insisted on a wheelchair in case he got dizzy.

I wandered around a bit, got some black licorice and a bag of Cheetos from the vending machine and settled in to wait. A wide-screen television hung on the cinder block wall, flickering with the bright neon colors of the local news station, showing the weather map of eastern Long Island. It was entirely obscured under a swath of the darkest blue. Snow.

I always liked the emergency room. I liked the white lighting, the scuffed floors. I liked the low hum of activity taking place somewhere unseen. I liked the far-away chime of the PA system. Whose voice was that? I wondered. Was there a woman in a booth whose sole job was to broadcast messages? Did she feel like the Wizard of Oz, always behind a curtain, directing an outside world without being seen? What a great job! When the next announcement sounded, I mimicked the droll voice: Dr. Martelli. Dr. Robert Martelli to the ER." My voice had no authority, so I tried again. And again. A whiskered man sitting alone in a row of connected seats turned his head toward me. His mouth hung open; a terrapin tongue lashed out over his bottom lip.

Jeopardy! appeared on the television. I rotated toward the screen, ate the last of the Cheetos, and challenged myself to a game.

Three sitcoms after *Jeopardy!*, Jimbo came through the double doors. When his eyes found mine, his skin visibly pinked. I knew then, right at that moment, we were meant to be together.

It didn't take long to learn his story: he was fifty-two. He lived with his mother. He had two television sets in his bedroom and four computers to monitor the horses and lay bets through OTB. He was known in online betting communities, a whiz at picking horses for Aqueduct, Saratoga, and Belmont Park. I learned all these things while we waited for the billing representative to process the payment to his credit card. His mother's credit card. "I'm on a leash," he said, signing the receipt. He'd amassed a debt, he told me, and his mother made him promise to stop betting online. She paid for his incidentals, whatever that meant, and his vast medical expenses.

Jimbo had sustained a serious back injury when he was just seventeen. He'd been asleep in the back seat of his father's car with his grandfather riding shotgun when they were blindsided by an SUV that sped through a stoplight. His father and his grandfather died at the scene. Jimbo was hospitalized and treated with heavy-duty pain medications. That's how his addiction began. I loved him immediately.

Luckily, he hadn't broken any bones.

"They wanted to give me Percocet," he said once we were back in the car. He reached into his pocket with great effort and handed me a square sheet of paper. A prescription. "But I managed to convince them to give me something stronger." Dilaudid. "Do you think you can get this filled for me?"

Of course I could. I pulled into the pharmacy parking lot near my house, leaving him strapped in the front seat of my car with the heat on Full.

When I returned to the car, he was shining with pleasure. He looked so soft, I thought he might be formed of dough. I handed him the prescription bottle and a squeezebox of apple juice.

"How'd you know?" he grinned. "I love apple juice." His smile revealed perfectly white, even teeth. Tears quivered in the rims of his glasses. He sipped neatly. His fingers were tapered like dinner candles, his nails were smooth and pale.

I took him home to my house because it's close to the hospital, and because he was foggy on his own address.

***

"Are you still feeling dizzy?" I practically carry him into the house, the full weight of his body leans against my own. My arm around his midsection pulsates with unfamiliar exertion. We make our way into the living room in the dark.

He groans, more of a sigh than a groan. That tiny sound, the slow wheeze of his breath passing through his throat and nose shoots a current of responsibility into my body. I nearly stumble with the new awareness of his need for me. I move my feet apart seeking a place of balance. I cannot fall; Jimbo is already injured and sore. I hold him snug against me. He mews into me, resting his forehead against my neck. His chest presses to my arm. Suddenly, I am struck by a confidence that has never visited me before. I know him. I recognize him. He is like me.

Blood speeds through the transit grid of my arteries and veins, my face is flushed and sweaty. The whole rhythm of my body accelerates, out of control, like the onset of a sneeze.

"Can we sit down?"

I kick aside the bag of knitting yarn parked on the sofa and wait for his legs to connect with the steadfast frame of the couch. I see a pair of scissors hiding between the cushions, points jutting upward like barbs. "Hold on." I lean past him and grab the scissors. I'd been clipping coupons.

His body sags, falling heavy into mine. He is dead weight, like a child who falls asleep on your hip. "Can you stand on your own for a second?"

"I can't." His voice is an airy whisper.

I drop the scissors and kick it away with my shoe. It skitters among the litter and then pierces its prongs into the wall. The sound startles Jimbo. He opens his eyes to smile at me.

"Oomph," we grunt in unison, falling onto the couch.

His eyes peer into mine. "Hello there," he says as if newly awake. His breath smells of licorice. Or maybe it's mine. We are comingled already.

"Hello there yourself."

He slides his feet out of his shoes and rests his heels on a bundle of clothes piled on the coffee table, my laundry, waiting to be washed. He burrows his toes into the tangle of clothes, digging them in deep like snails. He looks around, taking in the details of my home. The footrest of the reclining sofa is stuck in the extended position, banking at a funny angle thanks to a mishap I had with the vacuum. Balanced on the faux leather is my dinner plate from last night, crusty with skirt steak juice and the remnants of instant mashed potatoes. A dried puddle of coagulated fat adheres the plate to a flyer advertising a new LED reading light. Reading is one of my favorite hobbies. I like romance novels best of all, and mysteries as long as they're not too gory. 'The eyes need more light to read at a rate of one percent a year,' the flyer explained. 'By the time you're 60 you need around 100 watts or 1600 lumens.' I know a good offer when I see one. Two for one! I'll ask my mother to buy them for me. She values reading.

She'll be thrilled to support my love of books. That is one thing we have in common.

My mother. Wait till I tell her about Jimbo!

"Can I have something to eat?" His head rests on my shoulder. The warm skin of his scalp touches my cheek.

Energy comes at me like a train. "I'll make sandwiches." I jump to my feet. I'd been eager to try out the new panini press I'd ordered online. "Grilled cheese?"

Cooking is absolutely my favorite hobby. Cooking, gardening, sewing, wallpapering. My living room is busy with mail order catalogues and old TV Guides mixed in with Simplicity-Plus dress Patterns. The flattened pizza box I use as a pincushion is almost like a party hat, streaming with threads of mistakable colors.

I step over the plastic crate borrowed from 7-Eleven. My foot snags on a carton filled with cookie cutters bought at the wholesale baking exchange. I have every intention of experimenting with these new cookie cutters one day. I just haven't had the time.

My mother disapproves of my housekeeping. She carps about germs and ants and clutter. She objects to the fist-sized hole in the floor near the sink and the missing tiles on the backsplash above the counters. "It's worse than a bus station in here!" Her last visit ended with a battle royale as she'd arrived with bottles of Clorox and a pair of rubber gloves, determined to clean out my refrigerator.

I yank at the handle of the refrigerator and retrieve the eight-pound brick of butter that I was saving for the cookie experiment and several slices of American cheese. The panini press heats up. I'd finished a loaf of bread that morning before going to visit Plots—was it just this morning that Jimbo and I met?—but there is plenty more in the pantry.

I'd sacrificed the dining area of my little rambler and created a room-sized pantry with wall-to-wall shelves I'd bought at Ikea and assembled myself. My mother challenged my decision. Losing the dining room? What if you have a dinner party?

I listen mainly because she paid for all the furniture in here. Who needs a dining room? Other than family, I never have people over. I eat all my meals in the living room, on the couch.

I put butter on the hot panini press and listen to the sizzle.

"That smells good," Jimbo says.

I place the raw sandwich on the press, cover the Wonder bread with a thick layer of butter and close the lid.

My chest swells. "I didn't even do anything yet!"

He lets out a high giggle. "Well, it already smells good." He claps his hands in anticipation. "Do you have any Dr Pepper?"

I shake my head. "No, but if you want, I'll run over to 7-Eleven and get some." My deft fingers assemble another sandwich on the counter. This is all so pleasant, so easy. Do other couples find each other so easy?

"Nah," he says. "Stay here with me."

His sandwich is ready. Browned and crispy and shining with butter. I pluck it off the grill and quickly place the next sandwich inside. The cabinet is empty of plates. The dishes must be in the dishwasher, and I've forgotten to run it again. I lower the door to the machine and extract two plates. One doesn't even look dirty. I wipe it over my chest and rotate it clean against the cotton of my blouse. My mother would cringe if she could see me.

I cut Jimbo's sandwich on the diagonal, just for fun. "Ready or not!"

He answers immediately, as if we'd rehearsed. "Ready!"

I rub the second plate clean and scrape off some old food debris with my fingernail.

My mother had just given me some new dishtowels. "I was in Bed Bath & Beyond and I wanted to use up my coupons before they expired. Plus, you can always use more dishtowels." That is her way of telling me she doesn't like how I dry my dishes. She doesn't like how I do much of anything.

What she refuses to accept is this. This is me. This is how I like to live. I don't like to clean, so I rarely do that. I don't scour my kitchen after cooking a meal and I don't use steel wool on the bottoms of my fry pans. I don't scrub my shower with bleach once a week like she does. And, despite repeated warnings about sanitizing the sink or putting things away when they are not in use, nothing terrible has happened. In fact, a good thing has happened.

"Are you coming?" His voice is soft, a Brahms lullaby.

***

For so many years, I'd feared love. Not love as an emotion or a concept but love as a relationship. A pairing: a sail and a mast, for example. Two nouns that balance each other perfectly, needing few if any additional words to reach coherence. Would it ever happen to me? I did not want to be afloat, alone for the rest of my life.

My first pseudo-love experience involved a boy in the school band. He sat right behind me with his slide trombone. The slide trombone! I remember thinking, is there a more exciting instrument than the slide trombone? In rehearsals, I heard him blowing and puffing, the chaos of his playing rattled in my bones in a way I'd never known. The music was innuendo, the unison of our scores became feelings. His music stand was so close; the long slide of his trombone nearly reached the back of my hair. His 'oom-pah-pahs' vibrated in my ear as sexual suggestion. His low bass tones mewled for my attention. When the top of my bassoon clanged into the bell of his trombone, we joked that our instruments were attracted to each other—which I understood as male-female interest. He was heavy, like me, but the trombone was such a large piece of equipment, it required heft to balance the weight of the brass. At the end of the school year, we had sex two times, one right after the other, in the conductor's garish office. It satisfied my desperation to be loved and for about a week it allowed me to think of him as my boyfriend. I learned later that he only really liked me because I hung out with pretty girls.

I had plenty of male friends. Men who needed a ride to the airport would always find a willing partner in me. Men who liked to swim in my parents' pool. Men who saw me as a confidante. As a co-conspirator. As a friend. I saw them for what they were, and yet I also hoped the outcomes would be different. They never were. People are, in fact, what they seem.

My fears grew. Would I ever find a person who loved me for the joy of loving? I wanted a full life. I saw myself in the kitchen, always in the kitchen, teaching my children to use the sandwich press on their grilled cheese sandwiches, enjoying their pride at having succeeded in attaining the perfect brownness of bread in the pan. I saw myself hosting dinner parties and backyard barbeques. I saw it. I just never found it.

FOUR

Plots wants to change his name to Jefferson. He tells me this while I'm pouring a third of a cup of coffee from the just dripped carafe. One third coffee, two thirds heavy cream. Four packets of sugar. The mixture swirls like syrup.

"Jefferson Green," Plots explains, "was an employee at the Southland Ice Company in Dallas. At that time, they only sold ice. But Jefferson Green decided to provide customers other stuff like milk and eggs and bread. And so, the concept of 7-Eleven was birthed." Plots has a wad of licorice tucked in his cheek, which makes him over-salivate. His 'S's gurgle. His teeth are ringed in black.

I heat the milky coffee in the microwave and bring it to the counter.

"Born," I correct him. "The concept of 7-Eleven was born. Not birthed."

"Not only that," he says, ignoring my grammatical proficiency, "but we share a birthday."

"Who?" I take a hefty swig of coffee, scalding the roof of my mouth.

"Me and 7-Eleven," he says as if stating a known fact. "We have the same birthday. July 11. Get it? Seven Eleven? July 11?"

I select a roll of Sweet Tarts from the display rack and settle in on a stool. Plots always leaves a stool for me next to the counter. "How do you know that?"

He grins, showing lichen-black gums. "I've been doing some research," he points to his tablet. "The official birthday of 7-Eleven is July 11, same as mine."

I roll a single Sweet Tart along the side of my tongue, feeling the rough edge of the candy scrape against my teeth. Sweet Tarts and coffee are the perfect combination. Sour and sweet and creamy. "Sounds like a medical condition," I say. "Jefferson Plots disease."

"He was probably a genius," Plots continues. He's like this. He's an information junkie, and once he gets started on a topic, he needs to finish it or maybe his head will explode, I'm not sure. I never stop him. I like the sound of his voice too much to interrupt. Once, though, he totally grossed me out talking about bedbugs. He'd awoken one morning to a body swollen with red welts and a trip to the Doc-in-the-Box confirmed he'd been a hearty meal for a mattress full of bedbugs. "Bedbugs are teeny tiny little critters who bite like piranhas, sucking at your blood. Their first bite has a little anesthetic in it, so you don't feel any of the effects until after. That's the worst part, I think. Just imagine," he insisted on telling me all he learned about bedbugs, even though I'd plugged my fingers into my ears and sealed my eyes closed, "they hide in the bed, waiting for your warm body to settle in, and then they swarm and you don't even know they're there!" Plots can get over-enthusiastic about topics. He'll research anything. Unlike me. I prefer to 'learn as I go'.

I had nightmares about bedbugs for a long time after that.

"But he wasn't the progenitor of the store," Plots says.

"The what?"

"The person who came up with the 7-Eleven concept. The progenitor. Isn't that the right word?"

Plots likes to try out vocabulary words. He spends his in-between-customers time reading. He reads the comic books and the *Financial Times* and everything in between. Even *Hustler*.

"I think it's more like originator," I say, unsure.

"Well, he had that first idea, and then the ice company started selling these items at all their ice docks and *voila*," he waves a hand like a dancer, "the convenience store was born."

"Fascinating," I say. I don't have much to do today. I could stay here and listen to Plots talk, or I could go to my parents' house and see if there's anything that they want me to get rid of. They had a party last night and are probably over-run with leftovers. Plus, I am out of toilet paper. My mother always has extra toilet paper.

Plots is picking licorice bits out of his teeth with the corner of a business card left by a patron hoping to generate business for his next-door insurance business. "7-Eleven is the world's largest convenience store chain," Plots says. "A new store opens every three and a half hours! Can you imagine? There are even 7-Eleven stores in Taiwan."

"Are you interested in moving to Taiwan?" I joke. Plots worked so hard to get here to the states, to the land of opportunity. Even after he'd secured a sponsor, a distant uncle who agreed to sign for him, he'd waited nearly four years for a visa. He'd never dream of going anywhere else.

"You never know," he surprises me with his answer. "That's the benefit of working for a large corporation. I can work here in our little town, or I can transfer somewhere else. I have options. I have possibilities. You, too, could have options and opportunities, my dear Charlotte. All you have to do is apply." He points to the job application forms stacked neatly on a riser. "Fill it out and we'll be co-workers."

"Very funny," I say, tossing my now empty cup into the trash. "I don't need options and opportunities. I have a business to consider," I remind him. I've been tending a productive garden in my back yard, and the zucchini are almost ready to harvest.

"I'm thinking of applying for 'organic' status," I tell him. "I filled out that application. Well, I filled out most of it. It's long, so I left the second half for later. I'll need to clean up the yard a little before they send the inspectors over. Although I can't imagine they will object to all the dog doo in the yard. That's as organic as you can get!"

"True," he agrees, and offers a small frown. "What's dog 'doo'?"

"Shit. Dog shit. We call it dog doo. Don't ask me why."

"That's all you've got to do? Fill out an application?" He points again to the employment applications.

"Did you do research?" Plots asks.

"Tons," I roll my eyes so he can glean the weight of this project. "I've done hours and hours of research. I've been to the library, and I've talked to the owners of the local farm communities. Long Island is famous for its farming. It's not all ducks and oysters." I'd done virtually no research, but anyone growing up on Long Island as I did knows about the duck farms and the oyster beds. The little bit of reading I'd done came bubbling out of me. "There are over one hundred different crops grown on Long Island," my voice is strong and smooth, worthy of radio. "We have well-drained soil and abundant fresh water. Perfect for organics."

I sigh, so he knows how arduous this process will be. "There are tons of rules for organic farming. Rules and restrictions. You have to know about acreage and composition. There is soil testing and all sorts of stuff. It's very rigorous. Very detailed. Plus," I add, "it costs a lot of money. I'll need a composting set-up. I'll need a monitoring system and some chemistry things. I'm going to talk with a business consultant at the bank and find out if I'll need a separate bank account or charge tax or what have you."

Now that I've talked about the organic farming idea, I'm excited to apply for that status. I can't remember where I left the application, but I know that I'll need some seed money. It's only twenty miles to my parents' house. If I leave now, I'll get there by lunch. I lean around the counter and smack a kiss on his chin.

I never did ask for the seed money. I forgot why.

FIVE

"You are describing the romance novel version of love, little girl," my grandmother tells me one long-ago afternoon. I am watching her bake scones for her freezer. I am not sure what that means. How can a freezer be hungry? Doesn't matter. I am happy just to be in her kitchen. I spend almost every afternoon here, sitting on the stool, watching her glide from the sink to the oven and back, stopping to scoop out ingredients from the drawer of large metallic bins that are silos for flour, sugar and salt. "Real life doesn't work like that."

Her house abuts the public-school compound where my sister Celia and I attend elementary school. The land was once owned by the Shinnecock Indians back when they populated Long Island. Two hundred acres of farmland stolen from the native Americans who had been here for centuries. That's basically all I know about the Indians. I'd stopped listening after that. I don't care much for history. I don't see the need to unearth the past. I do believe the rumor, though, that the far playground of our school hides an ancient burial ground haunted by Indians who were displaced by the settlers.

We're walkers, Celia and me, passing our grandmother's house twice each day. In the mornings, we walk fast past the burial ground, Celia and the neighbor kids trailing behind me. As the oldest, I am in charge of getting us to the school on time. Like geese, we tromp past my grandmother's house in clumsy formation, waving to the turret that shelters her creaky-floored bedroom. In warm months, she cranks open a window and yells out funny things like, "Don't take any wooden nickels."

After school, we spill into her kitchen with the hunger of new chicks. She has cookies waiting with tall glasses of whole milk for us and all the neighbor kids. We jostle, chatter, fill our stomachs. When the other kids go home, Celia starts on her homework right away, but I like to sit on the stepstool and talk to my grandmother. We have a special bond.

"Why can't life work like that?" I can hear the whine in my own voice. But my grandmother doesn't mind when I'm petulant. She thinks I'm fantastic, no matter what I do.

"Oh, Charlotte," she turns to me and smiles. She has flour on her fingers. She always has flour on her fingers. "You have a lot to learn. But you have plenty of time. In the meantime, just trust me," she says, turning back to the mixing bowl.

I do. I trust her. I sit completely still and watch her.

She stands with her legs apart; her feet are already swollen inside the pumps that define her feet. Her stockings are loose around the ankles. Later, I will watch her tug them up and snag them in the little rubber clamps dangling from her girdle. She always wears a girdle, reinforced with metal stays that I like to knock my knuckles against in play. She holds a heavy spatula over the Sunbeam Mixmaster's bowl. "You are going to have a wonderful life," she tells me. "You'll have a family and a house and plenty of friends." She stops the automatic mixer and works with the spatula, lunging with all her might into the batter. Cooking is hard work unless you love it. My grandmother taught me that. She scrapes the batter from the sides of the bowl and licks a bit of the creamy froth off a finger. "You'll have a job that makes you feel wonderful about yourself," she is talking and scraping and turning the mixer back on. The noise fills my head like mud in a tire tread. What did she say? A job?

"I don't want a job," I tell her. "I want to be a mother."

She bangs the spatula against the side of the bowl. The scones are made in two halves, one batch will have raisins and one will not. I like the muffins with the raisins. I pluck a few raisins from the bag I'm balancing on my lap. My grandmother always lets me help with the cooking. She trusts me with that.

"Don't eat those," she admonishes me without looking. She has eyes in the back of her head, or so she's said. "You will be a mother," she assures me. "But first you must learn. Education is everything," she says.

I know what comes next. She is going to tell me about my grandfather. I shift on my bum, getting comfortable. A raisin falls from the rough plaid fabric pulled taut over my already developing chest. In fifth grade, I was the only girl to wear a bra, a detail that does not go unnoticed by my classmates. The boy who sits directly behind me snaps the strap across my back every time our teacher turns toward the blackboard.

My grandmother is ready for the raisins. I stand and carry the bag toward her.

"Your grandfather wanted to go to school, to get his education, but his father pulled him out in eighth grade so he could work in the family's general store," she talks as she separates out half the batter into a glass bowl. Her upper arm is taut with effort. "He was a smart man," she continues. "A really smart man. But he always felt cheated out of an education."

She turns and reaches out a hand for the raisins, and me. "You can accomplish anything you put your mind to." Together, we pour the raisins into the batter. "You know, you're lucky. You're a smart girl. You can really go places."

Go places? A raisin remnant is stuck on the back of my tongue, glued to the dry cave of my mouth. I don't want to go anywhere.

I run a finger around the rim of the mixing bowl and taste the muffin batter. It is salty and a little tart. "What if I don't want to go?"

"Go where?"

"You said I can go places. Where am I supposed to go?"

She holds out the spatula for licking. Her fingers wrap around mine. Warmth. Acceptance. She begins to deposit large blobs of muffin batter into the buttered tins. She works with machine-like precision, spilling nothing. "What if I don't want to go anywhere? What if I want to stay right here?"

She laughs a little bit, washing the empty mixing bowl under the faucet, her shoulders rolling gently under her apron straps. "You sound like Peter Pan!" She smiles and sings: *I won't grow up. I won't grow up. I don't want to go to school.*

"You didn't go anywhere," I remind her, "and you turned out okay."

Her hands rest on the edge of the farmer's basin sink, stainless steel and deep enough to submerge a ship, her fingers hang like talons. "This is not the life for you, little girl. You are going to get an education and meet new people and learn new things. There is a big world out there."

"I don't care about the big world," I whine. "I want to be like you. I want to have a house and a family and a big yard. And, if I get a career, I'll be a cook. Like you."

She looks as if I've admitted to committing a sin. Murder, maybe. And then, she sighs and flaps the towel at me, signaling a new mood "How about we play the piano?" she said. "You play. I'll sing."

I follow her to the music room, ignoring the fervent defiance lodged, like a canker, in the walls of my stomach.

SIX

I am trying to remember when Celia and I got to be friends. I was four when she was born. Right away, she had a heart defect that took my parents away; she needed special surgery in a hospital in the city. New York City. I stayed behind with my grandmother until they all came home, which was, I think it was a year later, but I've been told by my grandmother it was more like three weeks.

I am in second grade and full of information and ritual. The sixties are a decade of warnings. We practice how to Duck and Cover when the air raid siren sounds, and how to Stop, Drop and Roll in the event of a fire. We have an emergency exit plan for the household so we can all find each other after evacuating the house in a mad rush. I still don't know what all the panic is about. The only thing that ever happens in our neighborhood is that the basements flood when it rains hard. And once, the Madiero's house was hit by lightning.

Our house is ground zero for Thanksgiving dinner. My mother prepares for weeks, storing cakes and square pans of brightly colored casseroles in the downstairs freezer. My father brings up all the folding chairs stored under the stairwell. Celia and I are supposed to stay out of the way. We are in the basement most of the time, playing schoolteacher. I am always the teacher. I stand at a blackboard my father affixed to the paneling and draw instructive diagrams on the board with three colors of chalk. Celia, age three, is the student, sitting cross-legged on the cold tile floor. I pretend to instruct her, writing two plus two on the board and pointing with a sword made from twisted tin foil. Celia has yet to go to preschool. Her heart keeps acting up; my parents are "erring on the side of caution."

"I wanna go to real school," Celia whines at me from the floor. Her big eyes are full to spilling.

"This is real school," I tell her. "Just pay attention. This is an A," I point to the A. Then, the B. As a second-grade student, I possess the knowledge of the universe. My body is large with confidence.

Celia is going to cry. I can just tell. If she cries, she'll need to run upstairs and then I'll be all alone with nothing to do. I think quickly. "How about if you're the teacher for a while," I dangle the offer to her, holding out the big chunk of chalk. Celia will jump at the chance to be the teacher. "You can teach me something that you know." I rub away my careful lettering with the felt eraser balanced on the little metal sill.

Celia will not be able to resist. I wait for her to untangle her legs. She is very slow to rise. If she doesn't want to play schoolteacher, I will lead her in a game of Duck and Cover.

"Write something on the board," I tell her, "and then teach me about it." I plop down to the floor and stare at the chalkboard as if willing the writing to appear. "Draw a picture. Of something you love. And then I'll guess what it is."

Celia holds the chalk in a fist and draws a slow circle. "It's a circle," I say.

Celia giggles and waves her free hand, shushing me. She draws smaller circles around the big one, varying the shapes. Some are like toenails. Some are jellybeans. Her tongue sticks past her lips while she's concentrating.

"It's a dog's foot," I shout out. "An eyeball. A cloud."

She turns to me. Her face is the same color as the chalk, her eyes are far away. My spine sags forward over my crossed ankles. The game is over.

I take the chalk from her fingers and lead her up the steps. When we arrive in the kitchen, I say too quietly, "Celia doesn't feel good," and wait while the sea of happy voices parts and then recedes. My mother slides her hands out of the hot pads, her skin slinks away from the smiling hills of her cheeks. She is gray with worry. I hate this colorless color of my mother's face. I hate that her eyes are suddenly marble hard and super-shiny and that her mouth tightens into a lobster claw that hides her beautiful shining teeth from me.

My father's authority descends into the room like humidity, quiet and sure. All will be well, his presence has its own weight, the room becomes muted under his assurances. Celia dissolves inside a cocoon of adults. I am expelled and untethered.

I tumble backward, stumbling into a nameless and silencing void. The essence of my existence is erased as blithely as chalk from slate.

I want to know how she feels, how it feels to have the world collapse in a defense shield around you. It must be marvelous, I think, to have all those faces turned toward you in synchronous energy. Like a force field of good intentions, heating you under intensive rays. Is it pleasant, I might ask Celia, to have everyone looking at you like that? Do you feel special?

My head swims with thoughts that spin and swirl, no order can be discerned from the confusion or ideas and words and feelings. I am too young for that kind of cohesion. Instead, the questions mutate and divide and leech into the clear glass portions of my psyche. Celia needs extra care, I do not. I am lucky, I am told, that I am healthy, that I do not battle my own body for a simple heartbeat. I am lucky.

I don't feel lucky. I feel invisible.

One day I open my mother's make-up bag and find a beautiful green compact, swirled and shiny as the inside of a shell. Inside, rouge. Coral pink and smooth as pudding. I rub my index finger along the powdery surface; the shadow trail of my touch leaves a ghostly mark. The whorls of my fingerprint bleed filmy lines; I rub against the silk again. There is an edge of coral pink under my fingernail. I insert the fingertip into my ear and spiral it deep, reaching for the injustice that nags at me. Celia is sick. I am not.

My father will look into my ear later that night and discover a very red and angry inflammation. He will take me to his office, which is closed at night, and turn on all the lights while dismantling the alarm, and he'll use his medical equipment to examine me. He'll use his soft doctor voice, the voice he uses when patients call with emergencies during dinner and late into the night. He'll soothe all my bad feelings and hurt. He will use that voice to calm me as the paper drape underneath my bottom crunches in support of my suffering. He will shine his headlamp into my ears, nose, and throat. I will obey his soft commands to open wide, tilt my head, hold still. I will lap up the milk of his attention. And he will smile at me after his examination is complete, with a sadness in his eyes that I will never decipher and take me to Carvel for an ice cream sundae, and we will pretend as only children can do, that I am the most important thing in the world.

***

You can never look at your childhood with any sort of calculating meter. Always, our memories are flecked with bits of debris: snippets of conversation overheard from behind closed doors, moments memorized and then reordered according to our years or our influences. When did this happen? Or that? The child's memory is not discerning. Rather, it retains only what was absorbed.

My memories of childhood are like touched-up photographs. Perfect. Hues of pink painted on gray cheeks, scowls softened into smiles. Two little girls in matching dresses standing on the front stoop holding hands. In some shots, my mother stands behind us, coiffed with an up-do she had teased by a lady named Doxie (a hard name to forget) every Friday while we waited on the bench outside the beauty parlor licking ice cream off sugar cones and fighting over who got to ride in the front seat on the way home.

My mother ran our family with a singular mantra. No matter what, she would say in her sternest voice, "You are sisters. You will take care of each other. No matter what happens, you will be there for one another."

Family. It held her steady like the lifeline railing on a ship. Her grip was a constant. Family comes first, she'd say when one of us was caught leaving another behind. "If one fails, we all fail." She repeated that phrase—if one fails, we all fail—in every phase and stage of my development. I pointed out that, as the elder, I had far weightier responsibilities than my sister, who seemed to glide without effort, navigating the microcosm of our childhood with steadfast equilibrium.

"It's not fair," I often whined to our mother; her snake-tongue response stung. "No one ever said life is fair."

I wasn't afraid of her, my mother. Not exactly. But I did keep my distance. Celia was the one to challenge her. She argued, disagreed; she worked hard at tenderizing our mother, pounding out her hard-set dogmas and prudence. As a teen, Celia was the one who objected to the laws, forced my mother to accept that we could wear jeans to school, and that buying the school lunch instead of carrying the very embarrassing kids' lunchboxes like elementary school children was not going to stunt our growth nor rot our teeth. "She is so closed-minded," my sister complained of our mother, sure of my solidarity. She is? I wondered in silence, knowing better than to interrupt.

My father worked long hours, frequently at night, and that left her, our mother, with complete control over the household. Sometimes I overheard her talking to my father on the phone, filling him in on the status of their more worrisome child. *Charlotte got a D in English*, she'd report my failings in low-voiced concern, as if a low grade was a sign of impending trouble. And it was a harbinger of problems ahead, but I didn't know that then. I do now.

When he was home, my father assumed his throne, yelling about the water bill, the shoes left on the welcome mat, the back door left open so he could pay to heat the entire neighborhood. Father things. I was afraid of him and in love with him. A kind word from my father was as precious as an ice cream sundae, and in our family, it was just as rare.

They loved each other, my parents, and that signaled to everyone, and to us, that we had a stable and devoted family. We took car trips in summer and went one year to Puerto Rico in winter to escape the cold where my father taught us to ride the waves on our stomachs, arms stretched ahead to prevent hitting the sand headfirst. We were provided with absolutely everything. Music lessons. Gymnastics. Private tutors in math when I lagged behind in high school trigonometry. We followed each other, taking turns at the helm. Celia rose from her difficult beginning and succeeded marvelously; she had a career and a husband and a pregnancy. Who ever thought Celia would carry a baby! Her once fragile heart had mended, she barely remembered the long years of doctors and hospitals.

I remembered everything. And I also achieved. I had an apartment and a dog. I always had a job, though, despite repeated attempts, I never did find a career. I was happy. At least that is my recollection.

SEVEN

"I'm standing here in a full panic. I've tried on every dress I have!" I plop down on the bed holding the phone tight to my head. "The only one I like is long-sleeved, and you know how I sweat when I'm nervous. Even if I stuff a paper towel under my bra, I'll be saturated before we get past the 'hellos.'" I close my eyes and deliver the half-burned cigarette to my lips. My hand shakes. The hot stream of smoke in my chest calms me.

"Are you smoking?"

My mother misses nothing.

"No." I reach for the ashtray. "But I think my blood sugar must be low. My hands are shaking."

I fall back against the unmade bedding and languish for a moment in the cool cotton fabric billowing around my face. I never make my bed—a fact that pisses my mother off.

"What about the light blue dress we bought at Macy's?" She's on the right track. It is a pretty dress, in good-enough shape, long enough to cover the worst of my legs and cinched at the waist with a band of elastic. The saleswoman at Macy's recommended adding a leather belt to emphasize the waist and add a little bit of pizzazz. I love the belt. It has an oversized, faux-leather-covered buckle that helps my mid-section seem small. An optical illusion.

Jimbo's mother will like the blue dress. I've never met her, not yet.

But I think she will appreciate the V-neck and the modest-length. I lift my head. Where is the blue dress?

"I'm not sure it's clean," I say, scanning the length of the wall-to-wall closet. I'd removed the accordion doors long ago.

My stomach gurgles. I am either hungry or about to have diarrhea.

I slide off the mattress and kick at the collection of rejected outfits tangling around my ankles. I have a lot of clothes. I have about a dozen two-piece outfits that I wear for work at the courthouse. Professional dresses from size fourteen to twenty-four. I have two suits in each size, from eighteen to twenty-eight, for weddings and funerals. I toy with the idea of wearing a suit to meet Jimbo's mother. But then, I don't want her to think I am stuffy.

Of the dresses that fit me, the blue one is in the best shape. I am hard on my clothes. So many are torn or stained.

"Or," my mother continues, her voice straight as a hairpin, "you could wear the green dress with a sweater over it. It's supposed to snow later."

The green dress has a big hole on the lapel where a red-hot ash had landed and burned through. The sunflower yellow shirtdress has a French dressing stain despite multiple treatments of stain remover. My sexy black dress with the ruffle has a two-inch tear under the arm—that's the one I really want to wear. I feel good in that dress, but sexy is not the message I want to convey to Jimbo's mother. I could wear white. White is the color of purity. Unfortunately, the white wrap-around dress no longer wraps all the way around. I'm saving it, though, for when I lose weight.

There it is. The blue dress. Its hem pokes out from under a wicker chair that had lost its seat a long time ago. It's wrinkled and dirty, half trapped under a gardening clog clumped with putrid mud. Shit. I want to cry. "I can't do this," I tell my mother. This is a big day, an important event. I am going to fail and fail miserably.

"Lansings never say can't," she quotes the stupid family motto my father made up.

The light outside the window pales to gray. "I feel light-headed," I tell my mother.

"Splash some cold water on your face," she says, curt. Even through twenty miles of fiber-optic networks, her voice has real power. I go quietly to the bathroom and do what I am told.

My image in the mirror looks worried. I stare into my own green eyes and try to feel confident. "What if she doesn't like me?" The phone is on speaker. It's almost like she's in the bathroom with me.

"Nonsense," my mother responds immediately. "What's not to like? You're kind. You're lovely. You come from a nice family. And you have a job. You're every mother's dream."

My image responds to her praise, a flower turning toward the light. I want to believe her, I want to be lovely and likeable.

"Life is a balancing act, Charlotte," my mother is talking in her calm-her-down voice. I know it well. "Some days are great, some days are awful. In the big scheme of things, the overall picture is good, the scales of justice balance out. Be patient, sweetie, and let nature take its course. Okay?"

I nod, even though she can't see me.

"Balance. That's the goal."

I take the towel from the counter and press it to my face. A sleeve of Oreo cookies is hidden underneath. Did Jimbo leave these for me? Only four left.

I smile, remembering. Just yesterday, Jimbo was walking around with a palm-full of Oreos, eating and talking and walking around. He must have left them here for me, a surprise present.

He's always doing things like that. Leaving a half-finished glass of milk in the refrigerator, knowing I get thirsty during the night. At first, I'd inquired, "Why don't you put your glass into the dishwasher?"

"I thought you might want the other half," he'd said with a boyish grin. "So we can be sharing."

The cookie settles my stomach. I say goodbye to my mother and promise to call her on my way home.

"Feel good about yourself, Charlotte," she says. "If his mother has a brain in her head, she'll love you."

I slip the sexy black dress with the ruffle over my head and clamp my arm down over the tear. As long as I don't raise my arm, no one will see the ragged rip.

I knew something about balance. I used to sail a tiny Sunfish. It was more a long surfboard than a watercraft, just over thirteen feet in length and four across. The sail measures nine feet, but once filled with wind, it expands into a trapeze of incredible power, strong enough to project the fiberglass boat across the water's surface at reckless velocities.

My parents had signed me up for sailing lessons the summer I turned thirteen. All the kids in our town took sailing lessons down at the shallow beach at the edge of our community. I was at home on the water; I felt strangely serene. I learned to shift my weight as the sail came about, and how to adjust the tension on the line. It was like being on a see-saw or riding two on a bicycle.

Had I known that my life, not my happiness or my success or my contributions, but that my life itself would require as much renegotiation, readjusting, rerouting as sailing a simple watercraft, I would likely have experienced a normal, maybe even pleasing, voyage. But that is not what happened. That is not the course that was to be mine.

EIGHT

"A counselor?" My mother's voice was pinched in her throat. I could almost see the long lines of her esophageal muscles contracting around the words. "You want to be a counselor? Like a social worker?"

"I guess you could say it is similar to social work," I explained over the phone. "Plus, I have a lot of personal experience. God knows, I've been going to counseling since I was ten," I said, adding, "Thanks mostly to you."

"I suppose," she paused. I could hear the loose pebbles of her mind churning.

"I thought I could work in the school system. I could help students understand relationships and behavior. Stuff like that."

"What do you know about relationships?" she asked without venom. It was true, at thirty-six, I had practically no relationship experiences. Our small town limited the number of people I met as well as curtailed any wild impulses I might have had. My young adulthood had not panned out. I amassed only a few friends, kept to menial jobs that neither challenged nor complemented my future. I became timid, hiding behind the scenes, doing back-office work.

My weight increased. Finally, I got what my mother would call "a temporary real job." I was clerk in the county courthouse just a few miles from my house. In my job, I transferred stacks of closed cases to the basement archive storage unit using a utilitarian cart that I pushed through Staff Only hallways, using Private service elevators. I made some friends. One of the older judges took a liking to me. He sat next to me on the bench outside where I ate my lunches. He talked about his grandchildren. A few times, I went out after work with some of the other clerks and support staff, but they were mostly my mother's age with families and children and homes with years of memories.

More than a few times, I'd recognize plaintiffs and defendants in the courthouse, but they rarely noticed me. Once, I nearly ran the cart over the toes of a former classmate from high school. The slide trombone player. He came out of the restroom, his hands linked at the wrists, escorted by a uniformed officer.

"Hey," I said, casual as a stranger.

"Step away from the defendant please," the court officer warned.

Officers of the court were sort of like cardboard cutouts: they represented authority but had no real training. I had explored this option. Becoming an officer of the court was a significant promotion from court clerk, with a pay raise and substantial increase in responsibility. They always needed more female court officers. It was the uniform that ruined it for me. Court officers wore a blue suit, top and bottom where clerks wore just a simple brown vest over their street clothes. As an officer, I'd need a special-order uniform to suit my pant size. Either that or buy a men's size large and cut the length in half. Instead, I decided to remain with my cart.

The slide trombonist glanced down at me. His height hadn't changed, at over six feet he was an Ichabod Crane, bent over and much too skinny. Heroin thin, is the phrase used in the hallways and stairways of the courts. His eyes remained on my face for a long minute. I stayed still and said nothing.

The court officer tugged on his arm, trapped at the wrists bound at his groin. I remembered that groin, and the smell of his musk. My face burned and I wanted to turn and run away. He didn't remember me, I could see the vagueness in his eyes.

"Charlotte," the officer warned me again, moving his charge in front of the cart. "Step back."

"Charlotte?" he remembered. He lifted his handcuffs as if to wave, or cover his face, and showed me his terrible teeth. "You're the Charlotte from the bassoon section?" He laughed, a sinister sound.

I saw myself from the outside. Four feet ten, and forty-eight inches around, I am a beach ball with a head on top, melting slowly into the floor. The sensation of shrinking, disappearing, was a pleasant one, and I wished for it to last. No such luck.

"What the fuck happened to *you*?" His eyes scanned my size with a glint of real horror. Was he remembering how he'd bent me over Mr. Nelson's desk that day? His mouth slanted like a bolt of lightning. The tightness of his laughter lashed gashes across my heart.

"Come on, asshole," the officer pulled at his arm, nearly knocking the taller man off his feet. I turned toward the elevator and prayed for the doors to open. My reflection in the metal door reinforced all the self-hatred I'd accumulated over the past thirty-six years. The plastic buttons on my button-down blouse tried desperately to flee. They strained and twisted on thick stalks of thread tethering them to the flimsy gray fabric. White flesh bulged like balloons, swelling into the spaces between the buttons as if amidst the process of inflation. Old sweat ringed my neck. *Open the door. Open the door.* I chanted at the elevator to open. All the doors in this building were fortified with security teeth able to clamp each doorway closed in the event of an attack. I was under attack. A bead of warm liquid escaped my body. Urine.

I'd started leaking when I was ten. Within months I was in the pediatrician's office with wet pants and a frantic mother. "What could be the cause?" my mother wanted to know. I just wanted to disappear. "She never used to wet the bed, and now it's an every night occurrence," she leaned so far forward in her chair I thought she might pitch to the floor. I hoped she would pitch to the floor. "She already wears a sanitary napkin every day to school." Oh, great. Embarrassments galore. "What else can we do?"

The answer: Therapy.

My first therapist was a woman recommended by the pediatrician.

"Your mother tells me you don't want to go to school."

My mother. She's the reason I'm stuck here in an overheated office on a Wednesday afternoon instead of hanging out in my room and playing with my mice. I have this huge mouse habitat set up in my bedroom. A giant matrix of tubes and conduits and chambers, complex as a space station.

"Is there a particular reason why you don't like school?" Her voice is faux pleasant, as if she thinks she'll coax me to confide in her. What does she want me to confide? That I have nothing to confide? That I've done nothing so far in my eleven years of life to brag about? I don't like school. That's all. I'm sure the preference is not unique.

"Lots of girls struggle in school." Despite my lack of participation, she is still talking. She is not the first person to talk to me about how normal I am about hating school. My mother pretends to understand by filling my silences with chatter about her fabulous experience in school where she was ridiculed for her asthma and then lauded for her work on the yearbook. My father pretends "it's just a phase," providing plenty of medical documentation about the development of the human body, none of which has anything to do with me or my refusal to go to school. The principal promises that learning can be fun, and the counselor who sits at a folding table in the nurse's office gives me a book written for children called, "It's Perfectly Normal." I am thinking of all these manifestos and staring at the therapist's ankles, refusing to meet her gaze. As my best friend Peter likes to say: this is not my first rodeo.

Peter is a social misfit. Too tall, too dark skinned. People assume he's African American but he is more white than I am. His mother is

Irish for god's sake. Peter is oversized and clumsy. He has bad teeth and hair on the backs of his hands. Fodder for any upper-class boy. If the psychiatrist wants to talk about struggle, I could tell her about Peter, bullied by the neighborhood kids from the day we started first grade. His last name is Lanford. I am Lansing, you can see how we ended up seated one behind the other in every year of school.

"It's a time of transformation for so many kids. Maybe you've noticed that your friends are changing a little bit? Maybe the girls are becoming more competitive or more selective in choosing who will be their friends and who will not." She pauses, waits. "Why don't you tell me about your friends. Whom do you like?"

Whom? Did she just say whom? Who uses that kind of language?

She waggles her pen, balancing it between her thumb and pointer, as if experimenting with that optical illusion of turning a solid object into a malleable worm. I stare at the pen, waiting for it to soften.

"Tell me the name of one girl who you consider to be a friend." Her voice prods my memory. I will tell her about Mary. My next-door neighbor.

Mary's mother and my mother are on the Committee for Something together. They carpool to the meetings and talk on the phone about the agendas. I think Mary's mother is the chairman of this committee, but I don't know for sure. We moved into our house when I was six and Mary's mother and my mother decided right away that Mary and I would be friends.

"Mary," I tell the therapist, nearly startling her with my sudden vocalization. I'd been silent for so long; she must have forgotten the sound of my voice. Mary had the longest hair of anyone I ever met. She wore it in a thick braid that hung down her back like a horse's tail. When she was a baby, she'd had a devastating reaction to a medication that left one side of her body paralyzed. She walked with a limp, her left arm was useless to her, it dangled next to her side like a flipper. She was sensitive about that and insisted I stay on the damaged side when walking to school, so others wouldn't see her dead arm.

"Mary is a friend of yours?" she asks, clarifying unnecessarily.

I nod innocently and hold my snide lip from lifting.

"Tell me one thing you like about Mary," she says, relaxing her shoulders as if we're finally getting somewhere.

I tell her. "She has eczema."

The therapist's fleshy mouth straightens. She leans forward, keeping her knees and her ankles together. Her elbows come to rest on her thighs. She is too close to me now. The little room closes in around us, trapping me in my seat. I feel constricted, my sneakers squeeze around my feet. Even my skin feels tight.

I lean far back in my chair. The chairs are identical, a matching pair of leather armchairs with a big metal X as a base. My chair bounces under me; I assume hers does too. Maybe that's why she holds her body so stiff. To control the chair underneath.

She changes course. "Why don't you tell me about your room," she says. "What do you like to do in your room at home?"

My room! Now we're getting somewhere. I have the coolest room. I have National Geographic magazine covers glued to the wall beside my bed. I painted the ceiling with stenciled flowers and stars—some even glow in the dark. The mirror is framed with big plastic buttons that I glued around the edges. My favorite is a bright red button that says: Panic Button. That one makes me laugh every time I see it.

My parents say I can decorate my room any way I like, as long as it's safe. I don't even know what that means.

"I have a gigantic mouse habitat," I tell her. I am coming alive in my skin. My lids open wide, I feel the warm office air on my eyeballs. "I started with one habitat kit, and then I added more. I must have about fifty mice in there by now." Her face looks like a cave painting. Black-rimmed eyes. Red lips shaped as a kiss.

I built the habitat myself, using three sets of prefabricated plastic parts. One habitat was definitely not enough. And two seemed half-assed. Put three of them together and you have something special.

"What is it about the mice that you like?" She's afraid of mice. I can tell in the way her voice fights to get out of her throat.

I think that over. I love watching the mice dash around, and I especially love when they run on the wheel. "Mice are like people," I tell her, "only nicer. They like to run and play, and they don't need much. Food, water, and exercise. That's all it takes to make them happy."

"Does watching the mice make you happy?" I want to shout at her: *What a stupid question to ask a ten-year-old.* I have no reason to help her with our session. She and I are enemies.

"I don't know. I like them. They are always busy, always running. The more space you give them, the more they travel. Peter brought over his stopwatch, and we keep track of how long it takes a mouse to find a treat. They like nuts, obviously. But they'll track down just about any food you put in there. Raisins. Fruit. Lettuce."

She is writing in skittish, short movements, scratching the paper with the nub of her pen. "Who is Peter?"

"Peter's my best friend," I tell her. "We work on the mouse habitat together, feeding and making sure the mice are happy. He used to come over all the time to play with them." Peter had a favorite mouse, he called her Nancy after Nancy Sinatra. "*These boots are made for walkin', that's just what they'll do.*" I'd sing the song, jazzing my shoulders to the beat. It's a great song. Peter and I used to listen to it in my room, lying on our backs with our legs in the air and fake-walking our feet on the ceiling.

"Does Peter still come over to play?"

I suck my lip. "Not really. Not anymore."

"Why is that? Why did he stop coming over to play with the mice?" she asks.

It's my mother's fault, I want to tell her. She wants me to be outside. She says I'm spending too much time in my room with Peter. Too much time sitting still. Go out and get some fresh air, she yells at me. Ride your bike. Jump rope with Mary.

Mary's driveway is fifty feet from my window. The sound of her weighted jump rope snapping on the cement is relentless. Mary ties her jump rope to the handle of their garage door so she needs only one other person to turn it. She has five siblings, so there is always someone to coerce, or to bribe. Once she bribed me, promising to hold a place in line when the ice cream man came to the court where we lived, only to give it up to her crying sister. By the time I got to the front, the Good Humor man was out of Creamsicles.

"Well," I say slowly. I do not want to talk to this therapist anymore. I want to go home and close my door and seal myself in the dark. I like to be alone, is that such a terrible thing? What's wrong with being alone in your room? I worked hard to make that room a perfect den. I picked the posters, the pictures, the tassels hanging from thumbtacks all around. I hung fringe from the windowsills and a bead curtain over the dresser. Why couldn't everyone just leave me alone and let me enjoy living in my room?

Peter used to really like my room. The last time he came over, we made vanilla fudge then watched the mice play in the habitat. I put a blob of vanilla fudge in an empty chamber and we waited for the mice to find it, making verbal bets on which mouse would get there first. His mouse won. That's when Peter told me he didn't want to hang out with me anymore. He had a crush on some girl he met in church choir.

I tell the therapist, "My mother decided we are not allowed to hang out in my room anymore. 'No boys in the bedrooms.'" I let my snide lip curl.

I didn't tell her how my stomach burned with acid-emptiness when he told me about that girl, or how I hated him so much for telling me how he felt about her. It's not like I wanted him to like *me*, but I didn't want him to stop being my friend, which is what was about to happen. I didn't tell her how, that night, I filled my aching stomach with a full-sized, store-bought Boston Cream Pie my mother had hidden away in the small extra refrigerator, stowed under a shelf unit in our basement. I didn't tell her how I shoved all that freezing cold cream into my mouth with a wooden spoon, nearly gagging myself in the process. I didn't tell her how I hid the empty carton in the recess of the recycling bin where no one would ever see it. I didn't tell her any of that.

"And what about Mary? Are you still friendly with her?" Her eyes bounce to the small clock on the shelf near my chair. Time's almost up.

"Mary is afraid of mice," I tell her. That part is true. That has to count for something.

***

To my mother, I boasted: "I've been told, you know, that I am easy to talk to." I arched my shoulders back though she clearly couldn't see.

It was one of the county judges who suggested the career to me. He'd remarked on my *wonderful acuity* in assessing some of the odd characters that passed through his small claims courtroom and remarked in passing that I was a natural counselor. Those were his words. Natural counselor. Apparently, he thought I knew something about people and relationships.

There was silence for too many minutes. "Did we do something wrong?" she asked. "Is that why you're interested in counseling? You need to talk about how bad your mother was to you? Right?" She was not joking. Her voice lilted, she pretended to be jolly, but really, I knew better. She meant those words.

"You're right, Denise," I said. When she pissed me off, I called her by her given name. Just to irritate her. "I am choosing my career based on a need to complain about you." I let the sarcasm sit a moment. "Don't be ridiculous."

A twinge of doubt pulled at my lip. Is it possible, I wondered, that I'm looking for a vehicle to vent my personal pain?

"I like learning about behaviors and motivations," I said. "I like figuring out how people reach conclusions about one another and about events that befall and present to them. Counseling is like looking at a puzzle. Once you see the big picture, you can figure out a solution."

I heard the telltale quickness of her breathing. I knew she was still on the line, but she chose not to say anything.

"Plus, I am a good listener," I said. "You always used to say that."

I was begging. Begging for my mother's approval. And she was refusing to give it. I wasn't sure I wanted to be a counselor. When the judge remarked on my natural ability, the idea materialized like a file dropped into an Inbox so I decided why not? Plus, my parents loved education. This would be a good way to generate appeal. "The program is only two years. The classes are at night, so I can keep my job."

My mother should be happy I'm going to be a counselor. It's a real job. A career.

"I talked to Mary about it," I lied.

Mary went to college out of state, got her PhD in psychology, and opened a private practice in Rhode Island. My mother always liked Mary. Mary had potential. Mary was going places. My mother had a bad case of Mary Standards: Mary got an A on the math test, and I got a D. Mary wore her silky-soft long hair in a perfect ponytail, and mine was like balled-up dried seaweed. "Try and follow in Mary's footsteps," my mother coached. "Mary is a good influence." She always had a lot of information about Mary and other appropriate girls. She was like a party line for other people's successful children.

"Oh, yes, Mary," she perked up. "How is she doing?"

"She's perfect." That was not a lie. Mary had everything my mother wanted for me. A family. A career. A degree.

"So, anyway," I said. "That is why I called. To tell you I sent in my application. I forget how much it costs. I put it on the Visa card."

"You know, your father hoped you'd be a lawyer," her voice yawned. "Or a doctor. Are you sure you don't want to be a doctor? They unravel puzzles, too."

"No," I ignored the misuse of my metaphor. But I did smile. Unravel puzzles! I would have to remember that one to tell Plots. "I am sure I don't want to be a doctor. But thank you for your input."

"I just can't imagine how you'd want to listen to people's problems all day long," she said. A long silence indicated she was not yet finished. "Will you get a degree, at least?"

"It's a certificate. It's like a degree, only better." My sarcasm hit the target. My mother groaned.

"You must admit, it suits my personality perfectly. I'm caring. I'm sensitive. I'm generous. That's what you always say."

"That's all true, Charlotte. You are kind and caring and full of love. A wonderful person, all around, and I am very proud of you." Pause. "So, is that it then?" she asked. "You've made up your mind?"

"Yes."

"Well, then." She wasn't happy, but at least I didn't hear panic in her tone like when I got evicted from my apartment, which was not even my fault.

She began to relate to me the important news. My sister's morning sickness. My grandmother's bunions *and* hearing loss. The ignition on her car was acting up. "Your father is on the roof," my mother said in closing. "He's cleaning out the gutters. I half expect his body to come crashing down right in front of the kitchen window."

I thought about my father on the ladder, weighted by an overfilled toolbelt, goggles protecting his eyes. "Tell him how excited I am. Tell him to be happy for me."

I found comfort in communicating successfully with my parents. I almost felt good about that.

NINE

My mother's expression is perfect for Mount Rushmore. Stern, grim and flexible as a twig in permafrost. Her fork hovers over her salad, the tines are slick with balsamic.

My father sets his cocktail tumbler on the tablecloth and studies the last lick of rye clinging to the sides of the glass. This is our favorite family restaurant. Southern Italian, my favorite. Years ago, my father treated the owner's son who suffered debilitating esophageal spasms. At seven, he weighed only forty pounds. None of the medical tests proved illness or cause. My father warded off recommendations from other specialists to operate, explore, medicate. "Let's wait," he'd quietly insisted. He was a big fan of waiting. Unlike me, who prefers to jump into a situation with both feet running.

The owner approaches our table and shakes my father's hand. "How is my favorite doctor?"

My father smiled. "How's my favorite patient?"

"Good, good."

I can't wait a second longer. "I'm getting married!" I spew the news at him.

His moustache curves into a crescent. "A celebration!" He puts his hand on my father's shoulder. "Congratulations, my dear friend, and to all of you."

They look like mannequins, my family.

"Wonderful news, wonderful. Quanto meraviglioso." He graces a curious eye on my quiet family and pats my father's back with delicate vigor, like an obstetrician urging a baby to breathe. "All the best. All the best." He removes an empty appetizer dish and backs away. "I will tell the chef. A special dessert to celebrate."

I am getting married. I can hardly believe it myself.

"How exciting is *this*?" I nearly aspirate a crouton; a gulp of water washes my airway. "We are like the same person. We like the same things. He makes me laugh all day long." No one is eating the appetizers. I reach across and snag the heel of the bread from the basket. My mother and I usually vie for the heel. This time, I win.

Mike, Celia's husband is the first to respond. "Well, you are certainly full of surprises." He signals the waiter approaching our table, another round.

I don't usually drink alcohol. It doesn't agree with me. Or maybe I don't agree with it. Doesn't matter. I order an apricot sour and take up where I left off. "We are like Stan and Ollie." I paint a layer of butter on the bread and then sprinkle it with salt. "I'm Stan. I'm the one with the sense. He's just a happy go-along, perfectly content with whatever comes to him." I mimic the slapstick body language of Stan Laurel. It's all in the shoulders, that kind of silliness. Sometimes, Jimbo and I walk to the bedroom like this, emulating Laurel and Hardy. Too funny.

My mother has yet to move.

The apricot sour arrives and I clap my hands like a little girl, startling the waiter. "I'm getting married," I tell him. He smiles, approval.

From across the table, Celia beams at me. She is happy for me. I can feel it.

But I need more. I need the approval of my parents. They'd had a rough start with Jimbo. He was really sick the day they came for brunch and was unable to join us at the table. I'd invited them on purpose, to meet him, to get to know him. I'd made baked French toast and a fruit compote with berries that I'd canned after last summer's harvest. We sat around the kitchen table, a hand-me-down from my mother's house, and pretended to be festive in his absence. I had to leave the room every few minutes to check on Jimbo, who was tucked tightly into my bed, shades drawn. Given enough time, they would really like him.

"Are you alive in there?" I lean toward my mother, my blouse dips into a dish of olive tapenade. The miniature serving spoon catapults from the dish and lands in my lap like a guppy. Jimbo would have laughed at that.

I take a massive breath. I will keep talking until my excitement is expelled, that way I will be able to eat. Right now, I am just too enthusiastic. "Here I am, forty-nine years old and giddy in love. I'll have to plan the wedding sort of fast. Not that it's a shotgun affair." I laugh, and the sound of my own laughter makes me laugh even harder. I press my legs together. I could easily wet my pants. "Dad, you'll finally get to walk your oldest daughter down the aisle. Can you believe it? I know that you put money for a wedding into a trust for me way back when." He'd set aside a certain amount of money for both of us, Celia and me. When we were girls, he told us we could have any kind of wedding we wanted as long as it did not exceed the amount he'd earmarked. However, he reminded us repeatedly during our growing-up years, that he was perfectly happy to buy an extension ladder instead. In case we chose to elope. A joke. Or half a joke. I have already depleted the trust, but there is no need to talk about that. "I promise to stay within a budget. If I can. You know about my motto: Why do when it's so easy to overdo?"

Celia laughs at that. "An understatement."

My face is warm, my hands are jittery. This is all too good.

"I really can't believe it. I am so happy."

My eyes are on my mother who has yet to blink. "Are you super excited?" I ask her.

No response.

"Well," my father swallows the contents of his replenished rye. He seems about to continue, but nothing comes.

"You know how I've always dreamed of a big wedding. And now's my chance. Better late than never. Right?"

The waiter clears away the uneaten appetizers. Only my plate is clean. "And isn't this the perfect birthday present?"

My mother meets my gaze, finally. She takes a small swallow of ice water and blots her mouth with a napkin. "I must say Charlotte, you do know how to shock your mother."

I lean back and clasp my hands over my belly. "That's me," I agree, rambling. "Full of surprises. But aren't you glad I'm finally adding something good to this family? I only wish Jimbo could have come tonight. He really wanted to be here, to help you have a great birthday, Mom. He just couldn't manage it right now. He has a little bit of a bug. Nothing serious. But his stomach isn't right. He thinks he has ulcers and, dear God, he's complaining all the time."

I make googly-eyes at Celia who has her hands wrapped around a glass as if praying. "You know," I nod to show I am now in the know. "Men!" I finish the second apricot sour and lick the sugar off my lip. "I'm going to order a veal chop before we leave and take it home to him. He'll like that. And maybe a side of spaghetti." I need more bread. The waiter has removed the basket from our table.

To Celia, I say, "I hope they put candles on the special dessert. We are celebrating, after all."

***

He never actually asked me to marry him. Instead, we agreed to marry each other. We were positively gleeful, reciting our commonalities and listing all the fun we were about to have. Married! A dream fulfilled. I had a lot of friends then.

I considered my life perfect. Two quiet people sharing a prune Danish for breakfast, licking frosting off our fingers. Two bodies in the bed, side by side, watching television through glazed eyes. The images over time become less clear, obscured by medication and misuse. Was I happy? I don't remember thinking about being happy. I was married. My definition had just the one word. Married.

Sometimes, I'd gaze at my husband asleep, and I knew that if I woke him, I would have nothing to say to him. That didn't worry me, especially. All couples have blank spots between them, places where ideas do not coagulate, where thoughts are unwelcome. What would I have wanted to talk about, I really have no idea. All my wishes had come true.

The years bobbed, the tides rose and receded. We had some good moments when we laughed hard, delighted over bargains found, and reported to each other the status of our souls. I began to know him. His softnesses. His devotion. We were always together, never apart.

Jimbo understood pain. He'd lost his father and his grandfather. His mother lost her father and her husband. They were the last two survivors on an island of despair. Jimbo went to his bed, in his mother's house, providing for her a reason to live. She cooked his meals, delivered his meds. She deposited his inheritance money into his savings account and did not inquire further about his purchases or his wagers. She chose to ignore his mounting gambling debt. It wasn't until the bright yellow envelopes began to arrive, threatening letters and foreclosure notices that she accepted responsibility for his financial future, moving the remainder of his inheritance into a trust designed to provide a monthly stipend for twenty years. That was twenty years ago. Time was up.

TEN

I waited for the second ring to finish before taking a calming drag off my cigarette. My father never picked up on the first ring. Nor the second. *If it's important*, he used to say, *it will wait*.

"Henry Lansing." His voice was curt.

"Hi Dad." Mine was nervous, a sudden soprano.

"Well, hello there Charlie-girl." He hadn't called me that in twenty years. I saw him in my mind, leaning back in his leather chair and swirling toward the window of his medical office in mid-town, his tie hanging like a windsock from a hook. "What's cooking?"

Sometimes, not often, we had marvelous conversations. Joking and sparring and being silly. When he was silly, my father was just about the best person around. When we stood nose to nose, there wasn't another person in the world.

"Ah, a bit of the usual," I bantered with a familiar volley. "Stone soup and goose down pie." Once, long ago, when my mother was sick and I was around nine or ten, I'd made dinner for my father when he arrived home late. The meal was a failure: I'd burned a patty of ground beef and cooked frozen vegetables into a puree. But he'd praised my effort that night as if I'd prepared for him a meal worthy of five Michelin stars. I can still see him, trying to hack apart the patty with the side of his fork. It was solid as a hockey puck but he kept trying, pretending it was perfect.

That praise! How I hungered for his praise.

One time, before my grandmother taught me how to make my father's favorite dishes—Shepherd's pie, and stuffed cabbage, and sweet-and-sour fish—I overheard him say: "Charlotte can make stone soup and goose down pie taste marvelous." That was when I'd decided to become a chef. I almost applied to the CIA, the Culinary Institute of America, but the paperwork was seriously overwhelming, and the interview process distasteful: A clear impossibility.

"Sounds delicious," he said. "Save the leftovers for me."

I laughed. "I always do," I said.

He asked me about my car—a new starter had cured whatever was ailing the guts of that vehicle—and I asked him about his plans to surprise my mother with a trip to Alaska.

"Are you sure you should surprise her?" I'd asked in a whisper, nearly hoarse with the honor of complicity in his secret.

He had booked the cruise and was now working on flights. I urged him to spend the extra money on a non-stop flight. He was so frugal, my father. Even now, when he had everything, he still believed in economizing. He bought off-brand appliances and generic toiletries. He never paid for parking.

"Even better! We're flying first class!" He laughed, his big tenor laugh. "I figure, we have to work harder, your mother and I, to use up your inheritance."

My inheritance? "Well, wait a minute," I started. "When you put it like that, I can see a whole other scenario where connecting flights might be better!"

Such fun. We parried a while longer, until an incoming call bubbled its way into our lively repartee. At once, I wanted to pout and complain about the interruption. But I didn't have the chance.

"You sound good, Charlotte." His office persona had returned. "Is there anything you need? I mean, you called for a reason?"

A reason? What could I possibly say in the scant two minutes we had left? No reason, I'd assured him. No reason.

***

My father was not a hard man. He'd been born to parents of the Depression. His mother, my grandmother, hid coins under shelf paper so when the bread man came around, she could buy a loaf for dinner. My father was far more affluent than his parents. They owned a home and had two cars. My father, a physician, left the house every day wearing a suit. They were a typical American success story. Work hard and everything will fall into place. Never spend what you don't already have. My father had graduated high school two years ahead of his class. He earned his degree in medicine before he was twenty-two. By thirty, he'd started his own internal medicine practice, married the woman he'd met on a blind date, and had the two of us, four years apart. By every definition, a success.

His attention on me was acute. I did what I thought he wanted: I learned to sail, same as him. I planted seeds in the garden while he mowed the lawn and carried the bucket behind him when he emptied the dead frogs and slimy leaves out of the pool filters. I learned to play tennis and memorized the rules of pro football, his favorite sport. At the top of all his other hobbies, my father absolutely loved music.

Before the school year formally began, my father drove me to the high school with the printout of my class schedule in his hand. He helped me find my first few classes, helped me familiarize myself with the wide hallways and sky-lit stairwells. As we walked into what would be my homeroom, I felt my body contract. My neck itched and I imagined the skin was blistering in hives just under the collar of my shirt. My breath was noisy.

"Don't do that," my father said, holding one of my terrified shoulders still. "Don't overreact." Then, he looked over the top of my frizzy hair and smiled. "Hey, look," he said to me. "Here comes Mr. Nelson." The music teacher also taught at the middle school, and I was one of his favorite students. He was rotund, like a marshmallow-coated bowling ball. He held out his hand for my father's.

"I was hoping I'd find you here," Mr. Nelson said. His mouth was a slit opening horizontally above his many chins. From my vantage point, a few inches below and to the side, his neck looked surprisingly like a short stack of pancakes. "Come on," he said, turning. "The uniforms are this way."

Uniforms? I looked to my father for an explanation, but he was ahead of me, in stride with Mr. Nelson. Tweedle-Dee and Tweedle-Dum, I remember thinking.

My father called to me from inside the storage closet. "Mr. Nelson called earlier in the week," he offered a weak explanation, "and he said you could get your band uniform ahead of schedule." He held open a pair of cherry red trousers, wide at the waist. Special ordered, I knew immediately, and my heart rolled itself into a fist and began punching at me from the inside, slowly at first and then faster until my pulse was a drumroll rising to a crescendo.

When we returned home, my mother was in the den, reading. Anticipation leached out of her like licks of fire, pulling her to her feet. I realized she'd been waiting for us to return.

"Got it," my father said as if he'd just figured out how an equation was solved. He tossed the uniform, still attached to the double hanger, over the back of the sofa.

My mother held up the jacket, her eyebrows were taut umbrellas. "This is so exciting!" she gushed, and for a moment, I was able to share her enthusiasm. Yes, the uniforms were beautiful. Red and white, our school colors. The double-breasted jacket had two rows of shiny buttons spaced far apart. The shoulders were stiff and square, fortified from within. "Does it need to be shortened?" She posed the question to my father, who was already busy doing something else.

Of course it needed to be shortened. It was a men's size, Portly/Medium. The sleeves extended beyond my fingernails. The pants fell to the floor like theatre drapes. My mother stood near me for a moment, thinking, feeling the rough material of the uniform between her spiny fingers. "We can do this later," she said, smoothing my frazzled hair with a cool hand. I went to my room and closed the door, spending the rest of that day staring into the mouse habitat erected on my dresser and wishing I were dead.

ELEVEN

Mr. Nelson cleaves the school's crowded hallways like Moses crossing the sea. His voice is a cannon, his gaze burns through rubber. Wild hair rims the equator of his knob-head and hangs in a straggly clump, oily curls knot down to his collar. A Fu Manchu beard juts from his chin like a tusk.

Mr. Nelson greets the students by name, engaging each with a bit of conversation. "You been practicing?" "How's that fast ball coming?"

He even likes the kids who scorn the music department. Like Jerry, a square-headed eleventh grader who dropped a dead mouse into the horn of a tuba before marching band practice. Jerry was never formally identified as the culprit, but we all knew he did it. Mr. Nelson was seen talking to him later that week, outside the school in the student's parking lot, and we all anticipated a fistfight or a police report, but nothing like that happened. Someone said Mr. Nelson hired Jerry to work on an old ATV he had stored in his garage, but I wasn't there, so I don't know if it's true.

Mr. Nelson is quite possibly a decent guy but I've decided to hate him. I hate his cheery disposition and the confident way he maneuvers in the hallways. I hate the way he looks at me. Like he and I share a secret.

One day at band practice Mr. Nelson looks at me, right in the eye, and then makes an announcement. He is handing out new music. We are going to sight-read a Mozart concerto.

I am second chair, meaning, I am the second-best bassoon player in the band. Kevin Keeger sits to my right. He is first chair. He plays all the main parts, and all the solos. Kevin is a very good bassoon player. He is also the worst kid in our school. He wears his red hair in a big Afro, long before anyone knew anything about Afros. His fingernails drape over the ends of his fingers. Sometimes I hear them click against the instrument's metal keys.

One day, as we're soaking our cane reeds in little Dixie cups of water before rehearsal, Kevin leans over and informs me: "You probably don't even know this," he says. "But when you play, your whole face turns into a blueberry," he twists his reed. "It swells up, and your eyes bulge out."

I turn away but that doesn't stop him from reporting that my double chin grows to twice its normal size when I'm concentrating on the music, so I accidentally knock over his cup of water and we both watch as his reed skitters on the floor and comes to rest, finally, against the metal foot of our shared music stand. The tip of a double reed is extremely thin, extremely fragile. We both know without looking: The reed is ruined.

Double-reed instruments are fussy. They need to be warmed by hand and by breath; good players will massage the maple wood with careful hands, avoiding the metal arms and keys too easily bent. By far, the trickiest part of a double-reed instrument is, well, the double reed. Most everyone who plays a double-reed instrument knows how to make their own reeds. This is an area where I excel. I love making reeds. Honing the knife, wrapping the wire, and cutting through the cane. I lose myself in the craft, spending hours practicing with the mandrel in one hand and the reed knife in the other. I like to make several reeds at once, all of them wrapped in neon blue wire. I line them up on the windowsill to dry before tending to their tips. The tip is critical. Often, when I go to sleep, an army of reed soldiers lay sleeping overhead on that sill, their little blue uniforms spaced carefully apart.

I suck my reed in my mouth and make crazy eyebrows at Kevin, hoping for some sort of bassoon-comradery.

Mr. Nelson is busy with the sheet music. The pages pass from hand to hand, each person groans with real or feigned nervousness. When I see the title on the bassoon score, I almost jump out of my skin. The Mozart concerto in B Flat.

My father says I play a "mean bassoon" and I choose to believe him. He sits on the bed while I practice at the flimsy music stand bought at someone's garage sale. He applauds when I reach the end of a phrase and apologizes when I complain of his frequent interruptions. Music makes me feel good, as if I am part of something lovely.

My father also plays the bassoon, and he likes to take out his old instrument so we can play together. We have these crazy music sets that let you play along with a symphony recorded on a vinyl record. Music Minus One. We sit side by side, sharing the sheet music while a professional orchestra plays on the stereo set on the loudest volume setting. The Mozart bassoon concerto is one of our favorites. We listen to it on the phonograph, we play along, I can hum the familiar melodies without even looking at the music. I know it well.

"Miss Lansing," Mr. Nelson points the conductor's wand at my forehead. "Can you play for us the bassoon part beginning at measure thirty-five?"

He could call on Kevin. But he calls on me.

The bassoon Concerto in B Flat by Mozart. I know the notes, and yet my fingers refuse to settle over the keys. He has that effect on people, Mr. Nelson—he can make a normal person stutter. I will not let him rattle me. I rest the reed against my tongue, soothed by the familiar texture of the perfectly shaved wood. If the reed is candy, it would be a watermelon-flavored Jolly Rancher. I relax my fingers into position and take a controlled breath.

The nervous dread of every student in the symphonic band settles over me as I seal my lips around the reed. As far as band practice goes, this is the worst-case scenario. No one likes to play alone. And certainly not on a new piece of music. I rub my fingers against the keys as if they itch and begin to play.

What a feeling! The notes flow from my fingers.

The familiar music replaces my dread, I am consumed by the beauty of the melody and the vibrating comfort of my bassoon. My fingers are limber. My embouchure is sure. I hear my sound—it's lovely. The most difficult passage is ahead, a full three measures of triplets and trills. I am not afraid. I draw in a breath and glance up at Mr. Nelson. His face glows. I play. My breath warms the wood, my fingers manipulate the keys with such fluidity, I wonder if they retain the memory of playing this piece with my father. I play and play and feel the pleasure of the music filling my heart. My sound is mellow and rich. I love this feeling. I love the sound and the tone and the melody that bays from the bell of my instrument. Most of all, I love being the person making the music.

I finish, hold the instrument in place, not moving. A moment ticks, and then another. And then, I hear the scuffing of shoes on the school floor. Applause, musician-style. I am at once the happiest I've ever been.

Mr. Nelson clanged his baton against the metal music stand and smiled at me. Applause. Applause. My skin tingled. I knew my face was sweaty and likely blueberry hued, but I didn't care. For once, I didn't care.

The bell rings and I am still soaring. Mr. Nelson offers me a beatific smile and collects the sheet music. We are done with the Mozart concerto. Kevin practically throws the music into the hands of the oboist who sits right in front of us. He is mad. He hadn't brought another reed, so he had to wait out the remainder of the period with his bassoon across his lap, forty full minutes of turning the pages of the music for me. His irritation is potent as vinegar.

My high lasts throughout the school day and follows me as I cross the plaza outside, carrying my bassoon case in two hands. My heart is dancing. I feel impossibly tall, which is a real feat for a girl who never breaks five feet.

Wait till I tell my father about the solo! I walk fast, eager to get to a phone.

Kevin calls out. "Hey! Fat Charlotte," he sneers. "Bet you're feeling pretty good right now."

I am elevated with pride, and I don't immediately sense his nefarious tenor.

Kevin is sitting on top of his bassoon case, surrounded by a small band of boys. Tenth graders like me. And one senior, a kid I've known since kindergarten.

I am a walker. I'll cut across the student parking lot until I reach the main road. In five minutes, I'll be at my grandmother's house where I'll call my father at the office. He won't mind being interrupted. Not for good news.

The bassoon case bangs against my leg. I am almost to the curb when I hear them. Oinking. The volume increased, guttural and gross. Oink! Oink!

I will never tell my father about the solo.

TWELVE

"Did you ask him?" Jimbo was waiting for me, although you'd never know it from his posture. He was lying on his side, nearly fetal, tucked into a cavern in the couch. All around him, cushions swelled. The remains of the breakfast I'd made, runny eggs and sausage and bacon and ham, stained the dinner plate he'd shoved aside on the sofa.

I stood against the wall and closed my eyes. In my mind, my father's gaze held me securely. I wanted to remain there, in that image, with him. Taking care of me. Keeping me safe.

"What did he say about the trust?"

I opened my eyes. Jimbo's attention was on me; his eyeballs were glass river stones, smooth and slick. He mouthed at his own lips, like a sleeping puppy sucking at an absent teat.

"Obviously, the money is yours." Jimbo continued a sentence he'd clearly begun in his head. I peered at him and tried to grasp on to his thread. "They wouldn't have set it aside unless they meant for you to use it."

Oh, the trust.

When Celia married and I did not, my father moved the money, my wedding money, into a trust in my name. For my future.

"So? What did he say?" Jimbo focused his eyes on me, and I was immediately alarmed. What was that tight expression in his stare? Was he disappointed? Upset?

I needed a minute. I went into the kitchen and started the electric kettle and began to rummage in the drawer, making a lot of noise, hunting down a tea bag in the clutter of Jimbo's collectables. Bottle caps and pull tabs were the focus of his latest recycling scheme. *For every one hundred metal tabs and caps, you get ten dollars.* Previously abandoned collection items were like litter in the drawer: rubber bands, paper clips, expired Lottery tickets, twist ties. There were no tea bags.

I squeezed some honey into a mug and added the boiling water, watching the swirls eddy and still. A shake of cinnamon, a squirt of lemon juice, a teaspoon of brown sugar. My father's voice wafted from the sweet-smelling mixture, soothing, silly. The happy sound warmed my stomach. I said, "They're planning a trip."

"Who?"

"My father. He's planning a surprise birthday trip for my mother. She hates surprises, but he seems to think this one is a good idea. I tried to talk him out of it. But you know. My father is pretty stubborn."

Jimbo leaned forward, perching a little bit over the edge of the couch. His flaccid feet remained harbored like infants under the afghan my grandmother made for me. The skin over his skull shined like a stretched rubber mask.

"Are you okay?" I came closer and sat on the armrest at his feet. "You look like you're about to hurl." Jimbo loved that word: hurl. If he was upset about something, a funny word might bring him around. I sipped the honey-water and smiled, hoping.

"I could hurl." The words foamed from his mouth and hung, quivering, in the living room's stagnant air.

My stomach tightened. "What's wrong? Did you take your pain pills on an empty stomach?" Normally, I'd bring him a full meal before every dose of medication. I looked at the clock. I'd been gone more than two hours.

"I thought you were going to talk to him about the trust." He drew his knees up. His eyes stretched wide with disappointment. "How come you didn't ask him?"

He was right. I'd gone to my father with a purpose. A plan. Jimbo and I had rehearsed it. We'd fashioned my presentation after an episode of Judge Judy, one of our favorite shows, where a woman made a case against her benefactor for withholding funds in her name. The trust was in my name. I should receive that money. I should have stood up for us.

"I don't think your father is being a nice man," he whispered. "Maybe he doesn't want us to have nice things. I don't know." He coughed, choking on an accumulation of saliva and mucus.

The sides of my throat constricted. Was I doing something wrong?

"And now I'm so tense, I think I pulled a muscle in my neck." Jimbo reached for his medicine pouch resting near my hip. The zipper snagged; I took it from his struggling hands and opened it, displaying rows of identical medicine bottles held in place by elastic bands. Some of the vials were nearly empty, even though I'd just refilled them this morning. I always make sure he has what he needs in his medicine pouch. How many pills had he taken while I was out?

"Which one?" I asked.

He pointed. Xanax. I poured the tablets into his hand and handed him the mug of hot water. He set a few pills on the windowsill and swallowed the rest.

"I am supposed to be your first priority," he said, bleakly. "That's what my mother told me. You are supposed to think about me first. Me." He jabbed his dainty thumb to his chest.

I nodded. "I'm sorry," I said. "I didn't forget about you, about us. I just got caught up in his excitement over the birthday trip. Please don't be upset."

"I don't like to be alone," he whimpered. "That's why I got worried." His eyes bled tears. I blotted at them gently with the napkin I had tucked up my sleeve. His lips glistened. "There was no one here to take care of me." A droplet the color of ice slid across his temple.

He needed me. My chest ached as the tendrils of his love enveloped me slowly, creeping over me like the thin fibers of a web, braiding, knotting, securing its firm hold on its prey. I sat very still, entranced. This was all I ever wanted.

I set the mug down on the sill and pushed it far out of reach as if it were radioactive. Steam fogged the dirty windowpane; a plume began to grow on the glass. I knelt, close to his head.

"I am sorry," I leaned down and nuzzled his neck.

"Good. That's settled." He tried to snap his fingers, to punctuate his words, but his fingers slipped, the snap failed. "You are my wife. Not his child."

"Can't I be both?"

"No." There. He said it. The missive emerged like a bear from a cave, cruddy with the long wait and hungry for attention. The firmness of the word seeped into my skin and sent a shiver through my limbs. I was afraid. Of what, I can't be sure.

"Are you saying you want me to discontinue my relationship with my father?" I spoke very slowly, carefully.

"I told you," he released a spray of saliva. "I'm needy."

I remembered that. He'd said that. And I'd agreed—no, I'd celebrated those words. They were exactly what I'd wanted to hear.

"You are supposed to want what I want." He was quieter now, leaning back, speaking with oily ease; Xanax diluted his words.

"You take care of me, and I take care of you. This is the way it's supposed to be." He closed his eyes. But I knew he wasn't asleep. "You know, I knew we were meant for each other," he said. His pupils were molten ink. "From the moment when you rescued me outside the 7-Eleven. I knew we were going to be together."

There it was: the devotion I'd craved, the love I'd always wanted. I was so happy, I saw stars.

He took my hand and intertwined our fingers. "I felt it in my bones," he said. "I just knew! Like a sixth sense. Now I know how a pig knows when the weather is about to change."

A pig? He had to use a pig as his example? I felt the hairs on my arms rise in protest, but he'd already started to snore.

I sucked in a quick breath. I'd told Jimbo about the boys in school and the way they oinked at me. I'd told him. He knew! I pressed my lips and tried to assemble words of objection, but nothing came.

As his body filled with air, a blister of spittle jiggled on his lower lip and his soft palate purred. He was like a big, soft puppy. He just needed a little guidance, that's all. We hadn't been together long. We were still in our adjustment period. Plus, he had obviously overmedicated himself again. I watched his nostrils swell with every exhale. Was he asleep? I saw a crescent of white lens peeking through his faint lashes.

"Wife?" he called for me.

"I'm here," my voice was froggy.

"Come to me, wife."

My heart surrendered. I lowered myself to the floor, to my knees, and I crawled to him, leading with my chin and following with my whole being.

"I have a present for you," he said. My face hovered over his body and came to rest on his pillowy chest. His fingertips found my lips. I opened my baby bird mouth and accepted the feed from his fingers. First one pill, then another.

The room faded out, like a watercolor in a misting rain. The couch, the wall, the afghan; everything became speckled and blurred, and eventually I saw nothing but the effervescent light of dust motes floating in the late afternoon rays. I was quiet, on my knees, in the very posture of servitude, leaning into the couch that cradled my husband when sleep finally took me.

***

It was probably no surprise that I broke away from the ideal of my father's expectations with some dramatic result. Like many girls, my teen years were about dissent. I challenged his demands, refusing to excel in school and neglecting my chores. We argued, we debated. His stubbornness was matched by my stubbornness. I would not do what he insisted. I could not. And the harder he pushed, the farther I went. I got an amateurish multicolored butterfly tattoo on my shoulder. I wore tie-dyed peasant tops without a bra so that my double-D breasts flopped around like rabbit ears. I hardly washed or brushed my hair; it knotted into wooly ropes, dreadlocks, that I stuffed under felt hats covered in anti-establishment buttons. I smoked cigarettes and wore pink-tinted Janis Joplin glasses. I brought home disciplinary notices.

"What is going on with you?" He inquired, holding a letter in his hand. "This says you're going to fail math. I thought that was one of your favorite subjects."

"What do I need math for? Everyone has a calculator," I explained. "It's such a waste of time. Who cares about the Pythagorean theorem anyway? Have you ever needed it in your daily life looking down people's throats?" Treading on dangerous ground, I felt my blood accelerate, rushing to my head. Would he hit me?

He never struck us. Never, not once. Maybe that's what I wanted. Maybe I wanted a gesture of disconnection, a radical severing of the parental cord. I don't know. I remember having a constant hunger in my belly, an emptiness, always wanting for something. Wanting and wanting. I wanted to be thin. I wanted to be popular. I wanted love and friendship and success.

"How will you succeed if you don't study?" He'd challenge me. "You're never going to get a job if you don't try and learn something."

A job? I didn't want a job. That was not the graph I'd envisioned for myself. I recoiled against him with all my energies. I fought him, I raged against him. I decried his accomplishments and belittled his ideals. If we'd had a weapon in the house, we'd have used it against one another.

Finally, high school came to an end. My father's alma mater offered me admission even though I'd yet to submit my application. He was on the board of directors of the college, and he taught one class each semester in biology or anatomy or something like that. He'd gone to this small college because his parents could not afford a better school. I went there because my father was able to get me in. In fact, I didn't submit one completed application to any college. Years later, I'd find all the blank applications in my bottom desk drawer. I pretended to want to go to college. That was my mistake. He perceived I was capable of surviving in college. His was a costlier mistake.

THIRTEEN

My college roommate, Elayne, an exchange student from Togo, stayed up through the night talking with her boyfriend in French on her phone. She smoked pot out of an exotic-looking water pipe that she'd brought all the way from Africa. On her tiny and illegal cooktop, she heated spices that burned the hairs in my nose and cloyed to my skin. I smelled like smoked game meat. She and her friends from the International Student's Union hung out in our room, smoking and jabbering, their gleaming dark eyes skittering over me. I would have understood the insults in any language: *gros, laid, neglige, lent.*

Weed was the only good thing about college. Elayne stole a tray from the cafeteria and used it to sift through the stash, tossing stems and seeds onto the floor where I swept them up in a piece of notebook paper and threw them in the toilet down the hall. In exchange, Elayne kept me supplied with joints which became something of a lure. Men began to seek me out. "You have weed?" I was popular. I invited strangers to my room and pretended they were friends. I shared my supply with any man who looked interested. I was stoned most of the time. At first, being high blotted out my memories. The pain of rejection and ridicule melted away, and I had moments of happiness. But then, the high changed. I became consumed with the injustices of the past, and I focused on the hurt. The ridicule. The noises. The "Hey Hey Hey, Fat Albert" imitations.

In October of my freshman year, I stopped going to class. Any class. At first, I felt a little guilty when I watched the ant armies of students marching toward the campus. I pretended. I carried around my knapsack, I left paper in my typewriter. I went to the cafeteria and pretended to read a textbook while I ate tater tots and mashed potatoes and fried chicken and macaroni and cheese.

In November, I informed my father I would not continue with my education. Not for me. No can do. No way, man.

"You mean, you're giving up?" he asked, incredulous. He didn't like quitters. He liked people who overcame obstacles and fought hard against challenging circumstances as he did, being a child of the depression and all that. I knew he would have trouble accepting Jimbo into our family.

He thrived on facts. Sometimes, when I talked to him, when I approached him with a new business idea or with a request for money, he'd grill me like a courtroom prosecutor. What was I planning to do, how was I planning to do it? He wanted to know that I'd done my due diligence, that I'd investigated and studied each opportunity. Where I liked vagaries, he liked specifics, details.

I knew that he'd request a lot of information about Jimbo before he could begin to embrace him. I also knew that he would not approve of Jimbo's lifestyle. Our lifestyle. To avoid risking my father's aversion, I glossed over much of the technical subject matter. I wooed his approval, silently displaying my happiness as a peacock fans its feathers. Look at me, I strutted before him. I'm a worthwhile person, a loved person.

I thought he'd be happy to see me so happy. I thought it was obvious: we were a couple in love. What else could we possibly need? Sure, we had some problems. Jimbo was dependent on medication. But I could handle that. He had few skills, but I had enough for both of us. Years of living alone, a single woman alone, had prepared me to face almost anything. I thought my father would find my positions clever, my methods clear.

When they met, Jimbo made a good impression, I thought. He'd been polite, he used his manners, and he ate everything my mother put on the table. We had scones and coffee, even though Jimbo didn't like coffee. He was hypersensitive to caffeine. Another thing we had in common.

I'd prepared my father in advance.

"What do you mean he doesn't work?"

I explained. "He does some computer tech stuff that I don't really understand." I made a face like a woman need not understand her man's business. "Plus, he has money to live on. He has a trust. What more do you want?"

My father pressed on. "But what does he *do*?"

"Do?"

"I mean, if he doesn't work, what does he do all day while you're at your job?" My job. I wouldn't be a court clerk much longer. I wanted only to be with Jimbo, at home. I wouldn't tell my father that. He had an image stuck in his head: success and money and achievement. These concepts held him firm and made my father unable to appreciate anyone who lived differently. We agreed, my husband and I, to remain polite and nonreactive, to maintain the balance I'd worked so hard to gain. It worked, for a while.

But our battles continued. My father did not like the way we lived; our carelessness bothered him. "How can you buy another computer if you don't have any income?" he'd bark over the phone. I'd hold out the receiver so Jimbo could hear the rant, and we'd giggle as silently as we could at the old man's closed-mindedness. "You must keep up with the maintenance," he chastised me when a corner of the roof fell off. I'd known the squirrels were up there for a couple of years, but I did nothing to deter them from nesting in the eave. Eventually, they gnawed their way through the frame and dislocated the joists from the beams. "Had you been more cautious, this would have never happened," he admonished me as he wrote out the check. He paid for most repairs to the house. That was also part of our balance.

FOURTEEN

I am in charge of making the party favors for the guests at Celia's wedding. What an honor. I am creating a series of crepe paper boxes, one for each person, each a different color. Each box will hold individually wrapped, homemade truffles, probably four per box. Only the most skilled chocolatier can produce a perfect truffle. It's one of my specialties thanks to a job I had in a homemade chocolate shop back in the college town where I lived for a while. Truffles are the apex candy of all the chocolate confections. Plus, they smell like love.

The doorbell is a welcome interruption. My hands are cramped with overuse. It's Celia; I heard her car crunching on the gravel drive. I light a cigarette and lean back, waiting for her to come inside.

"Open up," she shouts.

"Just push the door!" I yell back. "It's open."

I have glue on my fingertips. I pat them together, playful. Celia has also been busy with wedding plans. She invites me to come along on all the wedding planning appointments, but I don't see the need. The last thing I want to do is sit in a room and talk about someone else's party. Even Celia's. Plus, she tells me everything afterwards, so I hardly need to waste an outfit when it's easier to stay home in my nightgown and do what I want. Sometimes, I do feel a little discarded. Like when they met with the caterer and talked about the desserts. I wanted Celia to ask me to make the desserts, but she never did, which surprised me.

She liked the hilarious figures I made out of chocolates. Chocolate horses on a rotating platform. Chocolate birds to clip into the floral arrangements. For a while I thought about opening a chocolate-making business, but I never followed up.

"You should have seen Dad's face," Celia reported back after a long meeting with the wedding planner. "The caterer showed up in a Rolls Royce." She told me about the samples, the choices, the tasting. "At the end, the caterer slid a piece of paper across the table to Dad. The price. He looked at it, and asked how many affairs cancel at the last minute. The caterer guessed, about ten percent. Less than ten percent of prepaid contracts are canceled. So Dad looked her dead in the eye and said, 'Do you do funerals?'" Just like my father, to consider all the possibilities for his investment.

Celia is shouting from the front stoop. "Open the door. My hands are full."

I shove a chair back and take my time standing. I fix a cigarette into the corner of my lips and shuffle toward the door. Celia will laugh at me. My ratty nightgown. My bare feet. Cigarette dangling. A vision, she'll say. I pop the door open.

Celia is standing on the stoop with a dog in her arms. Not a dog, but a puppy. Blond, shaggy, sleeping. "This is Albie," she says, pushing him at me. "Your birthday dog."

She plucks the cigarette from my lips and chucks it into the dirt. "You don't want to give your new dog cancer on the first day." She pushes into the house.

The dog's heart pitter-patters, his limbs are limp and soft. In fact, his whole body is limp and soft. My birthday dog? I don't nitpick that my thirtieth birthday is still four months away. She knows.

"What's the matter with him?" I ask, following Celia inside. She has a history of bringing me dogs with issues. A three-legged poodle-mix with a skin problem. A blind Irish setter. Dogs that no one wants.

The puppy squirms, but only a little bit. His body hangs heavy in my arms; one leg hangs down, warming my stomach. I jostle his weight. "He's heavy."

Albie lifts his nose as if responding to the sound of my voice. His snout presses on the underside of my chin. I smell his puppy breath.

"He's exhausted," Celia explains. "He had a bath and some vaccinations. He's had all his shots, for now." She has pages to share, official looking reproductions of medical reports and records. "You'll need these," she looks around for a clear landing place. The table is littered with craft materials. The kitchen counters are busy with ingredients. "I'll put these on your bed."

I sit on the couch with Albie tucked close. His fur lies in ripples, like the surface of the water when the wind is light. His ears hang from his head, velvety butterscotch drapes. He repositions himself, pulling his long hind legs forward. His belly is spotted and pink as a piglet.

Celia returns from the bedroom and observes the art project. "How is this going?" She asks, picking up one of the finished boxes and turning it in her hands. Glitter showers from her fingertips, cascading down like silvery mist. "These are so beautiful, Char. So delicate."

I run my hand along the dog's leg. The muscle is spongy like taffy, I massage his shoulder, his thigh, his foot. He has big feet.

His whole body wiggles. "Oh, you're ticklish?" I busy my finger in between his pads and Celia laughs as he tries to escape my lap. She kneels on the floor. We have all four of our hands on the dog's pelt.

I've been dogless for about a year, since Angel was hit by a car backing out of the driveway. I still have a Costco bag of dog food in the back closet.

"I thought he would make you happy," she says, rubbing his ears between her manicured fingers. His tail falls between my knees, he is belly-up, his limbs in swimming bliss.

I am happy. I am happy for her. I'm happy that she's getting married and I'm happy that she found Mike. He is a happy addition to our family. But there is a limited amount of other people's happiness that I can tolerate. I will have Albie for twelve years, until he gets some kind of digestive disease. He will die in my arms, in the back seat of my father's Lincoln Continental, en route to the animal hospital where the on-call veterinarian waits with a box of tissues imprinted with tiny dog bones in hand.

Buddhists believe that every day of life is worth more than all the treasures of the universe. I read that somewhere. But what if each day is unmemorable? What is there to gain by waking up anew to another day of sameness?

Celia is lucky: she wakes up happy. She has purpose. For me, there is nothing. Nothing.

Those who greet the day each day with anticipation are the lucky ones. They have purpose. They know their role. For the rest of us, there is nothing. Just the daily rhythm of the breath, the slow and somber pulse as we march toward our end. Because we are all going to die, if not now, then soon. Life is interminably hard, insufferably drawn out. Even the good days are not to be trusted. Happiness is borrowed, too quickly called back. Your allotment of happiness has been exceeded. Your credit line of appreciations is limited. You are not permitted the luxury of pleasantness, of confidence in a steady wind. There are gale storms just past the horizon line. And then, dead calm. Irons, it's called on the sea. Bleak and black and endless. Feel lucky if you do not possess that knowledge, if you are confused or confounded by my conclusions. Those of us who know are not meant for longevity.

FIFTEEN

Every morning, I went to 7-Eleven to get cigarettes and coffee, and the racing sheets for Jimbo. He loved the trotters. I didn't know the first thing about horse racing, so he promised to take me to the track one day. It didn't matter that one day never came. He shared with me his vast knowledge of horse racing as we sat, side by side, on the couch, watching the races on television. I was happy for him when a cousin invited him to the track. I listened to his assessments on the horses, the trainers, and the jockeys as I drove him to his cousin's house two hours away, soaking in his happiness. I didn't think about my current unemployment or not having friends or spending too much of my parents' money. I didn't care about the news or the weather or the traffic or anything outside of my cozy two-person capsule. I didn't mind that the garage was now full of Jimbo's favorite soda water—cases and cases of soda water stacked tall as walls—forcing me to park in the street. He liked it when I made cocktails of apple juice and soda water. I had what I wanted.

I was still at home when my mother called.

"What are you up to today?"

My head was still foggy from the night. I was not a good sleeper, but Jimbo had a sure-fire sleeping pill in his medicine kit, a specialty concoction prepared by his friend, an ex-pharmacist who'd lost his practitioner's license due to bogus claims of product distribution. I don't know what the sleeping pill's ingredients were. I didn't care. I felt a little bad about skipping my morning visit with Plots, but that didn't seem to matter either. I slept.

"I'm just coming around." I'd been outside already, smoking in my broken chaise, breathing in the decay and cigarette smoke in equal portions. All around, the yard looked bad. The flowering plum tree Celia bought for my fiftieth birthday had lost its leaves over the course of the year. Too much water? Too little water? I'd neglected to research the needs of the tree, something I used to do. I hadn't seeded the vegetable garden early enough this year, so the raised platform beds that my father helped me build lay barren and fallow, a graveyard of weeds and dilapidated fencing.

The toilet flushed. Jimbo was awake.

"I'm putting together a shelf for Jimbo's books," I told my mother.

Jimbo had a massive paperback book collection. Hundreds and hundreds of mysteries, romances, science fiction, and history books. I'd borrowed Celia's wagon to move Jimbo from his mother's house. We must have made four trips just for his books. I thought my mother would like him because he's a voracious reader, but she never said anything.

"I'm going to put it in the alcove under the window where my sewing table was," I said, moving past a pile of old newspapers that nearly blocked the kitchen doorway. My mother liked this sort of conversation. House decorating, reorganization. "I need to put all these books into some kind of order, or Jimbo and I won't have any room to move around. There are books everywhere, in the kitchen, in the spare bedroom. There are even some in the gardening shed." My mother bought that shed for me as a birthday gift, or maybe it was for Valentine's. Lars Belnoir, who lived two houses down assembled it in the back corner of my yard. Lars worked part-time at the CVS on Sunrise Highway. He knew how to do things. My mother paid him cash that I wouldn't have minded for myself.

Jimbo came into the kitchen wearing his favorite blue pajamas. I passed him a bowl and a box of Lucky Charms.

I held the phone steady with my chin and reached for the milk.

The refrigerator door was not set firmly in its hinges. When the door was open, the top bracket yielded a little bit, causing the door to tilt. I needed two hands to close it properly. I slid the phone into the pocket of my bathrobe and shut the door.

Her voice strained from my pocket. "What about your sewing machine?" she asked. My workstation was an incidental now, unimportant. "Where will you work on your quilting? You do such beautiful work. Don't give it up."

She so clearly did not understand. My life was so much better now that I wasn't alone every single night, watching reruns of old television shows and pretending to be busy. I'd spent the previous twenty years in the company of crafts. I knitted, quilted, needlepointed, and folded origami. I made macramé wall hangings and crocheted king-sized afghans. I beaded, collaged…I did them all.

"I don't need to quilt," I told her. In truth, I had already sold my sewing machine and spent the cash on a crock pot. Jimbo loved pot roast; his mother used to make it in a crock pot.

"Try and remember," my mother was still talking. I rolled my eyes at Jimbo and he passed me a Xanax, which I swallowed without water. "You have your own life. Don't lose yourself. Keep your hobbies. Feed your own interests."

My hobbies? The last thing in the world I wanted was more alone time to sew or stamp or paste. I'd had enough isolation. Enough one-sided conversations with dogs. Having another person in the house was so satisfying. I made the whole box of pasta for my super rich bolognaise sauce. I roasted a whole pork tenderloin, a full-sized roasting chicken. I'd stopped replenishing my Tupperware supply. With two people, there were never any leftovers.

Jimbo had never kept a home. I had to teach him the basics like how to turn on the dishwasher and how to load laundry into the machine. For a time, I thought he'd share some of these tasks with me, but I was wrong. I didn't care. It didn't matter.

If I brought homemaking into his experience, he brought a life of belonging into mine. I was finally included into the mainstream of We. God, how I loved that pronoun. We watched *Law and Order*. We're having lunch. We like spaghetti.

In Walmart, we raced wheelchair shopping carts side by side, and I commiserated with the checkout lady about husbands who don't remember to reload the toilet paper holder while Jimbo fumbled to find the proper coupons in the clippings folder. We shouted our orders into the drive-thru microphone, sets of two. Two cokes. Two pot pies. Two. Two. Two. Two is an even number.

Two is a number that implies balance. Two is magic.

We went to all our appointments together. We sat close together in doctor's office waiting rooms. We helped diagnose each other, reviewing symptomology and incidences in complicated conversations. We got most of our information from the internet. We shared the same issues. Pain. Distress. Nonspecific discomforts.

Jimbo introduced me to his pain management doctor, who was a friend of a cousin, and who wrote prescriptions for the lollipops that Jimbo loved. Morphine pops. Fentanyl pops. The pain doctor took care of all Jimbo's refills. All his therapies. We bought discount packs of spinal epidurals that we scheduled together so we could hold hands during the procedures.

At night, we rested together in bed, holding hands and watching television. I felt like I was finally able to breathe for the very first time; every pill was a revelation, every treatment a discovery.

I called him Husband and he called me Wife.

Wife! I loved the sound of that word! For the first time in my life, I was part of the club, an honored guest in the secret society called marriage. All the defenses I'd built up, the hobbies, the small friendships, the hours and hours of recorded television entertainment, were like sunfish boats set asea. Gone. Disappeared with all the mishaps and stories of my single life onboard.

I'd always believed that marriage was a happy place.

"I'm so glad I married your grandfather," my grandmother spoke with the satisfaction of a person who'd made good choices. Apparently, she'd been dating another guy when she met my grandfather. He'd stolen her away, she recalled the fairy tale element of their union. My grandfather had died at the best part of her life, leaving her alone for the hardest part, old age, and yet she talked of their time together with simple lightness.

"He used to surprise me every Halloween," she recalled. "He'd put on a rubbery face mask and go around the side of the house to ring the front doorbell. When I'd answer, he'd yell, "Trick or Treat!" He also used to drop her off places and forget to pick her up. And he wandered off every time they had company to the house, preferring the companionship of his dog and his pipe to socializing with people. But mostly, she'd been happy.

My parents did not share any of their marriage difficulties. I do remember one large container of flowers delivered to the house with a note in my father's handwriting that read: Anger makes wrinkles. "You get used to each other," my mother provided wisdom in small packages when we were girls. Maybe she confided in more detail to Celia who married at twenty-six and therefore had a need for more serious information. There was much I'd missed as a single person. I am sure I idealized my parents' marriage, but what child doesn't? By the time I got married, my parents had already passed their fifty-third anniversary.

My sister never suffered an unhappy married day. But then, it is possible that the difficulties she encountered were not shared with me. She was, in some ways, like my mother. Reluctant to share too much about her own issues What she did share were the insignificant mishaps, the minor snafus of living as a pair. Conflicts over paint colors. Unleaded gas in the car or premium. Small insults. Habits and tics of silly annoyances.

If I hadn't met Jimbo, I'd have never known what it means to absorb another person, to join as one. The secrets afforded to the married were at once offered to me and I soared. What a marvel, to be a couple! To share the air with someone, to sit quietly and listen to each other's breaths. I learned his sounds and he learned mine. His stomach percolated while he slept. His urine splashed in the toilet water like spring rain, delicate and intermittent. The patter of his pale bare feet on the laminate flooring was soft as ballet, for a pudgy man he walked with an angel's grace.

We kissed. We kissed and tickled and tumbled on top of one another. What had been a terrifying concept, that I would never be loved, became a known trust: he loved me. Jimbo loved me. And he showed his love in attention and hugs and in a constant consciousness of my well-being. "How do you feel?" he'd ask, and I'd answer, "I feel with my hands." This was our private language, our secret banter. It meant: I am so happy to be with you.

I loved making his pastrami sandwiches on wheat and driving him to his appointments. I loved watching his favorite television shows and learning how to read the horse racing sheets. I loved everything about him. That we could not have sex didn't really bother me. I welcomed him into my bed as you'd welcome a discomfited child who scurries under the blankets for shelter during a lightning storm. Come to me. Lie with me. Let me stroke your face.

Every night at eight, Jimbo calls his mother. They have a very strong connection. Indeed, they share an intense history.

After the car accident that killed his father, Jimbo took to his bed, in his mother's house. She cooked his meals, delivered his meds. She drove him to doctors' appointments and picked up his prescriptions. At night, she drew a chair up close to the bed and they watched television together. It was no wonder that she got a little persnickety when Jimbo and I started seeing each other. I was hoping she'd be happy for us.

That she will not come to our little wedding is a serious disappointment, but no matter how I press, he is unable to convince her. I am already planning the party. I want bowls of jellybeans on the tables, servers dressed in renaissance costumes, and an old-fashioned popcorn machine with a butter dispenser stationed at the entrance. Also, I'm going to pass out party horns so everyone can participate in the festivity. I already invited the tattoo artist who opened a business in his garage across the street and a few of my better neighbors. Plots will come of course. And Perla, my friend.

Perla and I used to see a lot of each other. We'd visit after work, sometimes we cooked dinner on Perla's little Hibachi grill. I was a bookkeeper then, balancing payroll, paperwork, and soul-crushing boredom in the rangy back room of a dental office where I hardly ever saw another person other than the office manager, who poked her head into my space occasionally to say *Hello* and *Did you find the amended invoices I left for you.* I could have done the job in my sleep.

Perla lived in a tiny house on a large property owned by her parents who were rich, I think, back in Mexico. They'd tried for a few years to fix her up with a husband from their country, but no one would have her because of her scars. She'd had shingles as a teen which left her face puckered and pinched from her forehead to her neck. One side of her mouth hitched up as if lifted by a pulley. Perla had a menial job, a receptionist I think, in her uncle's small appliance repair shop. She lived a quiet life, like mine. We had similar comfort zones, keeping mostly out of sight, satisfied with our homey crafts and our little survivals. But that was before.

One night, at eight, Perla called and asked if I'd like to go shopping at the discount bazaar with her on a Saturday, an activity we used to do together.

"I can't," I told her. "Jimbo doesn't like when I go out without him."

"So bring him," she said.

I heard him mumbling to his mother. "My legs hurt," I heard. "I can hardly walk."

"He has trouble walking."

"He can walk next to me," she said. "That way, he won't feel self-conscious."

I felt a momentary pang of missing the amusing banter of her friendship. Perla and I had a lot of good talks, we had some fun here and there. Mainly, we occupied each other's time when no one else would. But I didn't need her anymore. I'd shed her along with my single woman designation. I didn't need friends. I had Jimbo.

Perla was not letting go. "Just because you have a husband does not mean you need to ditch all your friends, stop having fun," she challenged. "Remember that Halloween party?" She made me smile. I loved parties, I always had.

"Remember?" she said. "God, we had the most fun!"

SIXTEEN

The front door to my apartment sticks. You have to push the key all the way to the hilt and then pull it halfway out before trying to turn it. I can usually get it to open on the first try, but not today. The cold air makes the lock stubborn. I lean back against the door, resting a minute. It's not much past sun-up, the damp fog of morning is still hovering over the gravel lawn. I've been shopping since before dawn at the 24-hour super store. Bags of groceries sag on the rain-wet stoop between my feet.

I bite my gloves off and try again. One day, I will bring my tool kit out here and fix this damn thing. Spray some WD-40 in there. I'm handy, like my father. The lock clicks open.

"You get up too early." Bentley, my neighbor, is in our parking lot, coming home from his night shift. He works security, guarding an impound lot near the airport. His holstered revolver jangles at his thigh. It's not a real gun. It's a taser. Bentley has taken, and failed, the police entrance exam twice.

"Need help?" He nods at the door. Bentley is a big guy, but defeat makes him seem small.

He shoulders the door and it falls open. My feet slip on the almost-icy cement. One of the grocery bags tears, spilling lemons onto the ground.

"Woah," Bentley says. "Easy there." Like he's talking to a skittish horse. He picks up a few lemons and hands them over. "What's all this? Storing up for winter?"

I slide a few bags inside, holding the door open with my hip. "It's for the party," I tell him. "You know. Halloween. You were invited."

"A party?" he asks, tentative. As if he didn't remember.

"It's Halloween Saturday," I say. "Costumes, candy, scary decorations."

Bentley considers the idea with a half-smile distorting his face. He's not handsome, not really. His head is a perfect square, his eyebrows transverse the flat panel of his face, extending nearly to the edges. If I had to call him a name, I'd use 'blockhead.'

"Who's coming?" he asks. He wants to know if Tabitha will be here, the woman who lives in the house on the other side of mine. I've seen him looking out his window at her, watching her walk from her car. Tabitha is thin and willowy, like Olive Oyl. She has a five-year-old son whose name is Darren.

"My sister and her husband and two year-old Jackson, Tabitha and her son. Everyone." I send my eyes around the court, indicating that all our neighbors will be in attendance. I know they'll come. I've had several successful parties. It's a great way to get to know the neighbors, and to meet all their friends who come along. Memorial Day, Summer Solstice Day, and a 4th of July party, which went a little awry when a drunk ex-Marine tried to set off a firecracker and ended up blowing off a finger.

"You gonna have beer?"

Yes, I nod. I'll have beer. And everything else. I've been cooking for a week.

By Saturday, the house is transformed. Torn black paper covers the windows, shredded at the edges as if mauled by animal talons. Rubber mats on the floor shriek underfoot. The lightbulbs have red cellophane dimming their luminousness, spider webs film across the doorway at chin height.

Celia and Mike are the first to arrive. They are dressed like babies. They wear white trash can liners as diapers, tied at the sides with duct tape, and they're both sucking pacifiers belonging to my nephew and attached around their necks with already-sticky candy necklaces. Celia has a quilted bonnet on her head made from a place mat. Mike has drawn tears on his face with a marker of some kind, and his T-shirt is scribbled with brown and gold squiggles that must be baby barf.

Jackson looks like a miniature groom in a tuxedo and bow tie already stained orange. At two, he is in full possession of his personality. He is determined, stubborn, and often furious. He's a lot like me. "I fed him before we came," Celia says as she pushes through the door. She passes Jackson to me, and I bundle him so tightly he groans in his sleep. Sometimes, when I hold that baby, I wish I could absorb him right into my body. I love him that much.

Mike leans in to kiss me. His chin is scratchy, and I can't help but giggle.

The kitchen light flashes on and off: I have the florescent fixture hooked up to a timer. The effect is dizzying.

An osprey-pitched scream indicates someone has stepped on a party mat.

"Holy hell!" the voice is familiar to me. In the doorway stands my neighbor Bentley, dressed as a cowboy, with a stud in his nostril and a tattoo creeping up his fleshy neck. "You call this a party?" He swaggers into the room, his head glides side to side like a lizard. A taser hangs from his belt. His eyes land on the table, laden with unnaturally colored foods.

Mike steps in, a barrier between the baby and the man. "Hey man," Mike says, rolling the pacifier to the side of his mouth like a stogie. "What's with the gun?"

I take Jackson into the bedroom and roll him onto the mattress. He gurgles in his sleep. I stroke my knuckle over his plush pink cheek. My whole world changed when he was born. I always wanted kids. I wanted a lot of kids. Eight, at least. Maybe more. I'd been planning my family since I was in third grade when the Trucillis moved in next door. All the houses on our street were the same: Center-hall colonials, four bedrooms, two bathrooms and a basement for when the kids grow into teens and want some privacy to play spin the bottle. The Trucilli's house was a mirror image of ours, but their kitchen was on the left where ours was on the right. There were nine children in that house, five girls and four boys, which, to me, made our family seem paltry. There were so many *people*. The persistent noise of voices, the constant negotiations. It was like being inside a rectangular beehive. I wanted that. I wanted to feel full of noise and people and food.

When I am with Jackson, I think about my life in a different way. I think about what I want for myself versus what I have now. I still want kids. I want to be married and to be a homemaker and to have a lot of little mouths to feed. I want to sew matching outfits from Simplicity patterns that my kids will wear on Thanksgiving and Christmas, passing them to their siblings as they grow, marking the passage of time in hand-me-downs.

Jackson makes a puppy sound, a little yelp in his sleep, and I lean down to breathe him in. I put all the pillows around him, creating bumpers to prevent a fall.

Celia joins me on the bed and we both look down at the baby, bathing him in familial light.

"Some of your other neighbors are here," she says. "The woman from Bewitched, with her son. From next door. I didn't hear his name."

"Darren."

"Darren," she lets that sit for a moment. "And there are a few kids poking their fingers into the green frosting on top of the cake," Celia says. "One of them is writing his name on the wall in frosting. You might want to get out there and make sure all your valuables are locked down."

Celia worries too much. These are my neighbors. My friends. Nothing bad will happen.

Jackson twitches, an adorable spasm. We signal each other, Celia and I, and tiptoe out of the room.

"What's in the punch?" Celia wants to know.

"Gin, juice, and a splash of peppermint schnapps." Also tequila and some Midori that someone gave me as a house warming gift, but I don't tell her that.

"It's mostly juice," I tell her, which is true.

Celia is talking with Perla, who is dressed in a colorful Indian sari. From the back, I can see the layers of patterned fabric draping elegantly across her rotund torso and the brilliantly colored sash that rings her waist at least four times. It's a beautiful costume and I hardly notice her construction site of a face. Behind her, a man in a dinosaur costume makes lewd gestures toward her, thrusting his hips like a bull. There's a man I don't know dressed as an unraveling mummy. There are two versions of the Statue of Liberty, a superhero of some sort and a guy in a neon-yellow construction vest, wearing a hardhat. I am Queen Elizabeth, complete with a tiara that I made myself, and a sash that says, "Her Majesty the Queen."

I love when people get into the theme of a party. It makes it so much more festive.

"Charlotte is a party animal," Celia tells Perla. "When we were young, she'd invite all the neighborhood kids to come over when our parents were out."

Perla laughs with her hand in front of her lips. Behind her deformed lip, her teeth are bad; she doesn't like to show them. "That sounds dangerous," she says.

As a teen, I never saw any danger. There were a few incidents where the crowd turned rowdy. John Burger got drunk and fell off the porch, a distance of three feet, and somehow broke his collar bone. And Charlie Durnett took Celia out into the garage to make out, which was totally against the rules. By the time I opened the garage door, he already had her shirt off. She was only ten. I made him leave right then and there. For the rest of that school year, he tormented Celia with a nasty nickname: Mosquito Bites. Somehow, our mother found out about that one and we didn't have any parties for a while after that.

Being the hostess of a party makes you popular. Everyone is attracted to the hostess, people seek you out to ask directions to the bathroom, to the backyard, or to inquire about the food. I am in my element when at the center of a party, offering food and drink, carting away empty plates. I love that kind of attention; I serve a purpose, I am appreciated. I look forward to hosting a party the way a dog looks forward to an afternoon walk. I crave it, I hope for it, I am at my best in it.

Except when it goes wrong.

***

It's the long-ago morning of the block party. I am so excited. I've delivered handwritten invitations into the matching mailboxes of all my neighbors. There are only eight cottage houses on my street. Five on the pipestem and three around the cul-de-sac. I am the middle house in the bell of the court, dead center.

I am going over the guest list. "I don't know what to do about the Creeds," I tell Plots. We are sharing a Krispy Kreme glazed cruller from the bakery case. "They have a long-time family feud with the Belnoirs across the street. They all hate each other." The store is empty save one terribly skinny guy staring into the iced-over freezer door.

Plots untwists a portion of the cruller as if unbraiding a rope. "Belnoir?" he asks. "Isn't that the guy who does odd jobs at your house?" A crystal of sugar sparkles on his pulpy lip. Plots has a remarkable memory.

"Yeah. I haven't seen him for a while. He's in training for a bodybuilding competition."

"I don't like him," Plots says.

"You've never even met him."

“Doesn’t matter,” he says. “We don’t have muscle men in my country.”

“Bullshit!” I rap my knuckles on the counter and pull out my BlackBerry. “Here it is. Bangladesh’s National Bodybuilding Federation ousted one of the championship contenders after he loses calm and kicks his second-place award off the stage.” I kiss some glaze off my fingertips. Plots and I entertain ourselves with bits of worthless trivia. Right now, I am ahead. “And you know if it’s on the internet, it must be true.”

“That’s Bangladesh,” he says. “I’m from Bangaluru!”

Plots finishes the pastry and then tilts his head back to empty a bottle of water into his throat. His Adam’s apple is gigantic. I watch it slide, half expecting the sound of a carnival bell to ring at its rise, a human high striker.

I want to snatch up the last bite of cruller and fill my mouth with its instantaneous pleasure, but the skinny man comes to the checkout counter right then and stands a pint of ice cream on our paper bag. “Hey,” he says, peeling four bills off a loaf of singles.

I read the label. Banana cream pie ice cream. “Is that any good?” I ask him.

“Don’t know yet.” He retrieves a spoon from the coffee bar and peels the cardboard lid off. He tips the pint toward me, offering. I shake my head and swallow back the screaming urge to fill my mouth with banana cream pie ice cream. The ice cream is a little melted. It slides onto his spoon like custard. “So how are you all doing?” His mouth is rimmed in white cream, and I realize he is going to eat the entire pint of ice cream right there.

“Is that your breakfast?” I ask him.

“Yup.”

Plots clicks closed the cash drawer. “S’mores is the best seller in that brand,” he says. “It’s got graham crackers and fudge and all.” Sometimes he sounds like a real salesperson. But then, I know he’s not.

Working at 7-Eleven allows him just enough money to pay rent on his one room studio above the Laundromat and to send a few dollars back to his family every few months. He doesn't love the job. It's just a job.

"What's your game?" the man asks me casually.

"My what?"

"Your game. You know. How do you roll?"

I looked to Plots for translation, but he only twitched his pulpy lips and raised a shoulder as if to say, you're on your own.

"I'm good," I say without much conviction.

"You work here?" he asks, gouging out another heap of ice cream. The pint is already half empty.

I point to the carton. "Do you always have dessert for breakfast?"

He nods. "I like sugar," he says. "What can I tell you. I'm addicted to sweets. Not all sweets. I don't like gummies or taffy or anything like that." He carves out another mountain of ice cream. I can't help but watch him move the spoon to his mouth. His eyes close slightly. "I suppose that's a good thing," he adds, looking at me with light in his dark eyes. "Because I don't have too many choppers left." He grins, showing a few, rancid-looking teeth. Two top teeth, or maybe three.

"Bananas prevent leg cramps," he offers this comment with the simplicity of long conversation. "A buddy of mine, a runner, told me that."

"Are you a runner?" I ask. He is light-boned and thin. He could be an athlete.

"Nah," he says. "Not unless I'm being chased." He tosses the empty pint into the trash. "So that party sounds cool. My friend plays in a steel drum band. Maybe you want his band to play at your place? What night is the party? Saturday?"

A steel drum band! I imagine a yard full of guests wearing floral tops socializing around a swimming pool. Of course, I don't have a pool, and my neighbors are more likely to come in undershirts and cut-offs than breezy resort wear. But still.

"That sounds great," I tell him despite the silent warnings emanating from Plots. I jot my address on the back of a Lotto form. "I live just up the road."

"Eddie," he introduces himself.

"Charlotte," I say.

On the day of the party Tabitha comes over to help me set up. She's the first friend I made in the new neighborhood. We move the long table from the kitchen into the main room. I hang strings of festival lights across the window and around the bathroom door. Her son Darren made a sign for my front door with a big happy face in brilliant magic marker colors that bled into the cardboard. He even stapled some ribbon to the sign, shiny tendrils wafted in blues, greens and silvers.

"It's beginning to look like a party." Tabitha stands back and surveys our progress. She is worried about her closest neighbor Bentley. She thinks he's selling guns out of his garage, but he told me he only sells auto parts.

"Why would a guy who wants to be a cop do anything illegal?" I ask Tabitha as we unroll a long sheet of cellophane. We affix a length of plastic to the wall, creating an instant cabaret feel.

"Stupidity," she answers plainly.

Bentley has a scar that cuts straight through his lips, separating one side of his mouth from the other. It looks like someone took a scythe to his face. He inherited his house from his parents, who either moved to Florida or were murdered in their beds. Different neighbors have different historical renditions.

"Let's just keep him away from Darren," she says. She's emptying the second bottle of grain alcohol into the punch bowl. "I don't want my kid to socialize with a future felon."

I don't bother to remind her that Darren's father is in jail. Or in the military. Tabitha changes that story with each telling. Once she told me she's not even sure who fathered him in the first place.

The punch bowl is surrounded by a moat of 16-ounce plastic cups stacked tall. We've filled baskets of pretzels and nuts and Fritos and Cheetos and M&Ms and Reese's individually wrapped peanut butter cups that fill every inch and corner of the table. Tabitha brought pot brownies. A corner square of chocolate is already missing from the pan.

In the kitchen, my best efforts are on display: baked ziti made with goat cheese because it melts better, barbequed ribs with pearl onions, cheesecake decorated in red and white layers to look like the iconic hat in *The Cat in the Hat*.

Tabitha passes me her lit cigarette. "How much did all this cost?"

I breathe the smoke deep. I have no idea how much I spent. I had so much fun buying the napkins and matching plates, the plastic serving spoons and big tin foil pans. I must have made five trips to Walmart and more to the grocery stores.

I hand her back the cigarette and wave away the smoke. "Okay, help me with this thing." I have instructions for the keg I rented in a paper bag. A full keg. Serves one hundred and sixty-five. "You read the directions to me." I kneel and follow her instructions.

The pump locks into place.

A man's voice startles us. "Don't forget to release the pressure after you lock it in." It's Eddie the ice cream eater. He looks less skinny tonight, somehow.

He grins and I almost flinch: I remember those teeth. "Want help?" He takes a step toward me and Tabitha falls away, disappearing with some mumble about changing her clothes. Eddie is obviously a keg expert. With one heavy-handed motion, he locks the tap.

"Hand me a pitcher," he says to me. His voice is authoritarian. I don't remember that about him. I pass him the watering can—the only container not in use—and watch as he pours off about six cups of beer. "You gotta let the foam out," he tells me without moving his eyes from the tap. The watering can is nearly foaming over. Eddie stands up and puts the spout to his lips and nearly drains the can. His free hand rests over his navel; he massages himself in soft circles. His tee shirt doesn't reach all the way to the waist of his jeans. I see a slice of white skin, some hair. A braided brown belt holds the pants in place. Without the belt, his pants would be at his ankles.

"My guys are right behind me," he says, dark eyes glazing. His stare is unsettling.

"Your guys?"

"The drummers. Where should they set up?"

Oh yeah. The steel drum band.

"How about over there?" He selects the one corner that's not set up like a buffet. Together, we move an armchair, shove aside the potted plants. "This ought to work."

The door opens, closes. "Hey."

Lars Belnoir fills the doorway, literally. He's preparing for an all-state bodybuilder competition, and from what I can see, he's making great progress. His chest is a wall wrapped in a white tee; his arms extrude tight sleeves that are surely cutting off circulation to his hands. I'm surprised he can move at all.

Eddie exhales and mutters, "Jesus. Who or what is *that*?"

"Comin' through." Lars stands against the wall, looking like a plain-clothed superhero. The steel drum band has arrived. Eddie moves like a squirrel, darting and hopping out of the way. When the instruments are set, he introduces me to his so-called buddies. "This is Calvin. And this is Hobbs."

The musicians roll their eyes. Eddie takes another swallow from the watering can.

"Friends of yours?" Lars asks. He's moved from the wall to the pass through and is carving out a wedge of brownie. "You know, I think I've seen that guy," he says. "Are you sure you want him in your house?"

I wave away the warning. "Go easy on those," I tell him, pointing to the brownies. "They're spiked."

The drums tap, uncertainly at first.

Darren charges into the apartment, fists flying. He always holds his hands in fists when he's excited. "Woah, brother," one of the drummers rears backward and points his sticks at Darren. "Keep the kid away from the equipment."

"He's okay," I stand between Darren and the drummer.

The hallway is a weight of voices. In comes a few Creeds, a few Rickeys.

"Who's the muscle-head?" Eddie is at my ear asking about Lars who is eating ribs out of the pan with both hands. He has a massive appetite. A few times, we ended up sitting on the stoop together, doing a lot of nothing, and I offered to cook a meal for us. I'd say we have had dinner together a few times, maybe more.

More people arrive. A lot of them are unfamiliar to me. I like that. I like the open house feel. There are probably twenty people here, mostly guys, mostly strangers. Everyone is laughing and talking and eating. The keg pumps without rest.

Plots shows up carrying a bottle of wine. I don't laugh at him about the wine. He's still trying to figure out the American way of doing things.

"Wow, Charl," he says with wide eyes. "Who are all these people?"

"Friends of friends," I tell him. "Pretty good, right?"

He leans his head down to talk without shouting. "You don't know most of these people, do you?" His voice is stern, and I fight back my irritation. Who is he to criticize what I do? He touches my shoulder. "I recognize one of the guys outside from the clinic," he says. The methadone clinic.

"Huh," I say, happy that he has a person to talk to. Now he won't feel so left out.

One of the Creeds is facing off with Lenny or Lester or Lefty Belnoir. I get all the L names confused. Their gestures are frantic, like geese scrambling across the surface of the water. Mayhem, confusion, chaos. I see the Belnoir kid jab a punch at the Creed kid. Lars lurks from the other side of the crowded room, his eyes are black marbles, I can almost see his biceps twitch.

Plots straightens to full height. “They are going to fight.”

I use that moment to move away.

“Did you make all this?” a young woman in a group of three asks me. Her paper plate struggles under a load of ziti.

“I love to cook,” I tell them.

“The cheesecake is to die for,” one says.

“I’ll take home all the leftovers,” another offers.

Satisfaction swells in my chest. I roll my shoulders back, inviting more air to enter my lungs. I am taller. My smile feels permanent.

The woman with the cheesecake points her fork.

“That guy is rummaging around in your fridge,” she says.

I do not want to leave them, their little beehive of appreciation. A shout, a scuffle, the women disburse, leaving their plates on top of the overfilled trash can.

The crowd parts and I see a clump of men engaged in a wrestling maneuver. Their limbs are entangled, their body parts are impossibly repositioned.

I approach the guy leaning into the fridge. “Need something?”

He stands and looks at me. “Who are you?”

“Charlotte,” I tell him. “I live here.”

He is stoned. His face is loose, his eyelids fight, visibly, with gravity.

“What can I get you?”

He is leaning heavy on the refrigerator door.

I put my hand on his shoulder. “Are you here with someone?”

“Nope.” We are shouting over the clatter of the drums. This was a terrible idea; I just now realize. The drummers are bad musicians; the apartment is too small for this much noise.

“Who invited you tonight? I mean, you can stay and everything. But who told you about the party?”

“Bentley.” He shrugs.

Oh, Bentley. "He lives next door." I scan the room. "I don't see him." The stranger shrugs again. His eyes flit from the kitchen window to the door, back and forth. "He's fucking," he says, looking at the door again. "In the hall."

Someone has dismantled the cymbals and is using them as sparring shields, fending off faux punches from a guy holding spare rib bones in each hand. The drummer is shouting something. I see Lars slide into the bathroom with a girl whose face glints with piercings, his eyes are slits of wrongdoing. Darren is drinking from one of the plastic cups and I throw him a scowl so he knows I can see him, a ten-year-old drinking grain alcohol. Where is his mother?

Bentley pushes his way toward the kitchen, fire burns in his eyes. "What the fuck are you doing here?"

He is shouting at the stranger bending into my fridge. I thought they were friends.

Bentley reaches past me and grabs the smaller man by the neck. His forearm is a formidable beam. "You owe me two large," he says through his teeth.

Suddenly, Eddie is near. "Hey dude," he says. "Chill out."

"Fuck you," Bentley snaps. His face is dark and hard. He moves in closer to his prey, pressing his nose under the man's chin. "Until you have my money, you stay away," he growls, low and dangerous. "Hear me?"

The pounding drum snares are no competition for the sound of real fury.

I am trapped in the kitchen. We are, all of us, just inches from each other.

Eddie claps his hands like a camp counselor trying to regain control. "Let's take this outside."

Bentley does not blink. "Step off." A warning growl from low in his belly.

Eddie surprises me, standing his ground. His body blocks the kitchen area. Even though he's skinny, he takes up a lot of room.

Bentley presses his body forward, shoving the refrigerator into the wall.

A gallon-jug of ketchup teeters inside the refrigerator, falling on a mostly empty three-pound bag of grated cheese. I buy in large sizes; that way there is always plenty to eat. Right now, there is hardly any real food in there. Just some cream cheese leftover from the cake recipe, and a few bottles of marinades and dressings. Usually, my fridge is stocked like a chef's kitchen. I see a carton of half-and-half on the top shelf. After everyone leaves, I'll fill my stomach with Frosted Mini Wheats dosed in half-and-half.

Tabitha emerges from my bedroom. One of the Creed boys trots out after her, a grin of achievement at his lips. Darren is passed out on the armchair, his feet turned inward. Someone has drawn a handlebar moustache on Darren's face in what looks like black ink.

The sparring partners have ceased their game and are fully involved in a battle of beer pong they've set up in the hallway. "Hey, man," someone tells me, "some old lady is out there complaining about the noise."

Tabitha sidles next to me. "Probably Maude Manley. I'll go see," she offers. She only glances at the two men locked in battle at the refrigerator.

Bentley releases his grip. The man falls like a puppet from cut strings. "Motherfucker," Bentley mutters. He turns, and then stops abruptly.

Eddie is holding a gun. Is it real?

"Hey man," Bentley holds his hands out, sign of peaceful intent. "We're all good."

Eddie looks at Bentley's huge mitts. Then, he extends his arm with the gun held flat. Gangster style.

"Gun!" Someone screams and suddenly everyone is in motion, running, waving their arms, pushing toward the door. Someone hauls away a steel drum. A toilet flushes, the bathroom door opens, the drummer runs out and chases after the drum, shouting in a language I don't understand.

The air feels heavy. I can hear voices, laughter, talking, shouting. I can hear grunting coming from the bedroom. I hear someone retching and coughing, I hear something splat onto the floor. I see the gun in Eddie's hand.

Eddie is stone faced. The gun is steady, pointing at Bentley's head.

"Everybody out!" Plots shouts. "I'm calling the police." His voice is a taut staccato. He lowers his gaze to Eddie and says, "You better get out of here." He watches the gun with cold fearlessness; I want to make eye contact with him, to shout to him that the gun isn't real, but I can see in his rigid face, he is unreachable.

"Get out." His voice is a command. Like a herd of buffalo, the crowd moves toward the door. Within minutes, we are alone.

Plots high-steps his long legs over an upturned side table. "You should never have allowed those men into your home," he says. His voice is cold, critical. He bends, retrieves a tuft of brown fuzz from a gash carved into the fabric of my sofa. "Do you know what this is?" He holds the material out like an offering. It is hair. Is the stuffing coming out of the couch?

I peer behind Plots' body. The sofa is long past ruined. Long slashes slice through the beige fabric. Did someone bring a knife?

Plots forces the hair tuft toward me, insisting I take the evidence from him. It's a ponytail, held tight by a familiar beaded ring. "This was sheared off your friend."

"Who?"

"The one with the arm? Mary?"

"What happened? Is she okay?" I spin around, as if to look for her. The house is empty.

"They assaulted her, pushing her down, making fun of her arm and her limp. They pinned her to the couch and cut off her hair. I had to haul them off her."

My throat is on fire. The contents of my stomach are battling and boiling. Soon they will erupt. "I didn't know."

Plots is relentless. "You are too trusting, Charlotte. All these people? They take advantage of you! They drank your beer and ate your food. They took drugs and had sex in your bed. This is very bad. Very bad. Look what they did!"

I look. Cellophane is balled up on the floor like tumbleweeds. The punch bowl is upside down, cups and plates and food and liquid form a floor of sorts. The window nearest the kitchen has broken in a starburst pattern, shards of glass point inward like reverse spin art. "You should take pride in your home. You don't know how lucky you are to have a nice place like this! Now it looks like a dumpster."

He paces in a small space; foam gathers in the corners of his mouth. "What will your landlord do when he sees all this?" Plots spits. "You'll be evicted. And then what? You'll move back home again?"

"I called the police," Plots says, turning his back. "But I can't be here when they come. I don't have my papers." He takes a grim look around. "I'll help you clean up tomorrow."

He disappears before I can nod my response. I drop to the couch and lean back, light a new cigarette and listen to the sirens screaming into the night.

***

"Your father and I are concerned," my mother's voice wobbled. "The last few times we saw you, you didn't look right."

"I can't help it if you don't like the way I look," I said. The phone was hot in my hand.

"That is *not* what I meant, and you know it."

"But it's true. You just said it. *I didn't look right*. What else can that possibly mean?"

"Now you're just being difficult."

Difficult? Yes, I was being difficult. I don't know why, but this is how my mother and I communicate.

"Okay then. Tell me. What is wrong with me now?"

Silence. I squinted, concentrating, trying to hear the grinding mechanism of her worry.

"We're worried, that's all. You are not yourself. And so we are concerned. Your father is *very* concerned."

I tasted bitterness far back on my tongue. Like acid reflux, or bile. Another criticism about how Jimbo had changed me. Resentment for this particular conversation was almost like another limb, fully formed and hanging heavy on my frame. I rounded the small of my back into the mattress to alleviate the pressure building there.

I wasn't an idiot; Jimbo was an addict. But that didn't mean he wasn't a good husband. In fact, the opposite was true. For two years, we'd grappled with his drug issues. His morphine addiction held him in irons. He was unable to fend on his own. But we were working together on the other drugs. His anxiety medications, his antispasmotics. The one course I'd taken in counseling came in handy. I was able to explain to him why it was perfectly safe for him to wait out a period of anxiety, to let the chemicals in his body right themselves. And it worked. A few times. He tried very hard, listening to my voice as I counseled him through some terrible attacks. Panic attacks. Anxiety attacks. Spikes of pain. I coached him, encouraged him to wait before taking the next pill or injection. Patterning, it was called. To create a pattern of reaction and response. It took time. There were setbacks. There were times he was unable to comply, deaf to my counseling voice, but the successes were mounting, we were making progress. We had plenty of time.

"Do not let him influence you," my mother warned repeatedly. "It isn't necessary that you adopt his habits or his lifestyle."

She was dismayed that I'd quit my job at the courthouse to be home with Jimbo. He needed me. And I was determined to make a marriage for us, a marriage that would look like the one my grandmother had, my mother, my sister. I had to help him acclimate to our new life, slowly. His mother babied him, never taught him to cook or fend for himself. He barely knew how to use the toaster. It was my responsibility as his wife to prepare him, to train him. It was fun. I liked being the instructor, the teacher. He was not a great student, not like Celia used to be when we play-acted in our basement. But he was trying.

"You can't put that many towels into the dryer," I told him, pulling a few items from the machine. "Just a few at a time, or they won't dry."

"I like it when you correct me," he said. He was lying on his back on our bed, watching me. "You are such an adorable housewife."

I'd dissolved then into a fit of laughing. He had such an effect on me, his compliments gave me the giggles. I got into bed with him and snuggled close. Sometimes he'd share his medicine, so I could enjoy the same relaxation that left him quietly smiling. Then we'd lie together, listening to each other's breaths. The words I'd use to describe how I felt in those hours and days are: symbiosis, calm, happy.

My mother sent me snips from the local newspaper. Job listings. "Wouldn't you like to work in the gardening center? You know how you love to work with plants."

Why would I want a job? "I waited forty-nine years to find a partner," I said, curtly. "I'm not about to leave him to work with some plants." I was never going to convince her that I finally had what I'd always wanted.

Anyway, Jimbo had taught me how to submit the forms for Disability Insurance. There was no reason at all for me to work outside the house. Easy enough to prove: Disability. Between his payments and mine, we made enough. And, of course, there was the trust. "For dire emergencies," my father had explained. As if there was another kind.

"Jimbo does not need you to take care of him." My mother was insistent. "He is a grown man. You need to focus on yourself. What happened to your organic garden? I thought you said you were working toward certification?"

I wished I'd never told her. But she was right: I'd talked about getting certified long before I'd even met Jimbo, and I'd had every intention of starting the application process. One day.

SEVENTEEN

I pressed a cool compress to Jimbo's pallid face, soft as an overripe melon. He sat on the bathroom floor, his face tilted up to me like a light-starved sunflower. "You are going to be just fine," I said to him. "I'm taking care of you. Tell me what you need," I coaxed him.

We'd been like this for two hours or more, I had lost track of the time. He'd awakened during the night to vomit, which happened sometimes, he explained, as a result of his medication. But this time the vomiting did not stop. In fact, it worsened. I stood by him, leaning on the sink, holding his head when the retching arched through him. He'd slept for a while on the floor, his face like not-yet-set clay on the plastic toilet seat. I stood over him, vigilant.

"I don't know." Tears tumbled from vulvar eyelids. His pupils were tiny dots of black. "I want to die."

"You can't die," I told him. "I just found you!" His leg was bent like a chicken wing; I tip-toed over it. "I'm going to call my mother."

He moaned. "Your mother detests me."

I reached out for the phone, balanced on a pile of towels stained orange with emesis. "She detests everyone who isn't like her." The phone was cold in my hand.

"She thinks I'm ruining you," Jimbo said. I set the phone on the sink.

"I was already ruined," I said, smiling.

He rose quickly to one knee and heaved, his lips puffed and yawed but nothing passed out of his body. I waited until the spasms released him.

My sister picked up before the second ring.

"How's it going?" Her usual greeting. We spoke to each other every day.

"Jimbo is really sick," I blurted.

"Tell me." I like this about her: she snapped into her role as nurse faster than a blink. I described his pallor and his lethargy and the violence of his convulsions.

"Sounds like a stomach bug," she said. "Get him to drink some water, or Gatorade if you have it."

She knew I had Gatorade in the house. I kept a case of lemon-lime Gatorade in my garage. Long ago, she chastised me for ingesting unnecessary sugars in the form of juices. I loved fruit juices—still do.

"He has a fever," I added. "Isn't it dangerous for an adult to have a fever?"

"At what temperature?"

I glanced at the thermometer on the sink. His temperature never rose above one hundred, but I rounded up. "Just over one hundred and one."

"Well. That could be serious," she acknowledged, "or it could be a simple case of dehydration. Have him take tiny sips of Gatorade and tiny sips of water. That will help calm his system and replenish his fluids."

She always knew what to do.

"Should I put a nitroglycerin tab under his tongue?"

I heard a fast breath suction into her throat. "Why would you do that?"

"Because he said he was having heart pains!"

"Do not give him any medication, do you hear me?" She dictated the terms of his care slowly. "Offer him sips of water. Water or Gatorade only. He will perk up right away with hydration. You will only make it worse if you add more chemicals to his system." She was quiet a while. We listened to each other breathe. "Are you okay now? You know what to do?"

I nodded even though she couldn't see me. "I'll get a cup of water for him to sip. He's all sweaty."

"He'll be okay," she cooed. "You are a good nurse. You can do this. Call back if you need me."

Her voice left the line. A snag of regret caught in my heart, and I soothed myself with wiping Jimbo's bald head. She was right. He needed hydration. A coffee mug, stuck in a circle of creamer, appeared on the sink as if summoned. I filled it with warm water from the tap and held it to Jimbo's wormy lips. He drank, burped, drank.

He leaned back and stretched his legs out, resting his head on the curb of the tub. "Tell me," he said, "how you were ruined before I came along."

Jimbo liked when I told him stories, even when they weren't true. None of my stories were true, mainly because I didn't have a life before I met Jimbo. I had small jobs, unmemorable apartments, lots of disposable interactions that I pretended were friends. For him, I created a new life story every time I spoke, borrowing from other people's lives, from gossip, or from television. None of them belonged to me. Except for this one.

"I was a leftover hippie with a button collection and floppy hats and iron-on patches on the back of my jeans. I was around thirty by then. Celia had just gotten married. I worked in a bookkeeping office, and I had a second- floor walkup apartment in a crappy part of town. In Fort Lee, New Jersey."

Trepidation strangled my breath, preventing me from speaking. I'd never revealed this story before, this true story. Jimbo's head rolled a little, massaging my thigh, giving me courage to continue.

I felt the vibration of his breathing on my leg.

"Beautiful downtown Fort Lee," I said, nodding, remembering. At the base of the bridge, a commuter pass-through to New York City. It was just far enough away from my parents, and dumpy enough to dissuade them from visiting. I'd wanted to be independent. If I had a goal, that was it. My job and my rent were exactly the same, equal in cost and status. I bought a bed from the Salvation Army. I found a half broken armchair parked on the street outside the bookkeeping office; I jammed it into the back of my Pinto hatchback and clunked it up the apartment building's steps, losing, somewhere, one of the wheels. After that, it was a rocking chair. I ate fast food alone in my car, watched television on a set my father handed down to me. I used to fall asleep with the television on to mute the noise of the streets, the traffic, the shouting.

"One of the clients of the bookkeeping place owned a mechanic's shop near the office, and I brought the Pinto to him for an oil change. We started to talk. He hung out with a group of townies who'd known each other from high school or somewhere, and he invited me to hang out. That's how I met Karl."

I stopped for a bit; my fingers soft in Jimbo's beard. Karl was cruel; he burned my arm with cigarettes, branding me, he said, as if I was a possession. A possession he didn't really want. He debased me with insults, calling me Beluga, which degraded to 'lugie' followed by lobs of expectorant hurled in my direction. Sometimes he invited his buddies to a spitting contest with me as the target. He always had weed and 'ludes and acid. He fucked me doggy style so he wouldn't have to look at me, but I didn't tell Jimbo that.

Jimbo's head was in my lap. My fingertips rubbed the crescent edges of his ears. Heaven.

He looked up at me. Like a baby nursing at his mother. Endorphins zinged through me, knocking me sideways. I almost swayed. I held onto Jimbo's ears for stability.

"And Karl?" Jimbo urged me to continue. "What became of him?"

This part of the story hurt to tell. Karl killed himself by slicing open his wrists in a bathtub full of water. The bathtub was in my apartment. I was the one who found him. I'll never get that image out of my head.

***

"You have to get the key back." Celia is feeling bossy. I like when she does this, bosses me around. It makes me feel loved.

Karl has been stealing from me. I can tell it's him because he leaves his crap all over the place. This time, he took a six-pack of ginger ale from the fridge, a carton of cigarettes, and the reading lamp from an end table. I didn't tell her about the cigs.

"He took the lamp?" Celia swirls her spoon in the chicken soup. We're in the diner. Our hometown. Outside, the rain obscures our cars in the parking lot. We are the only patrons here. "You taught him to read? Well, good for you."

Celia's face is tinted green, her lips are without color. When she smiles, she looks exactly like herself. At the moment, she is critical and sarcastic and she looks like our mother.

"Fuck you," I say, filling my mouth with peach cobbler. The Homestyle Diner makes desserts fresh every day. In house. I know because I'd considered a career as pastry chef; the owner would certainly hire me because my father is his doctor.

"You can't just let him use you like this, Char," she says.

I'd told her. Karl still sometimes crashes at my place; I come home and find him asleep on the futon. I like it, finding him—or his trash—in my apartment. The soggy bags from Burger King. The cigarette butts extinguished on the kitchen counter. Makes me feel like I am not alone.

I do not tell Celia that he brought a woman to my place and had sex with her in my bed.

"He's not using me," I tell her. "We're friends."

I am hoping Karl gets tired of this other woman. I want him to have a good feeling about me, so when he's done with this fling he'll come back. That's why I haven't asked him to return my key. It's a sign of welcome. Karl still shows up a lot, mainly to get his laundry. I have a load of dirty clothes in the back of my car. His and mine. I take our laundry to my parents' house to use their machines.

Celia's eyes are closed. Her lids are bruises.

"There's a lot you don't know about Karl." I use my finger to wipe up the last of the pie filling. "He's had a hard life. His mother…" I hear my own voice gurgling on, defensive and strong, but I am no longer listening. I am only talking. I do not want to think about Celia and her heart and her health. She is unwell, I can see that. But I do not want to talk about her. I do not want to worry about her. This is about me. I am the one who is alone. I am the one who is fighting to exist, to be heard, to be known.

Celia has to leave. She apologizes and hands me a twenty. I sit there for the longest time, feeling cheated. Celia was supposed to listen to me. She was supposed to help me. I throw the money on the table and go home.

The bathroom door is closed. I knock. No sounds. I push the door open.

Karl is in the tub. Naked, half submerged in water. His face is waxy, his eyes are strangely still. I sit down on the toilet and stare at him. He looks peaceful; his hands are crossed over his chest as if in slumber. Long skinny limbs lay crumpled in the tub, folded at edgy angles, climbing along the porcelain like rhizomes, his feet are tangled in the basin. The water reminds me of the camp activity where you dunk a knotted t-shirt into a bucket of dye, which was probably red dye number two, now that I think about it.

I don't know how long I sit there. A while. I have a very detailed image of him, every millimeter of him, etched into my memory. His overly extended Adam's apple. His curved, gray-brown penis. He has fungus on his toenails.

When death visits a young person, some say they have been robbed of a life. They conjure lost moments, lost pleasures never known. For some reason, we feel sure that somehow that young body would have known delight, known happiness if only they'd lasted.

I feel none of that. What I feel is envy. Karl, I think, is lucky.

***

"Even worse," I said, pressing the memory down. "Celia had a miscarriage that night, so everyone got super upset about that."

I remembered the phone call. My father's voice, the bleak words. My skull tightened. My brain needed more room inside. I saw all their faces: Karl in the tub, Celia and Mike, my devastated parents. My mind scrambled for an exit. I lit a cigarette and waited for the calm.

"Once, I saw a program on whales," I said. "Did you know they get hit all the time by ships on the ocean? The boats don't even know when they've hit a whale, that's how big they are. The whales get battered by the ships. Hulls scrape against their flanks. The propellers gouge out hunks of their flesh. That's me. Gouged out. Battered."

Jimbo had fallen asleep, I was almost sure. I set my feet flat and pushed my body forward, toward him, until the top of my head pressed into the soft side of his body. The air was thick with terrible smells, but I pressed closer to him. I had a need to touch him, to attach to him. He moaned, moving slightly as I pushed myself closer and in my mind I watched him grow larger and stronger, a sunflower captured with time-lapse photography. I watched the confused and overmedicated cells within his capillaries assemble themselves into orderly columns, soldiers marching in perfect unison. I imagined his heart flexing like the bulging arm of Mr. Clean.

And there, on the floor of my bedroom and with my head half-draped under a bit of cotton reeking of vomit, I was startled by the sudden realization that my days would come to an end long before

I had a chance to live a life. I was sure. I would not survive beyond this point of resolution. The damaging propellers of my past were still there, still turning, churning, hacking away at me, as if my destruction was necessary to restore balance in the universe.

I reached past Jimbo's slumbering body and put my hand around the prescription bottle nearest the edge and emptied its contents into my mouth.

EIGHTEEN

"You are being transferred to the psychiatric service." The nurse eyed the IV apparatus hanging near my head. "Do you understand?"

I let my head fall heavy toward the wide white of her uniform. As far as I could tell, in what little I could see past her, the other emergency room bays were vacant.

A thin sheet covered my body; only my head was exposed. Like a swaddled baby. I felt no need to answer.

She departed with a flick of the privacy drape, as if snapping free a roller shade. If she'd intended to pull closed the curtain, she failed completely, and I was offered a panoramic view of the core of the hive.

Past the points of my toes, the central nursing station re-enacted the boarding of Noah's Ark. Two nurses in white conferred behind the chest-level barrier, side by side, heads down. Two orderlies in green paired off near the far wall. A duo of pink scrubs—laboratory technicians?—took inventory of a metal cart, opening the wafer-thin drawers one by one, metal scraping on metal, and counting aloud the contents within. The clock on the wall read seven o'clock. Change of shifts.

There is a utilitarian harshness to the Emergency Department, a mechanical, rhythmic dependability that I have always found appealing. Like being inside of a great machine, the sheer functionality of the place was like a balm to me. I closed my eyes and listened to the steady thump of my heart beating quietly from deep inside.

A warm body neared the bed. “Hey, there.” A soft male voice urged my eyes open.

An orderly. With a bald head that glowed in a halo of light. He looked sort of like an alien.

“Don’t worry, you’re going to be just fine.” The gentleness of his voice drew tears from my soul.

He smiled down on me. Oh, how I loved to be cared for, to be safe and tended in this place.

“Try and wake up.” He jostled my arm.

I nodded obediently.

He leaned over me and whispered. “Your labs are back,” he said. “The doc is reading them now. It shouldn’t be much longer.” He hovered there a long moment, as if considering his words. What would he say?

I studied his soft chin, his scanty beard. He’d tried to grow a moustache but it didn’t take.

“They are going to admit you,” he said, moving down to squeeze my toes through layers of thin linens. The intimacy of his hand anchored me, and I felt more myself at that moment than in a dozen years gone by. The pleasure of a stranger’s touch sent a wave of optimism through to my bones. I will be well handled, I knew, in this place. My body will be positioned and scrutinized and replenished. I will sleep sporadically, lightly, in the direct observation of a health professional. I will have no pain; I tightened a fist, feeling the tug of the IV line affixed to the back of my hand. All would be well. I could let go.

NINETEEN

"You know what they're saying, don't you?" asked my father.

Much as I wanted to answer, my lips would not cooperate.

"That you and Jimbo are a pair of junkies." His voice was a jumping bean, bouncing off the gray-green walls.

Where was Jimbo? I wanted to glance into the hall but the door to my room was closed.

"You've been to the ER five times in two years." His head swiveled like a marionette. "Your chart is marked across the front: Frequent Flyer." My father's lips were tight. "Tylenol overdose that nearly destroyed your liver. Extreme agitation," he read from the chart, "extreme lethargy. Your lab tests are flagged with these little red tags: Warning: Drug Seeking." With that, he coughed, a weak little sound.

I admit that his breach of emotion surprised me a little bit. Normally, my father's voice is a strong bass, full and dense with expectations. But here, standing along the rail of my bed, he sputtered much as a motor engine sputters when the fuel has run out. "Charlotte, listen to me. This is not a game. Jimbo has a high tolerance to all his medications, all his drugs. But you do not. When you take medication prescribed for him, you're killing yourself. Is that what you want? To kill yourself?" Spittle has accumulated in the folds of his mouth. "Charlotte, are you hearing me? Your mother and I are terrified that we are going to lose you."

He shook the bed rail, jerking me on the mattress. The overhead light jiggled comically. His hands released the rail and I watched the hair on his knuckles as his fingers peeled away. My mind screamed, *Don't go, Don't go*! He toed the leg of a chair, pulling it close, and sat with an audible "ugh."

"You were a delightful child," my father said so quietly. I worked to follow his voice. "Caring and sensitive. You had this eagerness in your face, like you just couldn't wait to experience whatever came next. And when you started school, you immediately made friends. Our house bustled with the cackle of little voices, eating snacks in the kitchen, playing games downstairs. That's why we finished the basement. For you and your friends. To have a place of your own."

I loved that basement. I wanted to tell him how much I loved it, but he was staring at the wall beyond my head, memories deep in his eyes.

"Your mother and I did the best that we could as parents. We made sure you had everything: books, music, toys, love. Always love. We love you, Charlotte. I hope you know that."

I felt a headache brewing behind my eyes. Jimbo had these great headache tabs that dissolved under your tongue. I couldn't remember the name.

"Your mother got her teaching degree largely because of you, did you know that?"

I did not.

"You were learning so fast. She was fascinated by the way you absorbed information, sifted through thoughts and feelings. You were perspicacious and so very clever. She took classes at night so she could be with you all your waking hours." He sounded proud. "She used to take you to the library when you were still in the baby seat. She'd bring your blanket—remember that ratty old blanket that you took everywhere?"

I did. It was pink, or maybe apricot colored. It was soft as fleece but was made of plain cotton. Everything in those days was cotton. I kept that blanket next to my cheek, holding it tightly with one hand

and hooking it over my ear for additional security. During the night, I later learned, my mother would disentangle the blanket and put it through the laundry while I was sleeping.

"She'd bring your blanket and some toys, and she'd put the baby seat, with you in it, on the floor near her feet. She used to say you and she studied for exams together."

The blanket disappeared before kindergarten. At first, it got smaller. And smaller still. Eventually, only a two by two-inch square remained. The disappearing blanket was one of my mother's techniques: gradual acceptance. Every few weeks, she cut the blanket in half and then in half again.

"You were inseparable, did you know that?"

I did not.

"You and your mother. You'd cry when she left the room, even for a minute. When she went to the bathroom, you'd wail until she returned. No one could comfort you. Not me. Not your grandmother."

My grandmother. My mind bounced in and out of memory.

***

"What's this I hear about you not going to college?" My grandmother passes me the peeler and nods to my hand, get busy. A full bushel of ripe peaches sits at my feet, the smell of sticky sweet is like ether, forcing my mind to quiet. Here, in this kitchen, I am most myself. At home in my skin, I am safe here, with my grandmother standing over me with her apron tied in a bow and her knee socks sagging. Joy permeates the walls; the room echoes with love.

And yet, here stands my grandmother with a decidedly disapproving gaze.

"Peel." Her command startles me. Her voice crackles. Is she angry?

I pick up the first peach and run the blades over its fuzzy skin. "These peelers need to be sharpened," I tell her, demonstrating. She ignores me. There are a lot of peaches in a bushel, and I feel a little intimidated. This job will never get done. Not that I have anywhere else to be. My high school classes end at noon and, as a Senior, I have no homework or assignments. I am basically free until dinner.

For a while, I had an afterschool job in the clinic where my father is the Chief of ENT. Ear, nose and throat. It was temporary, a six-week stint filling in for an employee on maternity leave. I filed away test results and made reminder phone calls to people with upcoming appointments. I liked that job. I was good at it.

Grandma pulls the big soup pot out from under the counter and places it on the stove. We are making peach marmalade. "That's just about the craziest news I've ever heard! Not going to college!" She stands with her hands at her midsection, elbows pointing out like wings. "Your grandfather is rolling in his grave. He wanted badly to go to college. His father refused, he needed all the boys to help him in the store. Only the youngest was allowed to leave the business. Only your great Uncle Bill."

I stab the peeler into the side of a peach. "I know. I know this story. You told me a hundred times. Only Uncle Bill got to go to college. Sheesh!"

She pinches the lobe of my ear, tugging my head none too gently. "Don't be wise," she warns. "You are lucky. Your father can afford to send you and your sister to any school you want." She retrieves a second peeler and pulls a chair near. I am on the step stool, perched on the rubberized top stair. I have been sitting on this stool since before I have memory.

She bounces a peach in her palm. "What are you going to do if you stay here?" She asks, peeling the delicate skin away from the fruit with a graceful stroke. "Are you going to work in your father's office for the rest of your life? Is that what you want? To be a receptionist?"

"You sound just like my mother." I follow her hand motion, peeling, sliding the blades over slippery peach flesh. "There is nothing wrong with office work. Why do you and my mother look down on that? It's honest. It's important. You can't run an office without quality help, right? Why does that have to be the worst of all jobs for me? I like it there. I'm comfortable there." I gesticulate, a dramatic flail of my hand, and a glob of peach flies from my peeler and splats against my grandmother's apron. The noise surprises us both and before I can apologize her head falls back and she releases a roar of guttural laughter. She is a great laugher, my grandma.

We are halfway through the bushel, paring quietly. After a time, she says, "Don't let fear keep you from your dreams, little girl."

I don't know where the tears come from. One minute, I'm silently congratulating myself for peeling the entire skin off a peach in one long strand, and the next my eyes are blinded by hot water.

"I don't have any dreams," I tell her.

She reaches over her shoulder for the dish towel and uses it to wipe my face. "Nonsense."

"I don't. Not anymore." I try to stop the emotion that seems intent on consuming me. I no longer feel my feet or my legs. My arms are gone, my body is a container for the pain I am about to spill all over the remaining peaches.

She puts a sticky finger under my chin and forces me to look at her. "This is just fear talking, little girl. You listen to me. You were born to do great things. From when you were the littlest baby, I knew you were special. Don't let your fear influence you. You're supposed to be afraid. We're all afraid for heaven's sake! Look at your old grandma," she put her hand, still holding a peach, over her heart. "I'm afraid of thunder! How about that? I have to force myself not to hide in the bathroom when the storms are overhead!" The peach slipped from her grasp and rolled down her belly, dropping soundlessly into her apron pocket.

"Damn," she swears, retrieving the fruit. "I'll need to clean my ring," she says, showing me. Her engagement ring is pinned inside her apron pocket. "This will be yours one day," she says. "I'm giving it to you. As a wedding present."

My throat is so dry it hurts to swallow. "I'm probably never going to get married," I tell her. It's my worst fear. And my biggest expectation.

"Pish posh," she says, forcing another fruit into my hands. "You have no idea what the future holds."

We've been depositing the peeled peaches into a bowl the size of a bathtub. My grandmother picks it up by the handles as if it has no weight at all and lifts it to the kitchen table. "Bring the last ones here. I'll start the slicing."

At last, we are ready to cook. The peaches are in the soup pot on the stove. She tears open a five-pound bag of cane sugar and upends it over the slices. No wonder I love her marmalade! "Now, add water," she tells me. "Pour water until the level reaches the knobs."

"The knobs?" I turn to her.

She points at the bolts that affix the sturdy handles to the sides of the huge pot. "The knobs," she says.

"Don't you measure?" I ask.

"This is measuring," she says.

I start to pour the water into the pot. "What if you use a different pot?"

She waggles a finger at the stove. "Watch what you're doing!" she says. I've spilled water over the stove. We both watch the little puddles sizzle and then evaporate. "Focus on what you're doing," she says. "That's the answer to all the questions. Just focus, do your best, and everything will work out."

TWENTY

Everything did *not* work out.

I tried to fit in, I really did. I tried to support myself. I had a lot of low-level jobs, back-room jobs like bookkeeping and making appointments and counting inventory. Sometimes I made enough to cover my rent. And when I ran out of money, my mother sent a check to help me out. Sure, they were all crap jobs. I ran the cash register at a pizza store, I was a receptionist at a roadside motel while my peers graduated from college and took jobs with capitalized titles. They married and reproduced and drove Volvos and Town Cars that shined with potential.

I disappeared into myself. I moved in ever-smaller circles, keeping low and sharing little. I had my family. I pretended that was enough.

It wasn't enough. I got tired. Tired of minimum wage, tired of television commercials showing beautiful people finding pleasure in water skiing and horseback riding and cozying up on the couch in front of a fire. I got tired of hoping.

"You were always too sensitive," my grandmother once told me. "Even as a child. You cried at every little thing, as if every moment hurt you personally." I was probably in my early teens. She was teaching me to knit. We sat close together on the sofa in my grandmother's living room with the television on low. "Try not to let every bad thing affect you. Remember, God gave you two ears, so you could let things go in one ear and out the other," she coached me over the clicking of her needles. My hands worked much slower, but they kept moving. I was good at crafts.

"You have to be careful," she said, knitting furiously, "not to overreact. That's a trait you share with your father, only where he gets angry you get sad." Her needles stilled. "Someone in the family once said, you were never the same after Celia was born, but that is not at all true. You are what God made you. A terrific sister. A wonderful friend and a loyal companion." She jabbed her elbow until it connected with mine. "You can be happy," she said. "You can learn how to be content with your life," she explained as if I would ever understand. "It's a process. You have to work at it."

I didn't want to work at it. I didn't want to work at anything.

TWENTY-ONE

We were waiting for the transport to the psychiatric floor. I'd never been there before. I was sort of looking forward to it.

My mother slipped into the room. "Celia wants to talk to you," she held out her cell phone. "Are you awake enough to talk? She's angry. You'd better take it."

Celia? Angry? She hardly ever got angry. I put the phone to my head and grunted.

"What the fuck, Charlotte." Her words were wet. I pictured water spraying from her lips. "I thought you said you were feeling really good. I thought you said you were doing great. Didn't we just have a good conversation? Why do you have to scare the shit out of everyone? How can you be so selfish? Other people have problems, too, you know." I waited, listening. I'd never heard this tone in Celia's voice before. High-pitched, too loud. It was a screech, really. She sounded like our mother.

"I'm sorry," I said in my calming voice. I wanted to tell her I'd just misjudged something. I was so tired from sitting up all night with Jimbo. I didn't know what I was doing.

"What is the matter with you?" Celia wailed. "Don't you know how important you are to me? Don't you know that I depend on you, I need you. You can't be this reckless. You're putting yourself in real danger. Think about me, Char," she said.

My mother took the phone away and snapped it closed. "It's a good question, Charlotte. What about us? Did you think what all this does to us?" Her lips barely moved. "What about me?"

***

I am thinking about Celia. It's a murky memory. My father and mother are in a whispery huddle in front of the custom-made valuables cabinet, a floor-to-ceiling wall of mirrors with a hidden door that opens at the slightest touch. This is where they go to talk *in private*, out of earshot of the children. Into the corner of mirrors, not five feet from the kitchen sink. If I wanted, I could read their lips from multiple locations including the front hall, the bathroom, and the kitchen.

I hear my father agree to something. My mother's tone lilts. Is she nervous?

In the mirror, my father's face is eager, his blue-gray eyes welcome whatever my mother is transmitting to him. My father does not have what you call a 'poker face.' He can't get through a joke without breaking up before the punch line. His eyes harden into marbles when he's angry and soften to cream puffs when he's not. He lifts his wrist, checking his watch, and his eyes find mine in the mirrored reflection.

"Hey Charlie," he says. No one calls me Charlie except my father.

I am working on a craft project in the kitchen using Gardener's Eden Twist Ties. I love this stuff. I wrap a length of wire around the stems two and three times, making sure the green wire is perfectly flat. If you do it right, the wire is invisible. Whoever realized that twist ties, plain coated wire, had applications beyond clamping off stinky garbage bags was a real genius. I tuck the end piece into the cleft between the naked stems.

I've created a corsage. I rinse the petals under a gentle spray with the faucet and then place the flowers on a paper towel to dry. I open the junk drawer in search of a safety pin. I rummage in paperclips and postage stamps and pencils with no tips.

"In the sewing kit." My mother is so helpful. I already know that the safety pins are in the sewing kit. I was hoping to find one lone pin so I wouldn't have to walk all the way down into the basement.

I find a safety pin. Back at the sink, I wrangle the base of the pin into the tight band of wrapped twist tie, forcing the thin metal all the way through so that the locking mechanism is exposed. This will work, I smile at my own ingenuity. I have made a perfectly professional corsage.

"You almost ready to go?"

My father is taking me to a movie. It is the night of my senior prom.

Celia is going to the prom with Peter, who used to be my friend. Peter and I never had anything romantic between us. We'd been in every class together, in every grade. We joked that we'd end up one day in the same nursing home. We weren't even really friends. We'd just been thrown together so often, we sort of got used to each other. Like cousins.

My father stands behind me, watching. I so rarely see him standing still. It feels weird to have so much of his attention. "You gotta love a Clint Eastwood movie," he tells me, rocking onto his toes. "This one's a comedy," he says. "Not a gunslinger western." He loves a western. Sometimes, during the night when I can't sleep, I find him in his big chair in the den watching old western movies on television. Those are the best nights; I curl up on the couch and watch with him. Those nights I like to pretend we are the only two people in the world.

There are only a few confirmed couples in my grade, not many. We move more in groups. The burnouts smoke cigarettes in the Pit, the designated smoking area outside the building, between the trash containers. The arts kids spend their free time making posters and conjuring themes for school events that lend well to decorative flourishes. The music kids are inaccessible because they carry their instrument cases all day. Peter is a rarity: he's one of those kids who bridges several groups. He plays the drums in the band, and he carries his sticks in the back pocket of his jeans, which is very cool. He has Jackson Browne hair and wears John Lennon glasses. He doesn't smoke, but he hangs out in the Pit while we suck away at our cigarettes. In the fall he runs track. And he also holds the record for the 5k in cross country.

Peter had broached the subject of the prom two weeks before the tickets went on sale. "You going to grace this event with your presence?"

"Prom? Nah." I knew he wasn't asking me to go to the prom with him. He and I would never deign to attend such a lame event. We were walking home together after band practice. Peter twirled his drumsticks as we walked, like a parade marshal.

But maybe he was.

"I thought that wasn't your scene."

"It isn't," he agreed.

"A bunch of us are meeting at the overpass," I told him. The overpass is a clearing beside the railroad tracks that runs through our town. It's a favorite hangout for the young and truant. "We might go over to Friendly's." A big night. Get high at the overpass and then wander into town for a double cheeseburger and a banana barge. Sounded good to me.

Peter scratched his armpit using the tip of a drumstick. "Well, I might go this time. Since it's our last one." The sticks weaved between his fingers like a baton, twirling. "So it'll be cool if I take Celia?" It wasn't a question. "Since you don't want to go."

I went with Peter to rent his tuxedo. He kissed me afterwards, saying I was his best friend and pretending he couldn't have figured out how to pick out his prom suit without me. But he and I were just friends. So it was okay.

My mother is puttering in the valuables cabinet pretending to do something. The shelves in there are lined in felt; putting the formal wear away is like reaching into a tomb. Soft and warm and uniform in color, the drawer is my favorite part of the vault. It has little slots for the knives, and you just slide the blade of each knife perfectly into its own little parking space. The dishes have felt dividers in between each porcelain plate, keeping them from touching each other. Crystal glasses and fragile serving pieces have predetermined positions on the shelves, aligned and spaced carefully to avoid any possible clinking. When I was little, I thought the valuables cabinet would be a great place to live.

I hear footsteps from overhead. Celia is moving around up there, getting ready.

"Celia!" I bellow as loud as I can. "Celia, come down."

"I'm almost done," she screams back.

"Just come down now, for two seconds."

"Can't you just wait until I'm finished?"

My father is mumbling something to my mother. I feel the vibration of their voices as I pass the mirrored doors. "Just come to the top of the stairs," I tell her.

She is dressed in a tight blue sheath, like a violet lily with a pair of bare feet.

"Can't you see I'm not ready!" she barks at me. "I have to do my hair and I can't find my shoes. What do you want?"

I show her the corsage. "In case that loser Peter forgets to bring you a corsage," I hold it high so she can see. It's beautiful. Glistening. The irises match her dress perfectly; people will think she picked the dress just to match the flower.

When we get into the car, my father says: "That was really nice, what you did for Celia."

TWENTY-TWO

A clown head poked into the doorway, sideways. It was Jimbo, wearing a mask. "Where's the party?" He bobbed the plastic head around, making fun.

He came fully into the room and slid the mask off. "The prodigal husband returns," he said, plopping into the chair my mother had vacated. He exhaled. "Whew. I almost didn't make it back. I took the wrong elevator and ended up in the bowels of the building. And let me tell you, it's not pretty down there."

My spine relaxed into the mattress.

"I ended up at the morgue." He pretended to shiver. His soft jowls wobbled; he was trying to make me laugh. "I was going to peek in the door, but I was afraid I'd see someone on the table, in the middle of an autopsy. Can you imagine if there was a body lying there, having its head sawed open? How gross would that be?" He stuck his tongue all the way out. "You'd think I was used to gore, what with all the *CSI* we watch."

I nodded at him. It was true. We watched *Law and Order* and *CSI* and all the crime shows. We especially liked the marathons, one show after another.

"The morgue?" my father asked.

My mother whispered, "That is exactly what we were worried about."

Jimbo ignored them both. "I rode back up in the elevator with an orderly who looked like Lurch. I couldn't help myself. I said, 'There are a lot of sick people here.'"

The first laugh came out like a burp. It burned my throat a little. I tasted the loamy salt of charcoal on the back of my tongue. The second laugh came easier.

Jimbo laughed along with me. "A lot of sick people here." He slapped his knee. "Get it? That's so funny. It kills me every time."

Choosing between doomsday parents and a joking husband was a no brainer. My eyes settled on Jimbo. My parents backed away, their gray gloom blended into the wall until their broken frames and pinched faces disappeared entirely.

Jimbo scrunched into bed next to me and grabbed a pad of fat at my hip. "Well," he said, hunching to suppress a giggle, "they seemed tense."

The warmth of his body coaxed me out of the morass of my withdrawal, my mind scrambled to focus outside its own crushing headache. He poked a finger into my belly, tickling me. I began to chuckle. The jiggling of my torso caused Jimbo to laugh, and then we were both bellowing like drunks in a bar.

Jimbo banged a spoon on the bedrail, flinging a rainbow of green Jell-O onto the floor and we laughed harder, yelling and carrying on. A nurse popped her head around the edge of the doorway, and we tried hard to quell our glee but we had very little success. Jimbo did that for me. He released me.

TWENTY-THREE

The mirror in the Walmart dressing room is a flatterer, makes me look better than I really look. I turn to one side, noting how the sundress cascades over my ass. I've lost weight.

I come out of the dressing room.

Celia is balanced on one leg, like a stork resting a limb on the low rung of the shopping cart. Her anger has long evaporated. She has brought me to Walmart to cheer me up, and it's working.

"Hey," she says, looking up. "That looks really good."

I twirl like a girl and smile with some apprehension. I am still feeling shaky, a little unsure. Leaving the hospital always sends me into nervousness. "Turns out, the hospital is good for the figure." I am not sure how long I was in there before Celia signed me out. Could have been a few hours. Or days. My head is still foggy on the details.

I almost feel lucky in this dress. I turn and turn again. "I must have lost eight pounds," I tell her with certainty. "Maybe more."

She meets my gaze. I'm stilled by the pain I see in her eyes. I've scared her. I feel sort of bad about that. I'd had a horrible headache, I told her, so Jimbo gave me one of his pain pills. I guess it was too much for me. Jimbo had called 911 when he couldn't wake me. The ambulance driver had called Celia, waking her in the night. Her name is listed in my phone under ICE: In Case of Emergency.

She was at the hospital when I arrived, holding my hand as the emergency room physicians shouted questions at me. Questions I heard but was unable to answer.

How much have you had to drink?

What did you take?

How many pills did you swallow?

They'd filled my stomach with charcoal and Celia held the bucket to my chin as I regurgitated the muddy mixture in the yellow plastic basin. Yellow. I remember thinking, who decided the colors for a hospital setting? Yellows and greens and grays. Terrible colors. Colors that make you feel sick.

The dress is pink and yellow, with a swirl of blue around the elasticized waist. "That looks really good on you," she tells me.

I center the V neck between my breasts and tug it low, exposing the long line of my cleavage. A wrap-around style is always good on me. "Jimbo likes when I show off my bust," I say. "He says, 'If you've got it, flaunt it.' Don't you love that about him? He thinks I'm beautiful."

"You are beautiful," Celia says, and I think I see water fill to the blue of her eyes.

"Horse shit," I say, laughing now. "You're just saying that to make me feel better."

"That's true," she laughs with me. "But it's not to make you feel better. I have to think you're beautiful because you look like me! And I look like you."

This is only half true. We used to look alike. When we were girls, we submitted our photographs to the Wrigley's open call for twins for a brand new Doublemint Gum campaign.

"Double Your Pleasure, Double Your Fun," we say in unison and, for a moment, we are schoolgirls again.

Celia's smile warms me. "Thank you for not telling them," I say, searching her face for the softness I know so well. She turns away.

I slide back into the dressing room. "I'm buying all these dresses,"

I call over the saloon-style shutters hanging askew. "And I want to get a case of seltzer for Jimbo."

"Is he feeling any better?" Celia's voice is timid. I'd already blasted her for criticizing Jimbo. *He couldn't even pull himself together to go to the hospital with you*? Her disbelief splotched red on her face as she stood next to me in the hospital bed, gripping the bedrail. My hands hung from restraints. Suicide watch. Again. My skin was delicate as a marshmallow heated over a flame. She shook the bed. I hurt so much I half expected to see black char on the backs of my fingers. We didn't talk for a few days after that. This shopping spree was our retail reconciliation.

"He's fine. Just needed a good night's sleep. He was just scared. You know." I push my way through the saloon doors.

Celia pushes the cart close. I drop the dresses into the metal basket and blow the hair from my face. "He's a delicate flower, my husband."

Celia almost smiles.

A large woman in a floral muumuu pushes past Celia, nearly knocking her into the cart. I help Celia make a U-turn and follow her and the cart toppling with clothes, out of the dressing area.

We share a quick wink, she and I. All is well.

"You know," Celia says as we wait in one of the long lines for the cashier, "I said I'd buy you a dress to celebrate your recovery. One dress. As in singular. I didn't mean to offer a whole new wardrobe."

There is, in truth, an entire wardrobe in the cart. Dresses. Shoes. Nightgowns and underwear. I even found a pair of jeans that fit. "No problem," I tell her. "Jimbo said I could buy whatever I wanted. He's a good husband," I say.

The carts roll forward, we are like horses trained to move in tandem. One cart stops at the conveyor, the rest of us glide to a halt, one behind the other.

"Are you sure you can afford all this?" She asks, eyeballing the two largest items in our cart. The stainless-steel crock pot will not break the bank, but the toaster oven is nearly one hundred dollars. "Maybe you should pick a different toaster oven."

"Nonsense," I shrug one shoulder. "I've always wanted one of these. My toaster oven is a standard four-slice machine. This one is not only digital, but it has a convection oven. How cool is that?" I take a Coke from the refrigerated kiosk.

"That's full of sugar," Celia reminds. "Don't you have to be more careful with your diabetes?"

I take a swig, holding her stare. "Pre-diabetes."

The trail of carts rolls forward again. Tail to nose. Tail to nose.

"And anyway," I tell her, "Jimbo is paying for all this. He told me so. I put the whole thing on my credit card, and then he pays me back in cash he gets from his trust fund at the end of the month."

"You guys are something," Celia says, shaking her head. She is not angry. Not exactly. Her eyes are wide and dry, as if she's trying to understand a hard math problem. She doesn't blink. I shove the cart a little, startling her.

"We're trust fund babies." I shout it out.

In my pocketbook, I have the invoice from my hospital stay. Twelve thousand dollars in charges and fees. We do not have twelve thousand dollars. And I knew we'd never pay off this bill. In fact, there were dozens of bills in the ceramic mail jug inside the front foyer of our house. Bills that would have to be resolved one day. Jimbo didn't pay any bills. Before we married, his mother paid for everything. And now, I do that job. While I was in the hospital, our household electric was shut off. Lack of payment. I called the power company from the hospital and settled the balance with the help of my mother, who'd offered her checkbook. I didn't ask her to do that. She offered.

"Most often, that designation means you're flush with cash," Celia notes, wryly.

It is almost our turn at the cashier. "Oh, I'm flush all right," I joke, wiping my upper lip with the butt of my hand. Celia and I are both starting menopause early. We like to compare how badly we sweat.

The lady ahead of us is paying with coupons. This is going to take forever. I have to pee.

"Do me a favor," I whisper loudly. "Stay in line while I go to the bathroom." I hurry away, walking carefully in the new shoes I just picked out. The shoebox for these shoes is in the cart, filled now with my old shoes, despite my offer to toss it into a nearby bin of boxes. No one will even know, I told Celia, but she insisted we pay for the shoes and so that is what we are going to do.

The ladies' room is empty. I go quickly and then dash out without washing my hands. Celia has already checked out and paid for everything. She waits near the automatic doors, tapping her fingertips on the handle of the cart. Her nails are painted blue.

"Ah!" I remember. "I meant to buy blue masking tape," I pause at the cart, considering. The store is so big. The household section is about a mile away. "Nevermind," I decide. "I'll get it next time."

"Why do you need masking tape?"

"I'm painting my closet," I tell her. "My shrink tells me I need to keep busy, be more active. And the closet was really a mess. I guess I'd thrown up on the carpet in there, and no one noticed until after I came home from the hospital. It stunk to high heaven. Jimbo has no sense of smell."

We roll the cart to the parking lot and dump all the bags into Celia's trunk. I am not yet allowed to drive, though I've been cheating a little bit, but only to get coffee at the 7-Eleven and pick up the racing sheets for Jimbo.

"Thanks for taking me out," I tell her when we assemble ourselves in the front seats. "It felt so good to shop. It helped take my mind off my sciatica, too. They say it's good to walk when you have nerve problems, but who wants to just walk aimlessly? It's better to walk and shop. I'm sure you agree."

Celia twists the key in the ignition and slides her sunglasses over her eyes. “You owe me four hundred and forty dollars and eighty-four cents,” she says.

I have to giggle. I can’t help it. Spending money, anyone’s money, makes me silly. “Ah well,” I say. “It’s only money.”

“Says the woman who never has any!”

TWENTY-FOUR

"But we always have Thanksgiving at Celia's house." My mother and I were at a standoff.

"That's my point," I said. "She always hosts. Don't I get a chance?" I scanned my tiny dining area. It was a square space, slightly larger than a closet. A second-hand credenza backed up to one wall. Inside, the wedding china, a gift from Jimbo's mother, remained cushioned in its foam coffin, each precious piece wrapped tightly in plastic. Only three wooden chairs fit around the table. If we had a family dinner here, I'd have to move all the cartons of Gatorade into the garage, and Jimbo's boxes of books would have to go somewhere.

I sensed the fight going out of her. "Let's not make such a big deal of this," she said. "It's just easier this way. She has that big table and all the place settings. But if you want to talk to her about it, go right ahead."

Frustration made me antsy. I fought the urge to stamp my feet, for she would surely hear it, even through the phones. "I just think I should get a turn." I refused to relent.

Thanksgiving was a big deal in my family. When we were young, we shared the holiday with our cousins and grandparents. It was something to look forward to then; a festive reunion that lasted the whole weekend. A guaranteed good time. Last year, we'd arrived late due to a miscalculation in Jimbo's medications, pills taken too close to our departure time. I had to wait for him to wake up before loading him into the car. But we got there. Late, but present.

"But let me be clear," she had that chastising tone in her voice; heat prickled the back of my neck. "No one wants a repeat of last year."

I knew she'd bring that up! Jimbo had fallen asleep at the table and drooled onto the fancy tablecloth. So what?

Fuck you. That's what I wanted to say. Fuck you for insulting my husband. You never liked him! I'm not surprised he went to sleep, what with all the callousness you all showed him. No one talked to him. He was an outsider, like a leper. No wonder he wanted to be numb.

"Daddy never liked him."

Her retort stung swiftly. "For heaven's sake! Your father is trying the best that he can! And you don't make it any easier. Why do you feel the need to challenge him all the time? He loves you. Isn't that enough? What more does he have to do to convince you?"

I wouldn't relent. I enjoyed the banter, the rise in her tone, the increase of nasal vibration. Very bassoon-like.

My father sounded more like a saxophone. Low, deep, resonant. Even in a whisper, his sound reached my bones. "He's playing fast with the drugs." My father had pulled me aside after dinner last year, after the turkey was cleared away and the diners had splayed themselves around the huge stone colonial that housed my sister and her family. It was a beautiful home. Neat and pristine and full of nice things. Not suitable for me, but it was a nice house; no two ways about it. "You can love him without joining him. Don't let him convince you of anything. You remember that."

It wasn't as if I hadn't tried. When I came home from the hospital, I made Jimbo swear to wean himself off one of his meds. I didn't care which one. I just wanted to have some progress to report, something to prove he was making an effort.

"He's much better now," I lied. "We've been going to a new therapist, and he just remarked this week that he was very impressed with our progress." I kept talking, adding details to the fiction recounting how many sessions we've done so far (four) and what time of day is optimal for our appointments (noon, at the earliest because Jimbo is a late sleeper).

I did find a therapist, that part was true. And Jimbo agreed to go, so that was true too. But when it came time to make an appointment, well, we just didn't see the reason to waste a day.

I listened to her breathe.

"What's going on?"

She didn't answer for a long while. "Well, your father isn't feeling well," she said. This was news. My father was rarely sick, and I couldn't ever recall her describing him as feeling unwell.

"Stomach?" I asked. "I had a stomach flu the night before last and I was up all night with the runs. It's better now. But I must tell you, I was really sick." The door was wide open for a new course heading, and I charged through like a schooner at full sail. "Jimbo took such good care of me. He kept me company all night, bringing me water and Ginger Ale. Finally, he gave me a pill to calm my guts. It worked like a miracle! You put a tiny pill under your tongue, and *poof!* All the pain subsides! Like magic!"

She responded quickly. "What pill?"

Figured. It was just like her to ignore the great good news of my recovery and hone in on the insignificant.

"It was probably like Pepto, only stronger." The question of my poor judgment was a topic that we exploited with some regularity. In fact, we revisited it like clockwork, like that geyser in Yellowstone National Park. Bad decisions galore: that was me. Bad decisions on top of bad decisions. Interestingly, she was unaware of some of the serious bad decisions I'd made. She based her entire criticism of me on the few paltry examples that seemed perennially handy to her.

I wanted her to realize that I'd become an independent woman. But that was not the way we related to each other. No matter my age, we reverted to the old ways. She was back at the helm, I was left dangling, flapping in the wind.

"So, are you fine now?" she asked, already exiting the conversation.

"Yup."

"Good. Now don't take any more medicine!"

"Yeah, yeah," I said. "Tell Dad I said hi. What's wrong with him anyway?"

"Probably nothing," she said, rushed. "He is just not himself."

I laughed. "Who is?"

I felt nothing at that moment beyond a self-satisfied contentment with my own communication skills. I'd requested to host Thanksgiving, and I'd shared with my mother a quality scenario where I was able to manage an illness on my own. I would have thought she'd be thrilled. But rather than praise, she offered nothing to indicate that she was pleased with me. Nothing at all.

***

Jimbo was probably right. We should have boycotted the holiday at my sister's house entirely. He reminded me how badly I'm treated in the family and that I am too often the odd man out at family occasions. But some habits are hard to break. Every year, I cooked using produce from my garden. This time I'd preserved cherries, currents, blueberries, and kumquats. I wanted to show off my jellies, my squash, and my green beans. And, for the first time ever, I had harvested enough asparagus to feed everyone.

I had to go. We had to go.

Inside, I thrummed with expectation. I'd be sure to seat Jimbo next to my grandmother, on her good side, the one with the new hearing aid. She and I were so close. Whenever there was a family activity that required partnering, she was my partner. We shared a double room on vacations, sat together at weddings ensuring that the tables were filled evenly. She was not told of my small accidents, my hospital visits. I had not yet disappointed her, not completely.

I made the green beans with slivered almonds. I made cucumber salad with dill. My house was a mess, the sink was full of rinds and shells and seeds. I made squash soup that splashed orange all over the stove and zucchini frittata that filled the house with the overpowering smell of its four cheeses. I peeled and diced so many tomatoes for the caprese salad that my fingertips split. While Jimbo watched football, I made the desserts: cheesecake, cannoli, and gingerbread. When I couldn't sleep, I baked. When Jimbo napped, I baked. The oven was always hot, always ready. The whole house smelled like spun sugar. Blondies and caramel crisps, pecan sandies and mud slides. The work was exhilarating. I felt energized, as if I could work forever. Ingredients disappeared. I went through two boxes of plastic wrap. I slept hard with sore hands and aching feet and flour flecks in my hair.

Was I overcompensating? I didn't feel nervous. Well, maybe I was a little nervous. I needed this holiday to go well. I wanted so badly to have just one occasion where I felt like an equal, like a family member in full. Not an odd man out but rather a valued participant.

We woke around noon. I made extremely weak coffee and diluted it with cream. I carried two mugs back to our bed. Jimbo took an appreciative sip and then kissed the air as thanks. "Light and sweet," I said. "Just the way you like it." We sipped, moving our feet closer under the sheet until they intertwined. Our feet liked to be together. That's what Jimbo always said. I was thinking about how we would get all the food into the car when he started to burp in little hiccups. He patted his balloon stomach and burped again.

"Are you sick?"

"Maybe." He balanced the coffee mug on the plank of his chest and reached his hand to his night table. Without counting, he spilled the contents of a prescription bottle into his mouth and washed them down with a delicate swig of coffee.

"Don't drink that," I told him. "I'll make you some tea. Tea and honey."

"Heavy on the honey, honey." He felt well enough to be silly. I went to the kitchen and set the kettle on the stove. I needed him to be in good form today. I felt a sting behind my ear. Could be a migraine coming on.

Habit lured me to open the refrigerator door. I was immediately calmed by the sight inside. Rows of Tupperware containers filled with greens and reds and oranges were waiting for their own coming-out. A column of squash soup, like orange velvet, stood sentry on the top shelf. Ziplock bags of cookies and brownies filled the compartments on the door crowding out the milk and cream and eggs. There's nothing better than a full refrigerator. The kettle sang.

In the bedroom, Jimbo had curled himself into a larva. "Your tea, sir." I gave him my best English accent. He would look good today. I had put together an outfit for him: slacks and a shirt with a sweater overtop. He only wore tennis shoes because he said regular footwear bothered his bunions, but no one would notice his shoes.

I'd bought a new dress the day before at Walmart. I bought shoes to match. I turned on the water in the shower and waited for it to get hot. "Do you want to shower with me?" I used my 'come hither' voice, memorized from hours of romantic comedies and black and white classics.

"I can't."

I caught sight of my face crimped with tension in the unbroken half of our medicine cabinet mirror and I forced myself to stop and face my image. I loosened my lips, softened my eyes. The act of watching while altering my appearance in the mirror was a magic exercise; I felt calmer.

From inside the shower, I called out: "Come on in, the water's fine!"

False cheer. I was getting worried. "We don't want to be late. We're late. We're late. For a very important date."

Little ditties helped me feel confident. I have no idea if, as a child, my mother distracted me in times of distress with songs and rhymes. Maybe she did. I can't remember.

I toweled off and turned to the bed. "Hey, lazy bones! Get moving!"

He groaned. "I don't feel right." He put a hand over his brow. "I might have a fever."

"You just need a hot shower." I pulled the dress over my head. "It's nearly one. And we have to be there by three." This was a lie. I lied to my husband, something I'd sworn to never do. But I had no choice. My sister said that we should plan to eat around five. Five is much later than three, but I figured we'd use the extra time to prepare. We could sit in the car and review the personalities of each person, which would make Jimbo feel more confident as if he knew everyone better. I waited while he put on the pants and the shirt. He didn't like to shave. In truth, he had little facial hair other than the goatee-style beard. There was some brown-gray scruff on his jowls, but I felt sure no one would notice that.

I wanted the day to be a success, and I needed him to make a responsible entrance if only to prove that his last stumbling approach, when he tumbled into the foyer and lay, passed out, on the floor for two hours, was a fluke.

I loaded the car while Jimbo rested on the couch watching the Macy's Day Parade on television, wrapped in my grandmother's afghan. I would tell her about that later, about how cute he looked mummified in the yarn she so expertly knitted for me.

It was an easy twenty-minute drive. We did stop once, at 7-Eleven, to pick up the racing sheets, but that only took a minute. I left the car running in the parking lot and just dashed in to make the purchase and to wish Plots a happy holiday even though he didn't understand the national importance of Thanksgiving. Jimbo waited in the car, his head bobbing in the passenger seat of the idling car.

Celia came running out of the house as soon as she heard the car drive up, and in moments we were encircled by a swarm of relatives.

We unloaded the containers of food. Jackson opened all the lids before lifting them from the trunk, tasting everything with a teenage finger. He was my favorite because he liked doing what I liked to do: gardening, cooking, playing with dogs.

"Come in! Come in! We've been waiting for you! Look who's here! And on time for once!"

Leave it to my sister to bring up a past transgression. I let it slide. My mood was elated, her insult didn't even graze my skin. My grandmother signaled me with a crooked finger, and I kneeled on the floor in front of her.

"Hello Dolly," she said, and I arched up to kiss her. God, I loved her. She had an ability to see me, to see the real me. Not the damage or the mistakes or the small failures. She saw *me.* "Where is your young man?"

I laughed. "He is not young," I said. "But I'll tell him you said that."

"He's young to me."

My sister reached around my shoulder. "Look, Grandma, look what she brought. The pita bread that you like!" A triangle of toasted pita passed through to my grandmother who smiled as if graced with gold.

"I made it with rosemary this time," I told her. "From my own garden." Happiness swelled inside me as I watched her nibble the cracker. My heart filled, my stomach settled, I felt blood rushing through wide-open avenues in every limb and every organ, passing the richness of belonging throughout my being.

I felt rather than heard the change in energy behind me, emanating from the kitchen. Where there was once the mindless cacophony of chattering voices, a black hole of silence now filled the space. My grandmother's eyes lifted from my face, and I saw in them a preview of the spectacle behind me. Jimbo, it seemed, had appeared.

He stood in my sister's kitchen, leaning over the counter. I could only see the back of him. His feet were bare; he'd already taken off his shoes and socks. The hem of his slacks was caught under his heels. He rocked up onto his toes and heaved, vomiting into the sink.

The women assembled themselves quickly, snatching at the platters and open containers of food on nearby counters. My sister lifted the sacrificial turkey over her head and carried it away as if she were the grand marshal of a parade. My mother raced from side to side, passing by Jimbo's bended spine as if he were invisible.

"Seems you've married a drunk," my grandmother resettled her gaze on my face. I had to force myself to look at her.

"He's not drunk," I balked. "He woke up with a stomachache. It's probably food related. He's very sensitive to food-borne toxins…"

"Horse shit." My grandmother's expression hardened. "You've gotten yourself into a mess, little girl." Usually, I softened at the pet name. However, she looked like she'd rather squeeze the flesh of my cheek than kiss it. "And I'd like to know how you plan to get out of it."

Get out of what? I loved Jimbo, I loved having a partner, someone to sit next to at Thanksgiving. So he had some misfortunes; who didn't? It wasn't my fault that no one could accept him. My family was stubborn and closed minded and rigid. Who could possibly meet their expectations?

I wanted to say all this, but frustration closed my throat. Instead, I sealed my lips as fury boiled and shook inside me. I would not lose my temper. I would not share—even accidentally—Jimbo's story of pain and reversals. And I knew if I let my anger flow, I'd lose control of what I said and how I said it. I would not let that happen. I could not afford to lose her.

What if she knew it was not alcohol but drugs that ruled my husband? Would she still love me then?

"I'm all right." Jimbo stood in the doorway, addressing aunts and uncles and in-laws and cousins. "Just a touch of food poisoning." He waved a hand. Like the Queen Mum. "I'm going to go lie down."

I did not go into the kitchen to help clean up. There were plenty of concerned women in there, clucking like hens. Instead, I joined Jimbo on the couch and stared at the television, tuned to the Macy's Day Parade with the sound set on mute.

We do what is necessary, regardless of whatever great truths are revealed before us. I was with Jimbo. He was with me.

***

No one in my family ever thought to hold back their feelings about me. Why should Thanksgiving be any different? I was used to their bantering, their battering comments about my weight and my lifestyles and my appearance and my habits. A lifetime of insults, small and large, had created a callous around my heart, a shell of protection to shirk away voices of dissatisfaction. I barely heard them: Get a pedicure. Lose some weight. Use some make up. Is that how you're going to wear your hair? Alone, I was easy prey. Tell me what you think of me, my selfless expression must have read. Tell me how to make myself more loveable.

I did not measure up. Not from the very beginning. I don't even remember when I'd stopped trying.

My grandmother always looked upon me with affection. *You are beautiful*, her gaze assured me. *You are beautiful to me*. Her touch was always gentle, her smile unimpeded. Even when she was commanding, ordering me or chastising me, she very clearly loved me.

"Charlotte Lansing, look at me." My grandmother's voice was hard with consonants.

I was starting to feel better, looser. I sat next to her and watched the dessert trays passing around. I saw the cheesecake. The cookies. Someone had plated all the cakes and cookies. I saw the white pointy edges of a doily under the blondies. I helped myself to apple pie and pecan pie and a square of fudge.

"Charlotte!"

The Xanax I'd swallowed was beginning to take. I smiled and reached out a hand to rest on her leg, but I miscalculated, and my arm plunged into the vacant space between us. My chin connected with her shoulder and knocked the steaming teacup out of her hand.

"What is going on with you?" She dabbed the hot water from her already reddening skin. "I've never seen you like this," she spoke so quietly I had to lean toward her to catch the words. "Slurred speech. Shuffling gait. Are you sick, or are you stoned?"

I was not expecting to hear that word from her. Stoned. At first, I considered laughing. It seemed like such a fiasco, almost a swear word. I leaned toward her in camaraderie and felt myself tilting onto one hip, wobbling out of balance. It seemed as if the house itself had begun to heel, the room was atilt. I tried leaning away from her, searching for equilibrium.

Too far! I toppled sideways, lumping to the floor. My plate, still heavy with pie, upended over me. Then, the chair. A disaster.

I was on the floor, on my side, wedged half under the Thanksgiving table.

"Charlotte!"

"What's wrong with her?"

"Oh my God!"

Mike's hand reached me first. He grabbed my upper arm and held on. "Jesus, Charlotte." His words were skewed with dismay. Embarrassment. Chagrin. My dress was twisted around my midsection. The underwear I wore were Jimbo's. Shortie briefs. Much more comfortable than women's panties, but I wouldn't bother to share that with any of them. I heard screaming, chairs scraped against the floor. A plate clattered. Under the table, it was relatively quiet.

Mike had a firm grip on my arm. I had no choice but to move. He hoisted me, pulling, until I drew my legs inward and turned facedown, centered on all fours. Doggie-style. He yanked my dress down to cover my rump while I waited for the swaying seasickness to pass. A stroke would have been nice, I thought. If I'd had a stroke, there would be no room for embarrassment. No one would recall the fall and the mess if I'd suffered a stroke.

Above me, a frantic fray of bodies and chairs and voices agitated. I leaned back on my heels, kept my head down, dangling between my arms in child's pose.

My sister was at my side, reaching under my head, lifting my chin. "Are you hurt?" Her voice came to me as a squeak, too high and too tight. "Does anything hurt? Oh my God, Charlotte, what have you done?"

I was not hurt. Although I'd likely develop some aches and pains from the fall, but that would take a few hours to set in. I rocked myself back onto my heels. "I'm okay," I called out. In fact, I felt good. Really good. The men hovered overhead, waiting to be needed. The women fetched paper towels and started to clean up the mess. My mother put her palm to my head as if taking my temperature.

"Let me up."

I leveled myself on one leg, and then reached out for the chairs held steady with eager fingers nearby. I felt a sturdy hand under my arm, another on the small of my back. Be careful now. Take it slow. A hand under my elbow. Fingers smoothed my hair from my face.

When I raised my head, I saw only the distressed expressions and embarrassed tones, the rues and admonishments. A wide-angle panorama of disappointments, hovering in space. All focused on one thing. Me. The relentless calamity of me.

A trickle of urine slipped out of my body as I inched my feet around inside my sneakers. Red sneakers to match my red dress.

That pretty much ended the evening for us. Mike helped me to the car with Jimbo following close behind with the car keys dangling from his finger. At the driveway, Jimbo realized he was barefoot; he went back inside for his shoes and socks.

"Are you sure you don't want me to drive you home?" Mike asked.

"I don't mind." He reached across me to fasten the belt. "Or I could follow you in my car, how about that? Just to be safe?"

Jimbo hadn't tied his shoes. He shuffled toward the car, taking tiny steps, clumsy, as if wearing slippers. He was so cute. Like a bald Charlie Chaplin.

I gave Mike a half smile. He was a good guy. "Thanks," I said. "We're good."

Jimbo assembled himself in the driver's seat. "Here." He put a solid disk on my lap. "I brought you a plate of pie. They were going to throw it out, but I rescued it for you. Nothing wrong with it," he said. "I even nabbed you a spoon."

Jimbo was so considerate.

I balanced the plate on my knees and waved a hand to Mike who stood shivering alongside the drive, fingers tucked into his armpits. Mike was tall and straight and strong. A statue of a man.

Jimbo let the car roll backwards into the street. An undiagnosed rheumatism had frozen his shoulder and restricted his neck from rotating fully. He joked that, while driving he only made right turns, never left. That way, he spared himself the agony of twisting in the seat. He fumbled the gearshift into drive and released his foot from the brake. "*Off we go, into the wild blue yonder*," he sang the first line of the Air Force song as the car glided onward, and I chimed in with the second: "*Flying high into the sun*."

The lyric ended abruptly. Darkness tapped at the window. I saw my reflection in the glass, frizzy hair spun a halo around my head. *You are beautiful*, I conjured my grandmother's words and fought to prevent the image of her disapproving scowl from surfacing onto the glass. Her tone at dinner had scalded my heart. She'd yelled at me before, plenty of times. She had a strong hand, my grandmother, and she did not believe in unruly children. I'd been at the receiving end of her disciplinarian stare a million times, but tonight was different. She'd attacked me. Her rigidity startled me, I'd never been shunned by her before. I saw myself as a child perched on the stool in her kitchen, I saw us laughing on the couch in her living room, watching Doris Day movies and crocheting two ends of a single afghan together. We were symbiotic, we were two peas in a pod. She was my champion.

She was right to berate me. She was right to criticize. I was a disappointment and a failure.

I tugged at the fanny pack twisted around my waist. Its Velcro fastener was misaligned; the seams gaped at me like a lopsided smile.

"Turn on the heat," Jimbo said. His neck vultured forward.

Jimbo didn't like to drive. Besides having bad eyesight, he had poor spacial awareness and was unable to determine proximities with any accuracy. Basically, he was a bad driver. But that was okay with me because I loved to drive. We balanced each other out in the transportation department.

Dust blew across our faces bringing parched heat into the car. I opened the lid of the pill dispenser to an array of lovely colored tabs. Orange ovals. Purple circles. Each little square held its own collection of magic medicines. White for pain. Yellow for panic. Pink for anxiety. I plucked three or four tablets and set them on my tongue. All would be well.

The pie plate teetered. "Don't forget to feed the driver," Jimbo said.

I filled the spoon and guided it into his mouth. One bite for him, one for me. Like that, we finished the pie.

"Bet you wish I'd grabbed the a la mode!" he said, sticking his tongue all the way out. "Who knew pie made you so thirsty?" He was funny.

Jimbo drove with one tire breaching the center line; security bumps clipped under the tire with the regular staccato of a woodpecker. I liked the way the bumps felt under the car. Like they were marking time or calculating a distance. That is what I sought. Distance. Distance from the smell of warm bread and the playful sound of Jackson and Mike wrestling before dinner. Distance from the relatives and their marriages and their diets and their jobs.

Streetlamps buffered the sidewalks, some were draped already in Christmas lights. Thanksgiving night meant all the stores were closed. The towns passed like tankers, glittering their lights above the blackened sea.

I sagged in the seat, feeling all aspects of the person I was, the person my family knew, slide off my frame like ice cream off a hot spoon. Jimbo breathed through a slack-open mouth. I felt myself levitating, leaving my lumbering, cumbersome body behind like shed snakeskin seat-belted into place. I watched the road from this angle, laid out in a straight line now, the darkness on either side fading into black as the car lights charged forward. I was light, feeling silly. I wanted to laugh, to mark the instance of perfect harmony, of balance, but no lofty bellow formed. Rather, a bleat escaped my lips and penetrated the car's perfect silence like a hiccup. A bleat? What was that? I had suddenly become a sheep?

The bumps in the road had ceased thudding underneath. We'd arrived home.

TWENTY-FIVE

Celia never said hello, she started every phone conversation in the middle. "Talk to me," she said. "I'm waiting my turn at the dermatology place. Gotta take care of some personal maintenance."

"Sure." Months had passed since Thanksgiving, since my little spa vacation. That's how I thought about the hospitalizations, R&R. Celia and I never exchanged a word about either of those.

I lowered my weight onto the chaise and lit a cigarette. The backyard was a sea of wintered weeds.

The sun split the lawn in two. Like a Phantom of the Opera mask, half good, half evil. The dark half was cold and foreboding, the spare stalks of old grasses and weeds tinged gray in the low light. The sunny part was worse, illuminating the decay and disuse of each individual mound in an expanse of fetid boredom. I closed my eyes.

"What are you doing?" she asked as if sensing my mind's wandering.

"My taxes," I lied, leaning back. I did not want to think about the yard, the sun, the world's split personality.

"I can hear you smoking," she said.

"Make sure they check your ears," I responded. The ease of our banter was a welcome comfort on a still afternoon. "They're likely clogged with wax."

A squirrel sped by, startling me. She heard the change in my breath. "What happened?" she asked.

Sometimes her intuition came across as creepy. But not today. Today, I floated on her buoyant perceptiveness.

"Nothing," I said. Blah, blah, blah. "What are you having done?"

"I have to have my beard lasered, and then the age spots on my cheeks need to be sandblasted off." Say it like it is, sister. She had a way of stripping away all the decoration and exposing precisely what was below. "I wanted to have a skin tag removed before it grows into a horn, but they didn't have any time in the schedule for that. How did you manage to escape the genetic disposition of facial anomalies? You don't have any facial hair. And no sunspots. How do you explain that?"

"Simple," I said. "I never go out in the sun." It was not far from true.

"What's Jimbo up to?"

"He's watching the draft." He participated from the bed, with two laptops open and the television tuned to a sports station.

"Did I tell you, we've decided to go away for our twentieth anniversary this summer. Two weeks in Italy," her voice surged with enthusiasm. "Just think. Two weeks of pasta and chianti and garlic and olives."

"You? You're going to eat Italian food for two weeks?"

Celia kept to a strict low-carb diet. To her, pasta was poison.

"You're going to eat pasta?"

"Yes, I am."

"Aren't you the one who calibrates the nutritional complement of every item you put in your mouth?"

"One and the same," she announced. "I'm already in training mode. I have three months to prepare. No carbs. No sugar. I'm living on chicken and hard-boiled eggs."

I had to laugh. "For a girl who counts out exactly how many Saltines she's allowed to eat at one time ('six Saltines for only seventy-seven calories!'), you are the unlikeliest person to take a trip to Italy."

"Yeah, I know. It's Mike's idea. He loves pasta."

"Ah, what we do for love," I said.

I stared into the watery sky and smoked, thinking. Look what she had on the horizon. A trip to Italy. I hadn't been overseas since our parents took us to Portugal when Celia and I were both in high school.

A long spell of silence settled between us. Celia and I could be silent and together at the same time, that's one of the things I loved about my sister.

I heard Jimbo yell, "Fuck!" Guess his fantasy team lost out on signing a player. I did not understand his infatuation with sports, but that was okay. Couples didn't have to share all their hobbies, did they? A pang of lonesomeness throbbed in my chest.

"What?" she asked.

"What, what?"

"Something's off," she said. "You sound funny."

"I didn't even say anything," I say, flooded with the pure pleasure of intimacy.

When I was a teenager, I cried to my mother in self-pity: "I'll never have a daughter."

Her immediate answer: "You have a sister."

I had Celia.

I had Celia and Jimbo and a house and a car. What more did I need?

"So, you might as well know," she said. "I did something that is going to make you mad."

I ground the cigarette out on the broken cement. The patio needed to be resurfaced. It was cracked and shrinking, its edges falling away into the dirt. "Okay," I said, ready.

"Well, you know I've been worried about you. I haven't seen you in a while, and you don't always answer your phone, which pisses me off."

"Uh-huh."

"And now Mike and I are going away and I'm totally freaking out that you'll do something crazy."

"Like what?" I asked her. "What could I possibly do? Get arrested for growing weed?"

"Are you growing weed?"

I scanned the far fence. No. Nothing was alive back there. "Not anymore."

"I called that ER doctor," she said slowly. "The one you saw in the hospital last time. I just wanted someone to know that I was going away and that you were on your own."

"On my own?" I was not on my own, not anymore. I had Jimbo, and he had me.

"Of course, he would never breach your confidence, and neither would I," she talked fast. "I didn't ask him any questions or reveal anything, in any way. I just wanted to fortify the support system in my absence."

Silence.

"Are you there? Don't be mad."

I watched a tiny black spider skittle on a dead leaf. "I'm here." The spider traversed the edge and then disappeared around the leaf's underside. I wasn't mad. In fact, I felt completely content. Why wasn't I more upset? She'd gone behind my back. She'd intervened, invaded. I should have been furious. But at that moment, I was perfectly at ease. Maybe it was the Klonopin I'd taken an hour ago. I imagined Celia sitting in the waiting room of the dermatology clinic, waiting for a skinny, cold fingered technician to burn the uglies off her face, and I could only smile. Look at the differences between us. She was basically shackled to an examining table, and I was out in nature, free.

I often compared our lives, Celia's and mine, especially when I was single. Her life fluctuated with career and family, all that I wanted, while mine remained stagnant and yet her affection for me never changed. Celia was worrying about me. There was some satisfaction in that.

"Are you still taking the anti-depressants?"

"Yup." I'd been taking them since I was sixteen. Sure, they changed over time. Dosages went up, never down. Newer drugs were introduced and replaced and replenished.

"Promise me," she said. "Promise that you won't do anything stupid. Anything careless."

"Aye, aye." My acquiescence slid out as naturally as an egg slides out of a hen. Sloop. There. I said it. I promised. It was so easy, so simple to placate her. She was my self-decreed supporter, my ally in the family. She liked to think of herself as helpful to me, and I allowed her to do so. In fact, her friendship was very dear to me. But it was also separate from me. She left twenty years ago.

"I'm not supposed to tell you but…," she paused, and paused. "Well, Mom has been talking about an intervention. You know how you used to talk about Jimbo going to rehab? Well, she thinks *you* should maybe go to rehab. She said we're supposed to look for warning signs."

"What signs?"

"Like if you're sleeping too much, if you neglect your garden, if your voice sounds slurry."

"Fuck her." I spat the words like projectiles. "She hates Jimbo, that's it. She makes no pretense of even trying to like him. Forget accepting him into the family. You'd think that seeing her daughter happy would be enough for her. But noooo." My energies coalesced, compacting to an icy hard ball. "She is so superior. She does not like that I am, for once in my life, with someone. My attention is diverted away from her and Dad, and—here's what I really think. I think that Mom has suddenly realized that she is not the focus of my life. I think she is jealous of what Jimbo and I have!"

The conclusion was like a spark to tumbleweed. The tide reached its apogee, the moon of emotion was full. I felt it full on, a slap-in-the-face hatred for my mother that nearly sucked the air right out of my own lungs.

"I don't know, Charl," Celia started.

"Well I do," I interrupted. "And I'll tell you exactly what the problem is: all these years, Mom was secretly happy that I was alone. She always wanted me to live nearby so that I could take care of her, of them, in their old age. Think about it!"

"Well…," Celia's tone was hollow and deep. "You're making a lot of assumptions, Charlotte. I think they are happy for you. They just don't want you to get hurt. Or to disintegrate."

Disintegrate. My mother's word. She was always worried that I gave myself over to Jimbo, that I became more like him and less like myself. That I was disintegrating in front of her eyes.

I tasted the word in my mouth, its familiarity coated my tongue like syrup. It was getting colder outside. I slipped another little white tab into my mouth and let the noise of our conversation flutter in my head. Intervention? Bitterness flooded my mouth as the pill began to dissolve. I sank into the flimsy mesh of the chair, waiting for the calm assurance its elixir would bring.

"Anyway," she was cutting herself loose. "Here I go. Wish me luck."

I wished her luck and then disassembled myself off the rickety chair. I should replace it, the one tired chaise I owned. Jimbo never sat outside. At one time, I'd picked out a new set from Walmart but then we forgot about it. It wasn't as if adding outdoor furniture would convince him to enjoy the yard with me. I thought about pulling up a few weeds, the ones nearest my bare foot were tall as early corn, but I didn't really see the point. Weeds grew back, no matter what I did.

The sun crept lower. Soon I'd have to retreat to the warmed interiors of the house. I surprised myself then, with the realization that I did not want to go inside. I did not want to hear Jimbo's shouts as he interacted with all his internet buddies. I did not want to face the empty living room, the cluttered kitchen. There was so much work that needed to be done in the house. Cabinets were hanging crooked from broken and rusty hinges. The DIY floor tiles no longer stuck to the cement subfloor; they sat atop striations of dried glue, their edges curled at the tips like bats' wings. Carpenter ants had eaten a hole the size of a plum into the wallboard of the foyer. I'd emptied two cans of Raid around the wall's perimeter and wedged a wad of Brillo into the hole. I'd intended to hang wallpaper over the eyesore but a twinge of nerve pain in my neck while holding up the edge of the first panel convinced me otherwise; long shiny rolls of unopened paper, pink and green leaned like gigantic pixie-sticks in a webby corner.

I stood with my back against the aluminum siding, sheltered from the sun by a strip of overhanging roof.

Just then, I saw so clearly that my life was hurdling toward something absolute, something on the horizon, anchored in place and not ever to be moved. I could see the end. I knew my destination, where to set my sightlines, how to plot my course. I would turn with the winds, tacking and trimming, but the basic trajectory of my journey remained clear. That knowledge changed everything for me. I was overcome with a sense of pure contentment. Suddenly, I was empowered with an uplifting gust of domination.

A carpenter ant crawled along the edge of my bare foot. I crushed its exoskeleton into dust under my tread-thick heel and headed inside.

TWENTY-SIX

"Hi Charlotte." My mother's voice lawn-darted through weeds of my barbiturate tangles, agitating, invading. "Are you up? Turn on the local news. I just saw a trailer for the noon show. They're doing a story about your program."

My program?

"You know," she added as if she had X-ray vision. Could she see my confusion through the walls of our houses, across the towns, cleaving the jumbled space in between? Often, her intuition penetrated my disassembled thoughts before I'd had the opportunity to assemble them for myself. "Your therapy in the garden thing."

My therapy in the garden thing. Ah, yes. Therapeutic Horticulture. What a genius idea that had been! My interest in psychology had not waned; rather I'd forgotten about it altogether. I had been accepted into one certificate program about ten years back, and I don't really remember what happened to intervene. I think I just decided against being in school. The regimen, the demands. It had seemed too rigorous for me. I was very definitely afraid of failing.

I was already good at gardening; I was happiest when my hands were busy in the dirt, clearing away the complications of nature and revealing the path to the sunlight for all the little lives to follow. Gardening was easy. The plants never minded that I smoked or had thick crusts of callous on my heels. The garden did not coil away from me when I jumped from job to job, career to career. It was never disappointed. It made no judgments.

Sometimes, during the night, when I was unable to sleep, I'd pad outside in my nightshirt and visit my garden in the night gray-light, coaxing weeds to release their grip on the earth, caressing the tongues of the corn stalks. I hadn't tended the living menagerie of the garden in a long time. What was the word my sister had used? Fallow?

"Charlotte? Are you there?"

I made a snorting noise, confirming my existence. My head was swollen inside; I heard distant sounds, elongated consonants, woodpecker punctuations.

What had happened to the Therapeutic Horticulture idea? I had filled out the application but couldn't remember if I'd sent it or not. I remembered buying all the supplies through the online distributor linked to the application's website. The cartons, some of them the size of bathtubs, were stacked where the UPS truck had deposited them: on the gravelly side yard facing the street. Were they still there? I tried to remember when I'd last been outside in the driveway.

"I was thinking about making another batch of that currant chutney again, the one everyone liked at Thanksgiving." A black hole of silence, and then her voice reemerged: "Charlotte? Can you hear me? I hate this phone. I don't know how you and Celia ever convinced me to get a smart phone. What good is a smart phone when it's in the hands of a dumb user?" She laughed. I watched a swirl of butterflies dancing over my bed.

Jimbo's CPAP machine hummed a numbing melody, white noise. Thanksgiving? Current chutney? Smart phone. What was she talking about?

I let my head fall to the side. It was somewhere before noon, I could see the eleven glowering at me from the clock, but the other two digits were distorted, hidden by a sail of torn paper. What was that? A pamphlet torn open?

"I had a great idea just now," my mother announced. "Why don't you meet me at West Marine and help me pick out some fishing gear for your father's birthday. Do you have a gift already? Who knows, you may see something in the store that catches your fancy."

I stared at the clock and remembered. I'd been coughing. Jimbo said it sounded like a rumbling freight train; he said it interfered with his sleep. And so he'd quieted my cough with a small infusion of morphine. Obviously, it had worked. I'd slept a long time.

"And if you feel like it, we can get some lunch." Like water boiling, her words bubbled around and around. Lunch? What had happened to breakfast?

My mouth felt like it was full of sand. "Lunch?" I ground the word into two syllables. Luh-unch.

A stillness ensued. The quiet before the storm. And then, atonal words. "Are you feeling okay?"

"Sure." I broke the suction that held tongue to palate and tried to pull some saliva from the depths of my cheeks. "I'm fine."

"What are you doing? You sound distracted." She was not going to stop. "Did I get you in the middle of something?"

Yes. That was it. "I'm cooking." A perfect answer. Cooking was a hobby we shared, something we could talk about. I inched myself up against the headboard until I was half-sitting. I saw the clock: Eleven fifty-eight. Jesus, I'd slept over ten hours! I reached out a foot and prodded the mound that was Jimbo. In sleep, he'd mummified himself within the sheets. Only his bald head stuck out. A pupa. That's what he looked like. A new life, fragile and full of possibilities. His breathing apparatus was the perfect image of an incubator.

"What are you making?"

"Soup."

"Soup? I thought you made soup last night?"

I searched for a cigarette, swiping aside the evidence of last night's ministrations. Syringe. Torn plastic. Jimbo had torn open the vacuum-sealed pouch that contained the single-dosage vial of morphine with his teeth, making me laugh. "You're an animal!" I'd tickled his ears with my fingers, pushing the tips of my pinkies deep into the waxy caverns of his ears, in and out, in and out, an audacious massage that sent him, as usual, to giggling. I loved that sound, of Jimbo giggling.

I couldn't help myself. I giggled too. It didn't come out as a giggle, though. It was more of a gurgle. Overnight, an accumulation of mucous and dryness and irritation had pooled in my throat. I sputtered and coughed, and then spit into the water glass near the clock. I rocked Jimbo's body with my foot, urging him to wake. Tiny white lights of pain twinkled inside my eyes with every one of my guttural exhales. I guess I'd dropped the phone.

With one hand, I lit a menthol cigarette and coughed out its exhaust. "Ouch, ouch ouch." Slices of pain cut along my rheumy throat. "Charlotte?" My mother's voice came to me from far away. Where was the phone?

I bounced my ass against the mattress, hoping to unearth the cell phone from its nook between the heavy quilt.

I shook the bed again and felt Jimbo finally beginning to stir. "Wake up, husband."

He lifted his head and arched back like a newly born bird; he pulled the CPAP mask away from his face. It left a red octagon, the trace outline of a *Stop* sign, imprinted on his skin.

"Hello wife," he said, smiling. His caramel voice invited me to join him on his pillow, and I slid down, rolling onto my side.

The phone fell from the accordion folds of my neck. I'd forgotten all about the call, the conversation. I toyed with the idea of disconnecting my mother, as if by accident, but for some reason I lifted it, instead, to my ear.

"Charlotte, tell me the truth. Are you really just waking up at this hour? At noon?"

The panic in her voice released in me an immediate reaction of consolation. "Don't be ridiculous," I croaked. "I've done ten things this morning already." A lie. It sat comfortably between us.

I was at the helm, in full control. I delivered, to my mother, a practiced recitation of my schedule. I could not meet for lunch as *the guy* was due to arrive any minute now. To fix a leak, to repair the washing machine, to patch a hole in the roof. Lie, lie. Lie. Later, one of Jimbo's friends was coming over to watch the hockey game. A lie. While they watched the game, I was going to bake. Lie.

The dialogue pulsed with a slow thud of a drum, lie, lie, lie. I was convincing, offering all the things she wanted to hear. I was canning the last of the tomatoes, which was a lie. I'd given up on the tomatoes weeks ago; I just didn't have the strength to go out there every day and futz with them. So much work! What the birds didn't get, the worms did. So I left them there, browning on the vines, eventually drooping to the dirt.

I was planning a get-together for Jimbo's college friends—another lie but how she loved to hear that I was entertaining! How many people? What will you serve? If her questions were the nails in a coffin, my answers were the hammer, walloping down with virile enthusiasm, confining me, imprisoning me in my own imagined social life. I added details, and then added some more. This is what it must feel like, I wondered, to do heroin. One taste worked to solve the problem, and you wanted more and more and more.

Behind the rhythm of my words, I sensed slack in our tether; I became suddenly, dully, alarmed. What had I told her? Had I been at all clear headed, or more emotionally astute, I might have realized that my mother was still trying her hardest to believe I would be fine.

TWENTY-SEVEN

Celia picked me up in her battered Honda at noon. It was hot that autumn day, and we'd planned to go to the orchard and pick apples. We did this every year, just the two of us. Jimbo and I had been cooped up for nearly a month with a virus that had infected us both.

"It started with what we thought was food poisoning," I said as Celica bounced along the poorly paved boulevard of my small neighborhood. "We'd been to the seafood buffet that day, and both of us had fried clams. So it was either the clams or the scallops. Or the shrimp."

Celia lowered the radio and looked at me with one eyebrow tilted down. "Did I ask you for the list of physical symptoms?"

I had to laugh. Celia could always see through me. "No. I guess you did not. But I wanted to say how happy I was to be picked up and taken out! I feel like I've been trapped in that house forever," I lowered the window a fraction.

"No cigarettes allowed in my car." Celia used her control panel on her armrest to close my window. Celia had quit smoking when we were still in our twenties. We'd done it together, only she'd succeeded, and I failed. "You know, you really don't have to stay home and take care of him. He's a grown man. You shouldn't treat him like a toddler."

"I don't treat him like a toddler," I said. "For your information, Jimbo took care of *me* these last weeks, not the other way around. I was much sicker than he was. In fact, I think it finally settled in my chest, and I am pretty sure I had another pneumonia."

Celia made a tsking sound, corrective, putting an end to my illness review. "You're the one who brought it up. I wasn't going to talk about being sick."

"You're not sick now, right?" Celia signaled to change lanes. She was an overly cautious driver in my opinion. But that was her way with everything. Caution.

"Correct," I confirmed.

"And he is not sick either," She shrugged. "So why are you babying him?"

"I don't baby him! I just wanted to make him a sandwich before I left, so he'd have something healthy to eat when he wakes up later." I let that sentence slide out knowing it would lure her to comment. Like an ant to spilled honey.

"Healthy? What is your definition of healthy?" Where I had a weight problem, Celia had none. Where I craved comfort foods, Celia craved salad. Salad!

"I made chicken soup this morning, and then I made a batch of meat lasagna for us to eat for dinner. If he gets super hungry, he can eat the lasagna now and we'll have something else for dinner." I envisioned Jimbo sitting on the couch, legs crossed underneath his spare frame, balancing a bowl of steaming lasagna on his wide-spread knees.

"Lasagna," Celia repeated. "Lasagna is a health food to you."

It was not a question. And so I didn't answer. We rode a while, listening to the whistle of the car's aging chassis. Celia's car wheezed like an old hound: it rattled and coughed dependably as we traversed the county. Ours was farm country: peaches, corn, berries, and ducks. My first job had been at a duck farm, monitoring the health of the huge pond that filled nearly half of the acreage with natural waters seeping in from underground, invisible aquifers. We were driving past it now, Haynes Duck Acreage, when Celia mused, "Remember when you worked at the duck farm and I had a humongous crush on the owner's son? What was his name? Rand? Something like that?"

Rand. That was his name. She had a good memory, my sister.

Rand was my age and in my class at school. And he was beautiful. Tall and wide and bronzed from his work in the sun. One long ago winter, Celia told my mother about him, that she liked him, that she wanted him to take her to the prom. My mother scowled, trying to remember the scoop on the Haynes family, and when she'd exhausted that avenue, she'd rebuked Celia with a single sentence: "Does he even know how to read?"

My mother felt that farmers were below her, and that Celia and I should only aim for the highest targets. Don't be a nurse, she'd said, be a doctor. Don't be an assistant, she'd said, be the boss. I guess her prodding worked on Celia because she'd married a professional. He had a 'Mr.' in front of his name. For herself, Celia defied my mother in her own benign way; she'd become a cardiac catheterization nurse. A nurse, yes. But a *specialist,* my mother confirmed.

***

Back then, we moved in groups, and no one really noticed that I never paired up with anyone. On weekend nights, we'd gather at one person's house and then moving as a clod from basement to basement, drinking from the open liquor bottles in our parents' cabinets and smoking pot out behind garages where we were sure not to be seen. But I noticed.

There was a time when I thought someone really liked me; I certainly liked him, but it turned out he only wanted to get with Celia. We'd gone to the beach, the whole bunch of us. I'd lagged behind, hauling the food from the trunk when one of Celia's friends approached me with an accusation, angling her head into the sun. "Don't get your hopes up," she'd said, watching the guy I liked moving away from the car.

I didn't go to the beach after that. The heat made me break out in hives, and I didn't like the sand burning the soles of my feet. I did like swimming in the rivers that carved into the county's landscape. River water is cold, always. In some places, the currents are strong enough to tear the swimsuit top right off a girl, ask me how I know.

When I was thirteen, I was a River Otter. That was what the strongest swimmers in summer camp were called. River Otters. Or ROs. I lead a group of ROs across a narrow ravine, demonstrating how to cross and where to set down our feet on the far side. In some places, the currents are strong enough to carry a whole man downstream, but I was never afraid. I was a great swimmer. I had confidence, commanded a lot of respect. Campers, boys and girls both, vied to be on my team. I was the best of the ROs. Until one day when a fast current zipped past me, taking my swimsuit top along with it. That was the last time I wore a two-piece.

As a teen, I dreaded hot afternoons if only because someone was likely, eventually, to suggest a dip in the river and then I'd be faced with the indignity of a swimsuit. Sometimes I swam in my clothes, but the soaked, billowy shirts made it difficult to climb out over the rock sides. Celia wore Playboy bikinis, the ones that require a girl to wax off all her pubic hair before sliding the high-cut bottoms up. My swimsuit looked like an advertisement for Fat Girl Magazine, and the last thing I was going to do was wear it in front of anyone. Ever.

"I wonder what ever happened to him?" Celia asked, her thought still on Rand.

"I saw him in the A&P," I said. "Not too long ago."

"How'd he look?"

"He is much less gorgeous than you remember," I said. "He's an inventory guy now. He made that pretty clear in the two minutes we spent together. He's not a stock guy. He's an inventory guy. Big difference. Apparently."

"Apparently," Celia concurred.

"As if, at our age, anyone cares about a title," I said.

Celia chewed on that for a while.

"He's married. Lives near me somewhere," I lowered the window, and then closed it again, remembering. No smoking. "He went out a few times with my friend Kate. Remember her? Tall, heavy set? Too many teeth crammed into her mouth?" It was a good description of Kate.

She was a chocolatier, with her own shop. I helped her out a few times when she had a big order and needed an extra pair of hands. Once, we made two hundred chocolate carousel horses, centerpieces for someone's wedding reception. For a while, I thought about going into business with Kate. The way I figured it, I could make a lot of the chocolates in my house, doubling the amount of production. But Kate had insisted all the confections be made in the shop. She said it had something to do with her commercial catering license, but I always thought she just didn't want to share her business with me. And so we split.

"Kate said he's a real loser now," I pulled air into my chest with whooshing noises. I was dying for a cigarette. "She also said he had a really small penis."

Celia choked a laugh.

"He refers to you as the one who got away, in case you're interested."

Celia was quiet. I guessed she was thinking about Rand and the bliss of being the star of her childhood, a social butterfly flitting from bud to bud.

"What happened with the gardening therapy program?" Celia asked, startling me. Weren't we talking about Rand? "Mom said you dropped it. I thought for sure you would follow through on this one, Charlotte. What happened?"

When I didn't respond, she continued. As expected.

"You love everything about the garden. Why not try again? You love plants, you love the process of discovering a new strain, cross breeding. And you could have helped people! Isn't that one of the foundations of a sound mental health? Helping others? Isn't that what you told me?"

She was right. Every psychiatrist I'd ever seen recommended some sort of mentoring system. "You fortify yourself when you reach out to others." And I'd thought about that. I'd considered becoming a Big Sister, but I never got past the idea stage.

Celia was still talking. "Mom said something chilling to me the other day. She said, 'We are going to lose Charlotte.'" A tug of satisfaction pulled at my heart. They were talking about me. They cared about me. "She said she's worried that you are on a road to disaster."

She pulled the car into a parking space and swiveled in her seat, facing me. "So tell me," she said. "What happened? One minute, you're happy and optimistic, talking about a new program, a new direction. You were so totally enthusiastic. You had a jingle in your voice. You were buying all the books, investigating which courses to take and in which order. You sounded so…happy!" She paused, breathing. "Mom and I were celebrating this new chapter in your life. We were so happy for you. This was going to be the turning point. Mom said that. She said, this program will help you turn your life around, to find something that makes you happy. How did it all fall apart?"

How did it fall apart? I'd paid the fees for registration and bought all the gear required for the first year's courses. But then, I thought about taking classes and listening to lectures, being on a schedule determined by someone else, studying and taking tests, and I thought about all the stress I would suffer and the pressure I'd be under, and I thought about leaving Jimbo alone for so many hours at a time. So. I did what I do. I let it go.

She looked at me, right at me, and I saw it in her face. The flat and open look of disappointment. Her eyelid twitched, her cheekbones deflated. She finally comprehended my position: I would not do anything that took me away from Jimbo. I would not reach for goals outside my small salt-box rambler of a house. I would not strive to be anything but a wife. And I could see that this fully realized information crushed her.

"I guess it wasn't right for me," I said, my voice a familiar plaint.

She huffed, frustrated, and thrust open her door. "Can you at least get a refund on your enrollment fee?"

It was too easy to lie, the words slipped out of my mouth as if coated in oil. "I already did."

TWENTY-EIGHT

"What took so long? I thought you'd never come home!" Jimbo wailed from his usual station on the couch.

I checked my watch. "It's only been three hours," I said, holding the door open with one foot. "Did you miss me?" I smiled at him. Oh, to be missed!

His pale face practically glowed in the lightless living room; faux-wooden shutters shielded a brilliant late afternoon sun.

"I missed you. I thought were you never coming back." Was he going to cry? A dinner plate on the coffee table evidenced the remains of his lunch. A tip of bread crust. A smear of yellow mustard. A jelly jar balanced on the armrest was half full of a dark liquid. Iced tea? He had taken good care of himself.

Like a marshmallow, I thought. Unroasted.

"I had visions of a giant apple falling from a tree and bonking you on the noggin, knocking you senseless!" He tucked his chin, challenging me with the ridiculousness of his concern. A wife beater T-shirt sagged over his concave chest; arms hung on either side of his shapeless torso. My stomach gurgled with hunger.

"I *am* senseless. Just like you!"

He giggled. "Senseless, maybe, but not scent-less." He lifted a doughy arm and sniffed underneath.

"Come on and help me drag this bushel inside," I said, knowing full well he would decline my request. Jimbo was not much for physical labor. He said he'd rather watch me move around the tiny house unimpeded than interrupt my flow. He said he liked to watch me go from place to place, from where he rested to the kitchen, to the closet, to the bathroom. You're the ballerina, he'd joked, and I'm the orchestra conductor. "It's heavy," I added, encouraging him off the couch.

"How many pecks did you pick, Peter Piper?" he joked.

I would not contrive a retort. I was too hot, too tired, for nursery rhymes. I let the door slam. I stood facing the street for a long moment. Spending the day with my sister was a refreshment. We talked, we laughed. It was all so familiar. In some ways, she reminded me of childhood when life's questions were easily answered or rerouted, when needs were few but always met. Celia was my lifeline to my family. She, for the most part, understood me.

But then, what had she said? I pander to Jimbo. I let him sit on the couch while I do all the housework, all the paperwork, all the…work.

"Hello, yoo-hoo, wife!" Jimbo called to me. "Are you in need?" That was his question. The one thing he asked me, the question that inevitably led to a sure and satisfying interaction. If I answered yes, I was in need, Jimbo would quickly diagnose my related symptoms and determine what he could do to help. I liked that he was alert to my noises and my rhythms. He could be counted on for that.

I opened the door, leaned down, and dragged the flimsy wooden crate into the entry. "Can you help me lift it onto the counter?" I asked.

"I could, but then I'd probably hurt my back," he answered.

I hauled the crate into the kitchen and dragged it toward the sink. Mine was a tiny kitchen, with the basics fused side by side along the back wall. The sink was in the corner, nearly obscured by countertop devices. A Dutch oven, a toaster oven, and a Kitchen Aid mixer huddled near the refrigerator. The regular toaster, the Ginzo knives, and the set of knife sharpeners cluttered the main countertop. I leaned against the sink and put a forearm across my brow.

"Can you help peel the apples?" I asked.

"I can probably help the most by keeping out of your way," he answered.

I lost myself in the apples, in my grandmother's applesauce. I peeled and pared and sliced the apples into the big soup pot, just as she'd instructed me so many times. The apples, the lemon rind, the sugar. How much sugar?

My grandmother would not approve of the chaos in my kitchen. When we made applesauce in her kitchen, the counters were cleared of all ingredients and utensils, leaving only the things we needed. "A clean kitchen is a clean mind." I stirred, remembering.

***

Rain hammers on the ledge outside my grandmother's tiny apartment window. We are reading, passing a lazy day together. She moved to this unit in the asssisted living facility when her big house began to melt. That's how she'd described it: melting. The fireplace sat three inches lower than the floor, and there was a sag in the foundation at the base of the stairs. I thought the flaws gave the house charm. Turns out, they were fatal.

I arch my back away from the couch cushion and yawn with dramatic volume. My grandmother does not like rain. It depresses her. She looks up from her Barbara Taylor Bradford novel and winks. "How's your book?" she asks.

I am reading Stephen King. "Great." I'd share it with her after I'm finished, but she doesn't like anything scary. "But I'm getting hungry," I tell her.

She peers at me under spikey gray brows. My grandmother is not beautiful. She has a hook nose, and her lips barely close over a canine tooth that grew in on the bias. That's how she says it: on the bias.

"I just ate lunch."

"A spoonful of cottage cheese is hardly lunch," I tell her. I should have brought some applesauce with me. Or one of the tiny apple pies I made. Instead, I show her the fresh cut on my thumb. I'd sliced my own finger while hacking up the apples. I thought I might require a trip to the hospital for stitches, but Jimbo and I managed to bind it with surgical tape. I kept a fully stocked first aid kit in the hall closet. I had a lot of medical supplies: ointments, gauze, a suture kit, and a hemostat that I sometimes pinched around the stub of a roach to keep my fingers from burning. After we wrapped my thumb, Jimbo gave me a Valium to take the edge off.

My grandmother's eyes are steady, I feel their warmth on my face and neck. She accepts me entirely. Everything I do, everything I am, pleases her. My shoulders relax. My jaws fall open. I feel wonderful. As if I've taken a Valium.

I reach my arms up, stretching. "Do you want something from the kitchen?"

This is a joke. The kitchen is only a countertop near where we are sitting. The apartment is that small, you can reach everything from one location. How can she cook in here? There is a four-burner stove. A dishwasher. A refrigerator. Compared to her expansive kitchen back home, this one is a prison.

Back home. I still have trouble remembering that the house is gone. Emptied. Sold. This is her home now.

It was my father's idea. He said the house was too much for her. It was dangerous for her to live there alone. "Nonsense," was my grandmother's immediate retort. I loved how she did that. She ended a conversation with one word.

But he kept at her. He talked about the electric, the plumbing. Nothing was up to code, which was apparently important to him; he repeated it often enough. The roof needed to be replaced. The air conditioning unit was older than Celia. She gave in, eventually. Too soon, if you asked me. But nobody did.

"I'll make some toast." I stand, grabbing into the shag carpet with my toes. I love this rug; it used to be in her foyer. Gold and brown and partially bald in the corner where all the foot traffic used to pass. My heel snags in the wool fibers, shredding a thin thread from the mass. It trails behind my foot like a sailor's telltale. "Or would you rather have a muffin?"

I open the freezer. No muffins.

"Toast," I tell her. I drop a slice of rye into the toaster. This is the only item on her countertop. A toaster. "Do you even live here?"

"What do you mean?"

I take out the butter, and some store-bought cherry jelly. Store bought!

"I mean, this place looks like one of those For Sale models. Everything is too neat. It's sterile. You need some clutter."

The toaster chimes, jerks. The toast is ready. I take a little yellow plate from the cabinet and select a knife from the silverware drawer. Her knives have yellow plastic handles. Matching.

"Do you want jelly on yours?" I ask her. She is staring out the window. Her profile looks old. I don't like when she's like this. Quiet. The rain makes her quiet. I tap the knife on the side of the toaster. "Gran?"

"None for me," she says without looking.

I butter mine up.

"I need to take my medicine with food," I tell her, taking a bite. I can fit a full quarter of the toast into my mouth at once.

"Jimbo says, to get the best results with any medication, follow the directions exactly. But you know that following directions is not one of my traits." I lean a hip against the small sink and chew. "But this one is important. When I started with this prescription, I had stomach aches all the time. I was so worried; I had a full upper GI series just to make sure I didn't have any cancer or anything." I find some peanut butter in the microwave where she stores her extras. Cereal, crackers. Dry goods fill the sad little oven. I'll use peanut butter on my next piece of toast.

"Turns out," I tell her, "I have a pre-ulcer. It's not a full-on ulcer, but more of a sore spot that gets irritated over and over. After a while, the sore spot can turn into an ulcer. I have to be careful." I place a large gray-and-red capsule on my tongue and encourage it downward, undulating my mouth like a guppy sucking air from water. I chase the pill into my gullet with a big swallow of milk. Whole milk. She and I are the only people left on the planet who still buy whole milk.

"Smoking is probably making it worse," she suggests without the weight of guilt. She never transmits guilt. It's one of her skills.

I'd told her about the nicotine patch and the gum. I shake my head, the universal sign of defeat. "Neither of those worked. But now that you mention it, I am suddenly dying for a smoke." I laugh with a mouth full of toast. "I am so suggestible!"

I lather the second slice of rye with peanut butter and come to sit in the armchair next to my grandmother, balancing the bread on a paper towel. "In truth, the only things that have proved bad for me are alcohol and caffeine. Lucky for me." I lick some melting peanut butter from the rim of the toast, "I never liked them anyway. I am very sensitive, turns out. Even one real cup of coffee makes my hands shake." I gobble the remaining toast before any more peanut butter can drip off. "That's why I have half-coffee and half-milk."

She watches me dab my mouth with the crumpled paper towel.

Thunder rolls in the distance and we turn our eyes to the window. My grandmother's apartment faces south so she gets wonderful light inside all day long. Today, the sky provides no light, no warmth. Raindrops big as grapes striate the glass. "The sky is crying," my grandmother says.

"What?"

"That's what your Dad used to say when the rain came down like this. The sky is crying." She smiles at the memory and at me. "You're so much like him," she says. "Your enthusiasm. Your charisma. He was just like that when he was young."

I rest into the soft cradle of the chair.

"He also had some darkness in him," she says. "The rain depressed him, the dark sky, the way the sun becomes dilute behind the storm. He used to hide away in his room when the rains came. I always felt bad about that." Her voice is muffled by the downpour. "That he felt depressed. You don't want your children to inherit your bad traits."

I never really thought about it, but I'd obviously inherited depression from my father. "I inherited his hammer toe," I tell her. "Want to see?" I hold up my right foot and fan out my toes. My second toes on both feet curl downward. Hard callouses capped the toe-tops in milky white.

"Your feet need work," she says.

She's right. The soles are split and crowded with spikes of dead skin. I never bother with my feet. What's the point? "No one looks at my feet," I tell her.

"I'm looking at them," she says. "These are the only feet you have," she continues. "You're going to rue the day you didn't take care of them." She pulls her feet from her slippers and holds them out for me to see.

"Look at mine," she says. "All those years in high heels and pointy toes ruined my feet. See the bunions? The way the toes are deformed, leaning to one side? I wish I'd taken better care."

"Do they hurt?" I feel a cramp in my own foot. Sympathy pain.

"They do sometimes," she admits. My grandmother does not like to talk about pain. She's a stoic. She once discovered a thumbtack imbedded in her shoe, point-side-up. It had been there for weeks. When she finally turned the shoe over and found the tack, she laughed and said, "So, *that's* why my foot hurt all the time!"

I am the opposite. I feel pain, and acutely. Luckily, the pain clinic where Jimbo gets his treatments has been great for me. They gave me my own prescription for Jimbo's most reliable drug, OxyContin, and also, I've been having epidural injections in my spine to help with my arthritis. I am young for arthritis, but that's just my luck, to have early onset problems. Like my ulcer. And my spinal stenosis. And my nerve pain.

I want to tell my grandmother about the new treatment therapies and how I'm feeling well for the first time in forever. But I do not get the chance.

"How is your friend?" she asks into the quiet. "Potty? The one with all the ambition."

"Plots." My voice breaks.

"Yes, Plots. The man from Bangladesh? Is that right?"

"Bangaluru," I correct her. "It used to be called Bangalore but they changed the name. It's the third most populated city in India." I focus on the geographical information. "Bangaluru is a capital city in the south of India. The climate is perfect, the landscape divine."

Plots didn't like to talk too much about India—he said it made him sad—but somehow I'd managed to ask a lot of questions anyway.

Plots is going back to India. His wife summoned him, she wants him back. His leaving sits in my stomach like a brick. I can't even think about it. When he told me, a cold blackness oozed into my visual panorama and inked out the whole sun.

TWENTY-NINE

My father raises parrots. Macaws, to be exact. Macaws are parrots with long beaks that can pierce a hole in your hand if you're not paying attention. While we were growing up, the neighbor kids liked to come to the bird room in our house and my father would put on a show, demonstrating how he taught them to shake hands or talk back to him and then bow like a knight when hearing applause. I never liked the birds, or maybe they never liked me. I'm not sure which is factually correct.

I arrive at my parent's house and slam the front door behind me. From the basement, I hear Beatrice dancing in her cage. Beatrice is my father's Illiger's macaw. She is thirty-five years old, ten years behind me. He raised Beatrice from a baby, feeding her bits of food from his fingertips, kissing her when she nuzzled. Beatrice and my father have something like a love affair going on between them.

"Henry?" the bird sounds exactly like my grandmother. Intonation, timbre, the voice is a perfect imitation of my father's own mother, calling to her son. "Henry?"

"It's me," I quiet her by speaking. If she thinks my father is in the house, she'll screech and caterwaul until he appears.

"Is that you, Charlotte?" My mother is upstairs; I can hear the radio playing classical music in the sitting room. "I thought you were going to be here an hour ago!"

Beatrice has my mother's voice down pat. "Charlotte? Is that you?" she cackles from the basement. No doubt about it, she is an amazing bird. She not only imitates perfectly, she converses with alacrity, altering her words to suit the situation. "Charlotte," Beatrice beckons, "Come quickly."

I know her game. She wants to play. She wants me to let her out of her habitat and bring her upstairs to 'where the action is'—my father's phrase.

I drop my purse and head to the bathroom.

From the toilet, I hear my mother fussing around, putting away her knitting or whatever she is doing. She talks to herself when she's frustrated, and I hear the unmistakable sound of her low-throated mumbling.

"Your father is waiting," my mother shouts, emphasizing the word father. Like I might forget who he is.

"Your father is waiting," Beatrice screeches as if she understands. "Your father is waiting. Your father is waiting."

The music volume increases. I can feel the snare drum rolls throbbing in my belly three rooms away. Classical music is the one thing that calms Beatrice. Brahms, Wagner, Tchaikovsky, she likes them all. I recognize the music. Ravel. *The Bolero*.

"Where were you?" She stands at the open bathroom door. "I thought you said you were coming right over."

"I did," I tell her, flicking my just washed hands at her.

"Use the towel," she chastises me, and we both wait to hear if Beatrice is going to mimic the reprimand.

Silence.

The birds were originally my mother's idea. She wanted to lure my father out of his annual funk, a block of time she called the February doldrums.

My mother likes to retell the story: "Since the start of our marriage, your father has come to me at the beginning of every February and said,

'Well, Denise, this just isn't working out.' And then I'd lock myself in the bathroom and cry my eyes out."

I can picture her doing this, crying into a towel. She is small and, therefore, prone to weeping.

"And then," she brightens at this part of the story, "it was forgotten. Until the following February. And the one after that." The pattern was born.

One February, she bought him a Hahn's macaw, a small and easy-to-manage bird rescued from an unscrupulous breeder a few towns over. "All you have to do is talk to it," she said. My mother explained what little she knew. She had lists from the animal control people, how to care for the bird, how to keep it happy. She had even bought a bag of food for the little green creature. To say my father 'took to' the parrot grossly understates the results. At one time, he had twelve birds living in homemade habitats down in our basement. Macaws, rose-breasted cockatoos, Amazon parrots, and conures, the noisiest of the lot. After Celia and I grew up and moved out, my mother put a swift end to *The Dirty Dozen* as she termed them. She managed to oust all but one of the giant birds. Beatrice. My father's favorite.

"I told you." My mother points to the front door. "Your father needs to be picked up in town. Please, Charlotte. Get going. Now." She glances at her watch, holding her arm up and away like a railroad conductor. She can't see anything without her reading glasses.

My father's car is in the shop. I'm picking him up at an appointment and dropping him off at the car place. I don't mind this task. I love to drive, and I love to be alone with my father. I park the car about fifty yards from our meeting place, a corner opposite the bowling alley, finding soothing shade under a wide elm. Small brick buildings align on the grassy acreage, individual professional offices each marked with a plaque nailed to the right of the door. Medical offices.

It's hot today, my neck is sticky. Once, when I lost a lot of weight, I had a really nice neck. A single column, narrow and without stacked inner tubes of flesh obscuring its anatomy. I looked taller and, for sure, thinner. If I could fix just one area of my body, it would be my neck. I lift my head and swipe at the perspiration coagulating in grim rings around my larynx.

A door opens just beyond the passenger window, and I hear the suction of air conditioning released into the heat. The smallish building looks more like a house than a professional office. I see the plaque: Mr. Marvin Stuben. Psychiatry.

My father's voice is unmistakable. "Okay," he says to someone hidden behind the door. His big hand leans on the doorknob. "See you next week." I am staring at the age spots on his hand; a few seconds pass before I realize he has walked right past the car. He is headed for the corner, our agreed-upon meeting place.

My father is seeing a psychiatrist? Is that why his instructions were so specific: Park at the end of the street, he'd said, at the corner before the crosswalk. He didn't want me to know.

THIRTY

Jimbo came into the kitchen, startling me.

Cooking was meditation, I attained a state of contemplative peace in the process of preparation; maintaining control over the slippery egg yolks as the white albumen slipped through my fingers. My grandmother taught me this technique. The first time I separated an egg with my fingers, I panicked at the feeling of the raw egg—all that slime and slither swimming in my palm—and I released the whole mucous mess onto the floor.

I laughed.

"What are you making?"

"Fudge."

"Fudge is funny?" He poured himself a glass of seltzer and recapped the bottle, sitting in the one kitchen chair that did not wobble. "See? I'm staying out of the way." On the opposing chair, he rested the heels of his tiny pink feet, like two hairless hamsters.

I nodded my appreciation. It had taken a while for us to get here, for Jimbo to understand what I wanted, and vice versa. I'm not saying everything was perfect. But just then, it felt pretty damn close.

"Someone's in the kitchen with Dinah," Jimbo sang. His feet waggled to his rhythm. "Someone's in the kitchen I know-oh-oh-oh. Someone's in the kitchen with Dinah, strummin' on the old banjo."

We sang the refrain together while I poured the rich brown batter into a square tin, thickly buttered. "Fee, Fi, Fiddly-Aye-Oh."

I stretched my back and winced.

"Your back hurt?" Jimbo asked.

"It's okay," I told him, wiping my hands. The kitchen looked like a crime scene, gooey melted chocolate clotted in the mixing bowl, fine white powdered sugar splayed out in rows on the warped countertop, splotches of vanilla made a trail from the mixer to the sink. I should have put all the utensils and tools in a soap bath in the sink. I should have wiped down the counters. Instead, I turned off the light.

Jimbo was waiting for me in our bed. The flat screen television flickered its cool blues—one of our favorite shows. *Law & Order*. One of my favorite episodes. I'd seen them all at least twice.

Jimbo held the blankets open, welcoming me.

"Did you bring me a taste?" he asked.

"No tasting for you," I said. "You didn't help, so you don't get to lick the beaters." I tried to get comfortable.

He pouted out a bottom lip. "Be nice, wife," he joked. "And stop all that squirming! I can't hear the words!"

"I can't help it. My sciatica is flaring up."

Jimbo flopped an arm over to his night table and pulled on the drawer knob. "Here," he said, extending two fingers pinched around a small triangular pill. "This will help."

I swallowed the pill without water and worked the muscles of my esophagus, coaxing the tablet down. Jack McCoy made an impassioned summation while the jury sat erect, their lemming heads leaning toward the prosecutor in unison.

Jimbo reached for my hand. He unfurled my tired fingers and pressed a metal ball into the palm; he began rolling it around, pressing on the pressure points, rubbing the skin-warmed metal against the fleshy heel and padded joints. A palm massage. It was glorious.

"Want me to do the feet?" He offered, but I shook my head.

"Too ticklish," I admitted.

He trilled his fingers near my armpit, threatening a tickle, but I was too tired to respond. Instead, he laced his soft fingers in between mine and said, "Here we are together. Like peas in a pod. Like birds in a nest."

"Like rabbits in a hutch," I chimed in, familiar with this game. The medication oozed through my body and I smiled to myself. I'd wished for this my whole life, to lie in bed with someone I loved.

THIRTY-ONE

"Guess what?" I shouted to my mother. Her phone beeped once, signaling an incoming call. Don't you dare, I sent the threat via extra sensory perception. Sometimes that worked. She had a way of reading me, even if I didn't use language. I steered the car into the parking lot and twisted the wheel hard. Tires squealed, the turning radius contracted tight to the right. "Jimbo's mother is coming to visit!"

The shopping mall was not yet open; the parking lot was nearly empty. Across the median, a school bus idled, a great heaving carcass of yellow metal.

"It's the first time she will come to my house," I said. "Oh my God, I'm going to be so nervous! I'm nervous already, and I've only known about the visit for a few hours. Jimbo spoke to her last night. You know how he calls her every night at eight on the nose? Well, last night they talked for a long time—so long that I was asleep before they finished." Often, though I would never admit this, Jimbo succumbed to sleep while still connected to his mother, like a baby cooed into slumber. The previous night was no exception: with the phone leaning against his ear, he snored beside me while the dull drone of his mother's voice vibrated atop his pillow. I was half tempted to disconnect the call, but I knew better. He'd wake and continue the construct, lulled to childlike equilibrium by the abstract presence of her voice.

"Jimbo has been asking her to come for a long time. But you know," I said, calibrating my excitement with a hint of secrecy, "she's had some problems and didn't want to travel. Although," I exhaled, finally, releasing a gust of pent-up energy, "between you and me, I think she's just afraid to leave the house. That's where Jimbo gets it." I blurted the truth before I could reel it back. "From her."

My mother intoned a defense, but I didn't hear the words. Something about not blaming the mother for every little thing.

"So she's coming! I have a million things to do before she gets here."

An interruption. Logistics, dates. Impatience surged inside me; I stamped a foot on the floor mat. My mother interrupted with petty details. "When is she coming? And, where will she sleep?" The guest room was saturated by two years of junk. No one had slept over since my nephew's last visit, before Jimbo had recreated me into a married woman.

"When? I don't know when exactly. She misses Jimbo. That's the reason for her visit. That's what Jimbo told me," I said. "The important thing is, she is going to visit us for the first time in our married lives." I would have clapped my hands, but they were fully occupied with a cigarette in one and a diluted cup of coffee in the other. I was positively buoyant with expectation.

"I'll need to hire a serious cleaning service before then. Not that your cleaning person isn't fine. She is. But for this, I will need more. Like a professional company," I said. "Maybe they can do the ducts, too. Do they do that? Suck all the crap out of the air ducts? I saw an ad on television… Maybe I'll call them."

Ideas shuffled in front of me, inspired, mostly, from television commercials. I should refinish the floors and regrout the shower. Oh, the bathroom! I'd need to fix the broken handle on the toilet. You can't host your mother-in-law when you have an unrepaired toilet flusher! My mother-in-law. I had a mother-in-law!

"Do you think she'd like to have dinner together? I mean, with us?" She penetrated my free-ranging thoughts with an offer. "It might be nice to have a meal together. You could all come here, or we could meet somewhere in between, so you don't have to drive too far?"

The last thing I wanted was to take Jimbo's mother to my parents' house with all its conventional grandeur and status fixtures. No. I did not want that. Rather, I coveted the idea of hosting a dinner of my own. Cooked in my own kitchen. Served on the plates she'd given to us. "Take them," she'd insisted. We'd visited her three times since our wedding, leaving her house each time with a carload of hand-me-downs. We had her towels, frayed at the edges. We had her ugly vinyl placemats with oil-painting style depictions of hunting dogs and horses and men with rifles littering the dense forest. We had her unwanted dishes, her pots and pans, her old coffee maker.

"Why do you ask? Do you think I'm not capable of making a perfectly great dinner in my own home?" That is not what she meant, I was sure. Yet, I reacted in the most familiar of ways, fending insult where none was offered, to chafe at kindness as if it were poison.

"I know you can," she assured, quickly. "But I am just thinking. You'll be nervous, of course. Sometimes it's a relief to not cook." Her reasoning made sense. "And, best of all, there's no clean up!"

We laughed. The long threads of innuendo and insinuation might just as easily have tangled and knotted, but not this time. I might have taken offense to her suggestion that I do not like to clean. But I did not. Instead, I allowed her to mother me.

"Pick a place, and we'll meet you. It will be Dad's honor." The grace of her declaration affected me profoundly: my heart, my head, it was as if I heard a wonderful arrangement of music. Dad's honor. It meant that I would have the chance to make my father happy.

I had a picture in my head: a group of amiable people relaxing around a white-clothed table that evidenced a marvelous meal, half-emptied wine glasses glistening like charms in the warm lighting, spirits shimmering amber in highball glasses smeared with marks from sticky fingertips. Five people in a fancy restaurant, a fine-tuned vision.

"That is a very generous offer," I agreed. "I accept. We accept."

***

Jimbo's mother, Sylvia, sat with intractable posture, perched precariously on her chair, as if prepared to hear "Fire!" alarmed at any moment. Her dress was without color, her skin had no flaws or markings. Her head was shaped like a science laboratory flask, long and unforgiving. Hair trapped under a net taut across her scalp, no makeup, no jewelry. Her mouth remained hidden within a starburst of wrinkles convening at the center like a purse or a rectum.

"Well, this is a rare treat," Sylvia's voice was high pitched and thin, like the call of an osprey. "I so rarely get to eat in a restaurant," she said.

"It is very nice to get together," my mother said. "We are so glad to finally meet you, Sylvia." The voice was oil in a hot pan.

Jimbo and I had calmed ourselves earlier with Valium, so we both passed on the cocktails. Jimbo lifted his ginger ale in a silent toast. My parents drank martinis, straight. Sylvia had declined a beverage, announcing to no one that she would be "just fine with water."

"Are you enjoying your visit?" my father asked.

My mother lifted her glass and followed his lead. "What have you done so far?"

"Done?" Sylvia spoke without moving any of the fine muscles in her face. For a moment, no one realized that she'd responded.

I sat close to her, on her right, downwind. And so I answered for her. "Well, Sylvia's train was late coming in last night, so we brought in dinner from the Chinese place and just hung around. This morning, I showed Sylvia where I keep all the housewares she's handed down to us."

Jimbo put his hands on his belly as if satisfied. "Our kitchen looks exactly like my mother's kitchen! It's almost like a flashback! If only

Charlotte wore an apron and rolled her stockings down, my life would be picture perfect."

"Very funny." I plucked the lime wedge out of my glass and squeezed it at him, trying to splash him with citrus, but the flesh was already spent. Nothing of worth came out. "Anyway, we watched television, and then rested up for dinner."

"Do you like riding the train?" my mother inquired.

Sylvia answered simply, "No."

My father opened his menu. "So, what does everyone feel like eating? We like the spinach ricotta pie here and the veal piccata. And the steak."

"It's nothing fancy, really," my mother apologized. "Just good, basic Italian food." She would order the fish. Of course. My father, sensing a depression in my mother's countenance, waggled his empty class at the cocktail waitress and signaled for another round of drinks.

"Well," Sylvia lifted spider hands to the surface but did not open her menu. "I guess there will be something here that I can eat."

My father moved his gaze laterally, turning to Sylvia. "Tell me Sylvia, where do you live? Jimbo described it to me, but I can't picture the street. I know it's near the exit for the airport, Exit 63?"

Long Islanders relate all geographic information to the exits of the expressway. I grew up off Exit 56.

He continued in an even pitch. "I travel sometimes for work, and I have been lost too many times around there more than I care to tell you!" My father's laugh settled me. He sipped from the second cocktail.

"We are at Exit 65," Sylvia said. "Past the airport."

My mother harmonized. "Past the airport! How fantastic. You must get to see the kids all the time."

The kids? I wanted to blast her. I am not a kid! We are not kids!

"No, not really," Sylvia admitted.

My mother calibrated her words carefully. "When is the last time you saw them, then?"

"It's been a year or two."

"Two *years*?"

"That's a long time." My father rested a finger on the rim of his martini glass, stabilizing it. A passing waiter raised an eyebrow, asking if we needed a refill, and I nodded back. Yes, my wide eyes transmitted. Bring another martini. This one for me.

I answered for him. "We see each other. We visit Sylvia whenever we're in the area, don't we? Jimbo still uses all his old doctors, so we go there pretty often. That's where we get our Botox treatments."

My mother scowled. "Botox treatments? Like for wrinkles?"

"Same stuff," I informed her. "Different purpose. We use it for nerve pain."

"Who has nerve pain?" my mother asked, surprised.

"I do," Jimbo said.

"We do," I corrected.

The waitress, my ally, came to receive our orders. Fish for my mother, as usual, prepared without butter. My father wanted a steak. Rare. I ordered the fettuccini alfredo. Not the half-order, either.

Jimbo was rummaging in his fanny pack, so I ordered shrimp fra diavolo for him.

"Oh no," he said.

"What's the matter?" I asked.

"I can't find my antispasmodic!" He placed a handful of plastic pill pouches on the table and began separating them into two piles. I watched, thinking that the pills looked almost like Skittles. Some were shiny, some were capsules filled with beads of color. Each pouch was marked with Jimbo's writing but lots of the ink had smeared or worn off. He grabbed the breadbasket, spilled the salted cheese twists onto the tablecloth and then unburdened the contents of his fanny pack into the basket.

"Here," he said, pushing the basket to me. "We're looking for Donnatal."

I sifted through the bags with one eye on the cheese twists. A pitcher of water appeared between Jimbo and me, and I drew the basket closer to my chest.

"What are all those pills?" My father frowned at the colorful confetti in the basket. "Do you even know what they're all for?"

"Got 'em." Jimbo sucked in a breath. "Here they are," he poised the plastic bag for all to see. "Levsin," he said with a big smile. "Just as good."

Ice cubes tumbled into the water glasses. A plate crashed to the floor from somewhere far away. A chair leg scraped against the bare wood floor.

"Really," my father leaned forward and whispered to me. "Is that necessary?"

I focused on the chaos of the noisy restaurant, dulling my father's concern behind the voices and utensils and the smell of wonderful foods gusting past our table.

Jimbo lifted his head and asked me, "Is this my bread plate or yours?" He looped his fingers into the OK sign, confirming which side belonged to him. He moved the plate, and a tiny blue pill darted out and jumped along the cloth like a skipped stone "Hey you! Come back here!" Jimbo plucked the pill off the table and held it out for me. "An escapee!" He said, and when he leaned over to nuzzle me, he pressed the pill between my lips.

My mother's fingers pressed against her eyes as if they might fall out of their sockets. I wanted to warn her, she'd have blue eyeshadow on her fingers later, but I didn't say anything. Sylvia stared straight ahead. The two mothers, two bastions of control. I knew too well the force of my own mother and her relentless need to guide my life toward a more *normal* existence. Jimbo's mother operated from a distant approach, passive, impotent.

My father's eyes were on me. I would not look at him in this setting, flanked by a woman who refused to smile and my mother who wore optimism like a shield. I was trapped, I felt the tension of my own claustrophobia constricting my throat. I wanted this! I wanted this vision, of the families dining together. Other couples did this, didn't they? Hosted both families at the same time? My sister Celia entertained her in-laws, didn't she?

A lovely vessel of creamy noodles slid into my visual range. Long lengths of fettuccini noodles swimming in velvet. Dinner was served! I scaled my nose forward, projecting over the steam geyser rising from the plate. It was marvelous, the smell of butter and cream and cheese and pepper! I opened my eyes and met the blue eyes of my father. I smiled at him with the condensation of fettuccini alfredo shining on my face.

Sylvia had ordered the grouper. Grilled. It lay before her on its side, mouth gaping as if striving for breath. I looked at the fish, and it looked at me, and I was at once tickled beyond restraint. I laughed, coughed, and laughed again. The fish, I swear it, was looking at me! A fit of coughing ensued, and I reached for relief in a glass of water.

"Did you ask permission to drink from my water?" Sylvia's voice pierced the air, causing my fingers to release the glass.

A cloud of water cascaded over the luscious concentrate of noodles. At once, the waitress appeared with a cloth napkin to cover my lap. I used the cocktail napkin made of paper to absorb the tiny bit of water pooled around the inside edges of my dinner.

"I can't take you anywhere," Jimbo joked.

My father leaned toward me, peering into my bowl. "Is that all right?" he wanted to know. "Can you still eat it?" He knew exactly what to say. I wanted to put my arms around his thick neck and feel his chest against mine.

My father and I were cut from the same cloth. That's what my grandmother said. We looked alike, we talked alike. We both had unusual hobbies. We had some other things in common, but we never talked about those.

My mother, cool as Cleopatra, paused, waiting with the outer tine of her fork poised above the innocent food lying below. I felt the vibration of her disapproval as viscerally as one feels an earthquake, not a generalized foreboding or vague hint, but rather a definitive shimmy and jibe that stains the skin and leaves a scar in its wake. I shifted, tried to reassess. I'd taken Sylvia's water. That was my crime. The scope of the infraction seemed quibbling; her reaction confounded me. Was it the muddle in my own head that distorted the magnitude of my own gaffe? Or perhaps Sylvia herself overreacted?

I would apologize, that's the adult thing to do. The mature thing. I would express my dismay at commandeering her water glass and move to quickly rectify that misstep. No problem. No sweat.

I would have addressed Sylvia right then if it weren't for the grouper. She'd beheaded it, and the severed head lay hanging off her plate, gawking at me.

I had trouble manipulating my fork. It repeatedly slipped from my hand, plopping into the heavy pasta. After a time, the waitress, thank God, offered a large spoon for twisting purposes and I was able to maneuver the utensils in a more effective manner.

The once pleasing background noise of the little restaurant began to itch inside my ears. What was that instrument? A viola? It sounded like a child crying. I turned my head, hoping that a change of latitude might alter the way the music affected me.

My mother's hand touched my wrist. A napkin. "You have cream on your chin," her voice bubbled, as if transmitted through water.

I heard my father. I heard my mother. Everyone was talking. The rhythm of their voices lulled; I felt my head bob.

"Charlotte?" I knew that voice. That tone. My mother had focused her laser beam attention on me. I assembled myself, pulling my spine long and clearing the phlegm from my throat.

I was stoned. Without intent, I had overmedicated myself. I had to hold steady, to retain a degree of control. I wiped the napkin across my face as if scrubbing off a layer of soot. The napkin fell to the floor. I was soon to follow.

***

My first thought was, how lovely. How lovely to be insulated by white noise, cocooned in a swaddling blanket. I flexed my toes trapped under a protective shield and rolled my ankles in languid circles.

"Open your eyes." Who spoke? I refused. I was unwilling to learn about my captor, my keeper. I did not recognize the young male voice, but its tone was unequivocal: Trouble lies ahead.

I heard the voice again, but it had altered its trajectory. "Does she have a nickname, something only a mother might use?"

"I am *not* her mother." I knew that voice. I opened my eyes to Sylvia, a statue pitched on an unseen chair, shiny black purse balanced on her lap. Eyes of granite. Her features inanimate, a heron stalking her prey.

The surroundings were not entirely unknown to me. I recognized the rhythmic beeping of machinery; heard the robotic call, an announcement delivered in concord monotone. I was in the hospital. Thank *God.* I let my eyelids sink and I focused on the regular tones of the monitor, matching my breaths to the beeps, synchronous, dependable breaths.

"Charlotte, open your eyes." I sensed nothing tender in the male voice, nothing kind, so I declined, again, to comply.

A pin prick burned on my shoulder. He'd stabbed me! My arm jerked, my hand clawed open, ready to defend. A sudden surprising pain in my wrist stilled me.

I opened my eyes.

The man was a nurse, judging by the formal white shirt buttoned to his Adam's apple. He appeared waifish, slight of build. He stood at the metal guard rail with a tiny spike pinched in his long brown fingers.

"There you are," he said without a smile. He did not look at my face. "Good. I'm glad you opened your eyes," he said, over-enunciating the words, leaning heavily on the consonants. "I'd hate to jab you again."

I would retaliate. My bicep clenched; I would thrash out an arm. I jerked, and then winced as my wrist wrenched against a tether. I was tied. A prisoner.

"You are in restraints." He provided information. "You are free to sit up, if you'd like." He pressed a button somewhere, and I heard the hum of mechanics.

"Stop. Stop!" I screamed, but no sound emerged. Instead, a white blade of pain tore at my throat.

"We had to pump your stomach," he said. "Your throat will be sore for a few days." Sore? I tried to swallow; the charred flanks of my throat were glued together, like flies on flypaper. I fought for an airway. I could not breathe! A whimper escaped through my nostril.

He was cold to my distress. Rather than comfort, this nurse seemed determined to harm. He flashed a stunning light, blinding my right eye. Then, the left.

I arched back, pressing my head back. The bed was too hard, my hair pulled on the coarse sheet. Where was my pillow?

He noted my movements and clicked his pen a few times before jotting notes on the pad tucked into his pants' pocket. "Suicides are not permitted to have pillows," he said. Suicide?

Did he say suicide?

Suddenly, a severe shiver took hold of my body. I shook, seized. I was being electrocuted! My mouth pulsed, opening wide, encouraging air inside. Panic flooded my chest. I was drowning. Mute and without breath, I begged him with my eyes. Help me.

"That's the detox," he said. "You will cycle through the process of metabolizing whatever poison is still in your system. Before you can get better, you have to get worse." He was flippant, almost cheerful. My hands rolled into fists. I would pummel him.

"Release your fists." A parlous whisper.

I complied, if only to escape the look of treachery radiating from his face. He was angry with me, I could see that. But why? What had I done to him?

An eruption of red-hot acid spewed from my throat, like lava from a volcano. Vomit landed on my chin.

"I am required by law to inform you," he began a recitation that would last minutes, maybe longer, "that you have been determined a danger to yourself and are a ward of this institution for a mandatory forty-eight hours. After that time, your status will be reviewed, and the details of your release will be communicated to you. Do you understand?"

My throat permitted a thin retort. "No."

"This is your third admission to the psych ward, am I right?" He paused, and then looked down at me. *Down* at me. Disapproval practically dripped down the length of his bulbous nose.

"Fuck you." My voice was weak, but the message hit him hard as a boxer.

He compacted the note pad he'd been holding, pressing it to his chest like a schoolgirl with a book, arms crossed across the back. He turned to Sylvia and said, "I will be back later."

The pucker of her mouth moved. "I will not be here," she said.

At once, it hit me. We'd been at dinner. I was eating noodles. And then, I wasn't.

I adapted my posture to the angle of the bed, sliding lower as if to obscure the canvas straps that affixed my wrists to the rails.

Sylvia did not speak. She only stared at me. Mean eyes. She had mean eyes.

"Where is Jimbo?" I asked.

Sylvia stood and approached the bed. She wore beige, with little yellow sprigs dancing across the top. Or bees. Maybe it was bees. A row of buttons strangled the material closed, modest to the collarbones. She put her vinyl handbag on the bed near my handcuff.

"Jimbo has not been in the hospital for at least ten years," she said. Her mouth moved within its starburst as if she were one of the Japanese anime characters Jimbo loved. What did that mean? Her words ravaged inside my head. What does my inability to metabolize alcohol have to do with Jimbo?

I never did well with alcohol. It irritated all my other problems. And I had so many. A predisposition to diabetes and high cholesterol. Migraines, nerve pain, high blood pressure, low thyroid function, and some angina which I skillfully self-managed. Honestly, I didn't like to list all my infirmities. But sometimes it was necessary to remind myself that I was doing well, considering all that was wrong with me.

Sylvia gripped knobby talons around the top rung of the rail and rasped: "You are a toxic person." Bolts of ice shot from her eyes.

She was a falcon, hovering over her prey. Any time now, her beak would plunge into my flesh and tear out my liver. Help! My spine went rigid. I held my breath; the bitter grains of vomit burned against my tongue.

"You are going to destroy my son." She lifted the cheap bag off the bed and disappeared as if made of gas.

THIRTY-TWO

Jackson greets me at the back door of Celia's house wearing his too-small Superman costume over his pajamas. He is six.

"Mommy throwed up," he says.

"Yuck!" I scoop him up and gobble at his neck.

I catch sight of Celia in the kitchen. She stands in a distorted box of sunlight, captured through the small window over the sink. Her body is a brief shadow, a ghost.

"Hey," I say to her, sliding Jackson down my body and turning him toward his bedroom. "I'll get Superman into his clothes."

Jackson wears his Superman costume every day. He wears it to kindergarten; he wears it when he goes outside to play. Celia has given up fighting with him about the costume. Her singular victory is that he will not wear it to bed, allowing her a few hours to soak it in Woolite every once in a while, and lay it to dry. The seams at the shoulders are spreading apart. A half-inch of blue thread zigzags between the panels, desperately holding the material together. I go into his room and peel the costume down with great caution. If I ruin it, Jackson will disintegrate into tears.

Soon as his pajamas are off, Jackson darts under the bed. "Catch me, catch me, Annchar!" Annchar. That's as close as he can get to Aunt Charlotte. I love it. It sounds like an exotic faraway land. The island of Annchar. I grab his ankle and drag him like a caught fish into the open.

"Come here, you," I skittle his ribs, pretending to use great strength as I pin him to the carpet. "Let's get dressed. I have some great surprises for you today." We are going to plant flowers. Sunflowers, to be specific. I have ten, six-inch plants in my car, and a plot picked out on the side of Celia's house. I made a sign out of a piece of siding and I painted his name in indelible markers: Jackson's Garden. We are going to stake the sign in front of the plants when we're done.

At the mention of a surprise, he stills. I walk on my knees to his dresser. Celia keeps his drawers in perfect order. Shorts in one drawer. Shirts in another. Pants in the bottom drawer.

Jackson lets me pull the shirt over his head without too much squiggling. I thread his twig legs into the shorts.

"Brush your teeth," I tell him. "And meet me at the door. How many seconds do you need?" This is a game we play, where I pretend to time him doing something he dislikes. "Ten? Twenty?"

He races to the bathroom. "Don't forget to scrub the ones in the back!" This is a joke only I understand. He has just a few teeth, mostly in the front. I watch him climb atop the stepstool and rise to his toes to turn on the water.

I press my back to the wall just outside the bathroom door, hiding from his view. "Four seconds," I say. A challenge. "Do a good job, Jackson. Four and a quarter," I count.

Celia is seated now, arms hugging her narrow chest. I take a mug from the cabinet and lift the coffee pot. "Four and a half," I shout toward the ceiling.

There is no coffee. The carafe is dry.

"Hey, Sis." I plunk the coffee pot to the counter. "Are you out of coffee? You should have told me. I'd have brought some over." I'd come directly from 7-Eleven. I had my first coffee of the day with Plots.

Sounds of a little boy spitting into the sink. "Four and three quarters!" I sit next to Celia. "One day he's going to hate me for destroying his sense of time," I say.

Celia is quiet. She is so still, she might be asleep. "Hey," I nudge her with my foot. "Anyone in there?"

Tiny feet skitter along the hallway floor. He's done brushing.

Does she hear me? She doesn't react. Her eyes are open. I watch her blink. There is no mascara on her eyelashes. They are vague and nearly invisible. I am not used to seeing her like this. Celia followed a military-strict morning routine. Fresh cold water and a swipe of astringent followed by a base coat of tinted moisturizer from hairline to collarbone to even out her tone and add a peachy hue. I can hear her narrative in my head: A *swipe of rose-colored powder to accent the cheek bones*. Today she is pale as milk.

"Wait for me, Annchar!" Jackson calls from his bedroom.

I hear a clunk, a soft sound of struggle. I know what he is doing. My heart does a little flutter kick. "Time's a'ticking!"

Celia leans forward—her first movement since I joined her in the kitchen—and catches her head in her hands. I bend over to see her face. It is dry as powder.

"Hey," I touch her arm and she peeks up at me, shaking her head. She's fine.

Jackson jumps into the doorway, legs spread far apart. He is wearing his Superman costume, inside out. "Time!" He is panting, his cheeks are petunia pink. "Time!" He insists again.

"Twelve seconds!" I clap my hands. "That's a record, buddy. You are getting faster and faster."

His eyes look past me. His body sags inside the costume. "Mommy is sick today," he says, moving closer. He puts a dimpled hand at the nape of Celia's neck, grabbing onto a length of her hair.

He leans his face toward hers. "Where is your rowboat?" he asks Celia, his lips nearly touching her chin.

She puffs out a breath and pulls her lips farther, a smile.

"What's a rowboat?" I ask.

Celia pushes the chair back and drags herself to stand. When she turns into the window's light, I am startled by the color of her face. Or the lack of color. She is completely gray. Gray skin, gray eyebrows, even her rich brown hair, Warm Brown number ten, appears gray. "Yikes," I say, arching back as if she carries black plague. "You look like shit."

That she doesn't admonish me for swearing in front of Jackson gives me worry. She points to a sheet of paper taped to the refrigerator door. Jackson's artwork. A boat on the water, complete with a fish at the bottom and a sun at the top.

"He says my smile is the shape of a rowboat," Celia says, the first words she's uttered since I arrived. "See?" She points at the drawing and bares her teeth, pulling her mouth back as if posing for a dental scan. It is hardly a smile. But I get the point.

"Do you need me to stay?" I ask her.

Celia has turned toward the hall, toward her bedroom. She holds a hand up, as if waving goodbye.

Jackson has two hands on the doorknob. He is ready to go. His exuberance makes my feet light. "Call if you need me," I shout over my shoulder.

Celia has a miscarriage. Her second since Jackson was born.

I am wearing her apron, standing in her kitchen. Water is boiling on her stove. Steam hovers over the Farberware stockpot and accumulates on the tile backsplash, beading like smallpox. I swipe my upper lip with the quilted potholder, aware that I've just committed a germ crime. If Celia were in the room, she'd be pissed.

She is upstairs in her bed, with a washcloth over her eyes. She has had so many unsuccessful pregnancies; her body is tired.

I slide the pasta from the cellophane bag into the water, careful not to splash any of the water onto my arms. Normally, I'm not so cautious, but today I am feeling the weight of my responsibility as Celia's nurse and that responsibility elevates me to *professional cook.* I chuckle at that, remembering when I wanted to be a professional cook. A professional anything. This is where I belong. I am needed.

I made a good batch of soup yesterday. I brought two quarts to Celia's house for her dinner today. Soup is always better on the second day, after it's had a chance to rest. This morning, I skimmed off the fat using my coffee mug and then boiled the liquid down by an inch to create a dense and flavorful stock. It is delicious. I had a big bowl of that soup before I came over here.

I open Celia's pantry closet. Flat egg noodles, are the best accompaniment for soup. Celia buys No-Yolk noodles which have no taste and no nutritional value whatsoever. I stir her noodles into the water until the finger-long strands begin to relax. Celia's apron dangles from my neck, the wrap-around ties meet around the back.

Celia has a gorgeous kitchen: Moroccan tiles gleam from the walls, the counter is a nearly transparent fine marble that is usually so spotlessly clean, you can check your teeth in its reflection.

The timer rings.

I drain and rinse the noodles in Celia's ceramic colander and then overturn half of them into a large bowl. I'll save the other noodles for Jackson's lunch: noodles with butter, always the same. He'll be home from kindergarten at noon. The simmering soup pours out in a clumpy stream. I pluck a wedge of carrot from the soup with my fingers and slide it into my mouth. Excellent.

Celia's bedroom door is open. I carry the tray to her bed where her sleeping body is flat under the blankets. "Are you still among the living?" I ask in a sing-song voice stolen from some long ago television show. I am a 1950s housewife with a tray and an apron.

"Ugggh," Celia sputters. Only her mouth moves. The bedding is taut, unchanged from how I tucked it under the mattress hours earlier. She looks gaunt lying there. The white pillowcase makes her face seem yellowed, like old book pages exposed to the air.

"You look like an extra in a Vincent Price movie," I tell her. I set the tray on her bedside table. She has nothing on that table. Not a box of tissues, not a pencil. "Where is all your crap?"

"What crap?" Finally. She speaks.

"I don't know, how about a book? A magazine? A glass of water. Who lives like this? Even Mom has a pen and paper on her bedside table."

I wait for her to sit upright.

"I brought soup," I tell her and fix the blanket over her legs. Her nightgown is twisted around her narrow torso. Her eyes have regressed into her skull. I balance the tray on her legs and hand her the spoon. She inserts the soup into her mouth like a robot. No expression.

"Good, huh?" I say. "I made it special." I watch as tiny slurps of soup enter her angered body. "I started with a clump of kale that I stuffed into one of those mesh bags used for spices. Plots turned me on to this type of cooking, they do it in India all the time. You basically boil all the nutrition out of the kale, and then remove the leaves all at once. Genius."

A flap of celery leaf hangs off Celia's lower lip. I snag it with my fingernail and flick it into the trash can. "How's the soup?"

"Good."

"I'm making dinner for Jackson and Mike. I stopped on the way over to load up on ingredients. God knows you don't have anything useful in that kitchen."

She stares at me through vacant eyes. *Where are you, Celia*? I miss her. I wish she'd pop back into herself and fend off my insult like her real self. This hollowed out Celia was giving me the creeps.

"I almost screamed when I opened your spice drawer. It's empty! I thought you were the victim of a seasoning robbery. You don't even have a box of Kosher salt. How do you cook without spices? No dill. No peppercorns." I tug on the apron, loosening it from around my belly. "I'm making cranberry chicken for dinner. How many pieces will Mike eat?"

"Three," she says, finishing the soup. "Thank you, Char. That was really good soup."

The compliment is like chocolate frosting on the roof of my mouth.

She slides lower, turns on her side. The darkness under her eyes scares me. Usually, I am the one who wants to sleep away the day. "So tell me," she says, comfortable. "What have I missed?"

I pick up the tray. "Men have colonized Mars. There is peace in the Middle East. Oh, and, Donald Trump is President."

Her lips stretch. It's not a full rowboat, but it's something. I will let her sleep. She'll be better after she sleeps.

I stand in the doorway, tray in hand. "I must tell you, this housewife business is a drag," I say to her. "The cooking, the cleaning, the endless vacuuming. I don't know how you do it."

She smiles, a real one this time. "You're the greatest," she says. "I don't know what I would do without you."

I nod in agreement. "Neither do I."

THIRTY-THREE

Celia came to see me in the hospital. I was glad for the reprieve. All day, my parents had loitered around the room, tripping over one another, feigning support. No, that was not fair, nor was it factual. They cared; I knew they cared. But the constant buzzing of their busybody presence grated on me.

Jimbo was home in our empty house. He had the dog for company, but that was not enough. He was not good on his own. He needed me.

I was comfortable. I had a window air unit and a television suspended from the ceiling. I had my own bathroom; the other bed had remained vacant since I got here.

The orderly had refreshed my sheets; I had showered and brushed my teeth. I was no longer required to wear the hospital gown, but it turned out I liked the cool looseness of the hospital's cotton sheath. I'd begged an extra gown and wore it like a robe, ensuring my rear end was covered.

Celia was in exercise clothes, tights and a long T-shirt, probably Mike's. Her face was the color of oatmeal. She'd been sick a lot lately. After one miscarriage, she became anemic. Then she got the flu, which turned into pneumonia. Her doctor wanted to put her in the hospital, but she refused. Jackson needed her.

"Jackson wanted to come with me," she said, "but I told him to wait until you're home." She plopped into the chair. Standard hospital rooms featured an armchair that reclined like a La-Z-Boy. She didn't ask how I was feeling, nor when I was to be discharged. "He wanted to know when you'd be back in the garden."

I really did feel like Jackson was a little bit mine. I was present for every birthday party, every graduation, every event. I was his date to the school's Spring Fair, probably my highest honor of all time. I let my mind go pillowy and closed my eyes so I could see him. I thought if I tried hard enough, I could conjure his smell.

***

Jackson loved the sunflower garden. He'd check on the saplings, he watered, he weeded. He tossed aside debris that blanketed the garden patch. Celia told me. When he came off the kindergarten bus, he went straight to the garden. I think I remember that the plants grew healthy and tall but I don't actually have a visual of them. Did they really take? The sign was still there. But what had happened to the sunflowers? I should have paid more attention. I should have come over and tested the soil when Jackson was in school. Everything was dead because of me.

Dr. Essent, my psychiatrist, had warned me about this sort of thinking. I was supposed to be mindful of over-presuming responsibility. Like saying I raised Jackson, when I was really, in truth, just a marvelous and attentive aunt. I soothed him when he was a baby. I quieted him when he had croup. My shoulder was where he rested his tired chin. But Celia was his mother. She was responsible. Same with the garden. I helped plant it. That was all.

I was supposed to try and lighten the load, unburden myself. I was carrying too much weight. That was the cause of my collapse.

My husband didn't like my mother. My father didn't like my husband. My mother-in-law didn't like anyone. And I was in the middle, trying hard to crochet everyone together. I loved to crochet. I'd passed so many lonely hours crocheting blankets and scarves.

Before I met Jimbo, my nights were compacted with crafts: crocheting, mosaics, rug hooking, molding chocolates. I'd wall-papered the halls of my house, retiled the kitchen floor. Like my father, I was handy and crafty and productive. I had my own tool belt. My own soldering iron.

But then I had Jimbo and the need to keep busy vanished. No more art projects. No more home improvements.

I liked it here, in this room. I liked the constant thrum of noise from the world beyond the closed door. I liked the cool air and the warm contact of hands tending to me, taking my temperature. I liked how the food was delivered in a little TV-dinner tray, all the little servings compartmentalized. The diabetic menu was completely tasteless, but Jimbo brought some necessities from home to spruce up the food: salt, butter flakes, and mayonnaise to moisten the dry meats and turkey burgers. Jimbo bought his meals in the cafeteria where he'd load a tray with double desserts for us to share. He ate in bed, with me.

He'd moved the big chair so it prevented the sunlight from reflecting off the television, making it easier to watch our daytime programs. That's where Celia sat now.

"Hello?" she waved a hand. "I just asked when you'd get out of here?"

I shrugged. "Don't know yet."

Jimbo was at the dentist's. He had terrible teeth. But his dentist was a buddy he'd grown up with and he offered plenty of pain relief so Jimbo actually liked going. "A great way to sleep for an hour and come home with some new prescriptions," he'd said. I looked at the clock. Was I going home? Who was going to take care of me?

Anxiety wielded its way from my molars to my colon.

In our last session, Dr. Essent coached me. "Do not allow the anxiety to take you hostage," he said. He gave me a card listing the realities of anxiety attacks. I only remembered the first two.

Anxiety is temporary.

You can't die from an anxiety attack.

I was in no danger. I had nothing to fear. My neck itched with dread. I wasn't ready. I wasn't ready to leave. I needed to remain in the care of others. Just thinking about going home made my throat ache. I was not balanced.

Celia stood up and paced to the window, bent at the waist as if she had a stomach cramp.

"You okay?" I asked.

She turned. "I'm scared," she squeaked. When she was little, the neighbor kids called her 'hamster' because when she was frightened her voice shot into the highest register. The voice unnerved me. She turned her wide eyes to mine and I saw the ovals of water, tears, reflected in the morning sun. "You're scaring me."

An emotional sheet closed around us, wrapping us in an invisible capsule. Just the two of us. Charlotte and Celia. Sisters.

"I'm scared for you. Mom is scared. Dad is terrified."

I had never seen my father express fear. I wondered what it felt like, to witness that emotion. I studied Celia's face, searching for clues, but I found only pallor.

"We don't know what we are supposed to do for you," she said. "What do you need? What can we do?"

She waited, her eyes were severe on mine, but I did not blink; I would not break the bond. "Don't worry about me," I used my older-sister voice, hoping to convince her of something that I was not convinced of myself.

"The psych team said you're a candidate for their inpatient treatment program."

Inpatient? Wasn't I an inpatient already? I said, "I'm good here. I'm doing well. Everyone said so." I didn't know if that was true, but it sounded good.

"But you can't stay here," Celia said. "You are only here now because Dad called in some favors from the hospital Board. They approved an extension to your stay, even though you are not being treated for anything." She scanned the room, noting, for the sake of obviousness, the lack of medical equipment.

"I *am* being treated." The words levitated from my tongue. "I'm being well treated, in fact. My temperature is recorded. The lab draws blood. I have a million things going on here. And can't you see," I challenged her, teetering very precariously, "how well I'm doing?"

I'd washed my hair that morning, and I'd rubbed some Vaseline over my peeling lips. The hospital provided everything. The comb, toothpaste, even the Vaseline. It was like a hotel. And now they wanted to force me out? I did not understand. Why would my family steal me from a healthy environment?

Celia was starting to cry. Her jawline became soft, I saw the hint of a double chin loose above her neckline.

I would not back down. My shoulders squared; I filled my lungs with air. "Now you listen to me," I said to her. "I don't need your help. And I don't need Mom and Dad to come to my rescue. I am a grown woman. I can dictate how I want to be treated. And where." I ignored the glare steaming from her swampy eyes. Celia was not usually a crier, but I was not swayed by her weakness. I was entitled to the best care. I would stay here.

The door pressed open. A candy striper delivered my lunch. Turkey burger, lettuce, tomato. No bun.

I dismissed Celia, pointing my finger after the candy striper to the hall. "Go."

They were worrying about me. I reached into the canvas bag Jimbo had left at my bedside and pulled out a Kaiser roll. I slid the burger onto the roll. My parents were probably right now sitting at their kitchen table with their spastic hands tapping subconsciously on the marble, wondering what in the world to do with me. I squeezed a packet of mayonnaise onto the burger and rubbed it around with a fingertip. My mother couldn't eat when she was nervous; she'd probably shed ten pounds on my behalf already. Hah! I almost laughed. I was good for her figure. I'd have to remember to tell her that. If it weren't for me, her skirts would be tight.

My father. Well. That was different. I did not glory in the image of my father's worry. When I thought about him, my own stomach reacted. Acid burped upward; I felt its iron residue on my palate. I squeezed out a packet of ketchup. Not Heinz, I noticed, but Hunts. I only liked Heinz, but I'd make do for the sake of amiability. Ketchup and mayonnaise mixed together made Russian dressing. It would be better with relish but…

I layered the tomato but not the lettuce. Lettuce. What a waste of a food! My father liked to refer to lettuce, or any greens really, as grass. "I'll have the grass with Russian dressing." That was one of the reasons I never grew lettuce in my gardens. Lettuce or any of its cousins. It was all, as my father said, grass.

I sent my mind back to my parent's kitchen. By now, Celia would be at the table with them. They were listening to Celia's report on my condition, my state of mind. I took a bite of the roll and chewed slowly, dabbing at the clod of Russian dressing that pooled on my lip, my body a receptacle for their concern.

The best thing about being in the hospital was that I held no dominion over what happened here. Food came and went. Doctors came and went. Everyone wanted to talk to me about me, how I felt, what I thought. Attention was honey. Marvelous and satiating. I couldn't get enough of it.

THIRTY-FOUR

I promised to attend six outpatient sessions with Dr. Essent, that was our arrangement. Not exactly a standard therapeutic arrangement, but it's what he'd worked out with my father. I could have complete control over my recovery as long as I saw the doctor six times. Minimum. That was what I agreed to do. I don't really remember agreeing to anything, but there you have it. Agreement. So many things in my life happened like that. Papers appeared, signatures were requested, orders were recited, repeated. I pretended to listen. I pretended to agree.

In retrospect, I recognized my pattern. Hateful as it was to admit, I liked being told what to do. I feigned independence as a teen. I fought against every nuance of my parents' perceived control: What I wore, the condition of my room, the slipping meter of my school grades. I had my father's temper; I raged and stormed and spewed poison at the walls. I'd look into the mirror of his face as it filled red and shined sweat, and I knew I had his attention.

When I was younger, I tried to elevate myself according to my father's expectations. His attention was sunshine on a sunflower; I flourished under his gaze. I did not do what he *told* me to do but rather what he *wanted* me to do. I felt, as the oldest and the first to receive his nod of appreciation, that I knew what he wanted beyond words, as if his wishes were transmitted by osmosis. We were, for a time, symbiotic. I felt select, special.

When I'd learned of the terms dictated by my father and the psychiatrist he'd chosen, I acquiesced. I was tired of confrontation. I didn't know what I wanted, where I wanted to be, or who I wanted to be. And so I was compliant. And there was a pleasing calm between us for a while.

Celia had appointed herself as my compliance officer. She drove me to my outpatient appointments, and I sat quietly in her car, perfectly content to not see anything beyond the horizon; I had no interest in wondering what might be ahead. And that, again in retrospect, is a curiosity given the perceptive nature of myself as a child, self-diagnosed though it was.

Celia drove like an old lady. Within the speed limit, in the right lane.

"What's he like? Dr. Essent?" she asked. Sleet dangled lightly outside the car where we huddled in our coats, wishing for the heat to fan on. "I picture him like Einstein. Small, tufts of white hair. Am I close?"

"Hardly," I said, visualizing the red-haired behemoth who'd supervised my treatment. I didn't mind seeing him; in fact, I liked the quiet time, the cool unpressured atmosphere of his office. No one disapproved of me in there. No one felt disappointed.

"So he's tall?" she prodded.

His office abutted the psychiatric hospital that had been my home for almost two weeks. I looked out the window, at the bleak gray mud of March and smiled. That everyone cared enough about me to escort me to my appointments and to take an interest in my progress!

For so long, no one was remotely curious about my life. What could she possibly have to share, they must have thought. A single woman with no social life, no prospects, no dates. What could I have added to any conversation?

"He's not tall," I said. We were filling time. Talking about nothing. Leisurely. "Or maybe he is tall," I'd reconsidered. "I only ever see him sitting down. And when I was in the hospital, I was lying down so that's no way to judge height."

Celia fidgeted, punching the buttons on the dash for the heater. "Fuck!" she banged a fist. "I hate this car."

"I don't think beating the shit out of it is going to help," I offered.

She coasted around a corner and crept onto the Expressway. "It guzzles gas; it fails the emissions test every year."

"So," I lit a cigarette and cranked the window down. "Buy another car."

Celia barked at me: "Hey! Put that out!"

I displayed the cigarette, holding my hand flat, totally innocent.

"I said, put it out. No one smokes in the car." She merged into the middle lane. "If I can't smoke, you can't smoke," she said.

"I can't quit," I said. "I have no willpower, you know that."

"You're the most stubborn person I know," Celia joked. "If anyone knows how to exercise their will, it's you."

"I don't want to exercise anything. I am happy where I am." A Toyota Prius sped across the grime-streaked window. Celia flashed her headlights and allowed the car to pass.

"If a Prius is going faster than you are, that means you're going too slow."

"I'm going the speed limit," Celia said.

"We're going to be late," I said. "I'll tell the esteemed doctor that I wasn't on time because of your bad driving."

Celia laughed and then turned her soft face in my direction. She had our grandmother's nose; a ski slope with a hump at the halfway mark; it took up a lot of room on her small face.

Suddenly, her face appeared in a smear on the windshield. Her eyes, her strong chin tilted down. Like she was angry with me. Like she was disappointed.

She swiped a sleeve across her mouth and settled on a new subject. "What are you doing later this afternoon? Anything good?"

I knew what she was doing. It was a technique we learned in therapy. When a disturbing thought comes into your head, notice it, take an inventory of the responses felt around your body, and then set it aside. Think about something else.

"Laundry. Someone has to do the laundry. The pile is up to my head."

"Jimbo doesn't do laundry, I take it?"

"I can't get Jimbo to do anything," I said, surprised at the frustration in my tone. "He won't put gas in the car or go shopping for food on his own. He doesn't know how to put in a load of laundry!"

"Have you tried going on strike? What if you suddenly stopped doing his laundry? Wash your own clothes and give him a lesson on how to run the machines. Eventually, he'd run out of underwear, and then he'd figure it out."

She seemed so sure. "If I stopped doing his laundry, he'd take it to his mother's, and she'd do it for him!"

"But he doesn't have transportation! It's your car, isn't it? If you wanted, you could manage to be out in the car the very day he discovers he has to go commando all day. That might be enough to motivate him."

"My car is his car," I said. That is the coda of marriage: what's mine is yours and what's yours is mine. Jimbo and I recited that phrase to each other all the time. What's mine is yours.

"But Charlotte, there is a limit to sharing. Everything that is yours, that was yours before the marriage, still belongs only to you. Only you. Like the trust. The reason a trust is established is to keep it separate from other assets. We have a trust for Jackson that ensures his college education. No matter what happens to us, even if we lose everything, the trust remains for Jackson. See?"

Lose everything? Was Celia telling me that she was in trouble? I did not like the trajectory of this conversation. What was she insinuating? Celia was the stable one, the one without trauma. If she faltered…

I slid my fingers down my leg as if to scratch. My purse was on the floor. She didn't notice the rummaging, the searching. I found my target, a contact lens case, and palmed it, dragging it up my leg and into my lap. Jimbo had taught me this trick: store some pills in a contact lens case. It keeps them from breaking apart, and also your fingers can almost always find the case, even without looking. I turned to the window and touched a pill to my lip before swallowing it.

The car's engine sputtered, coughed.

"Don't you dare," my sister threatened, veering off the highway.

I leaned toward the wheel and peered at the dash. "Does that say you have one hundred and twenty-two thousand miles on this car?"

"Yes," she said, turning into the parking lot.

"You need a new car," I said.

She swerved to the curb, depositing me close to the canvas awning. "I can't afford a new car." She could. She just didn't want to spend the money. That was a difference between us. A difference, not a difficulty.

According to Dr. Essent, I was supposed to know the implied nuances separating those two things: difference and difficulty. Difference means not alike. Difficulty insinuates an issue that is almost outside my ability, something that requires great energy or effort to overcome. Difficulty required work.

We waved. Celia would wait for me, for the fifty-minute appointment, across the street in a Starbucks.

We'd decided that Celia would take me to my appointments on Mondays. That was the easiest day of the week for her to leave early. I liked being in the car together, talking about my treatments and sharing all I was learning about myself. She made a lot of jokes: commenting on how everyone feels somehow complicit in this situation, how nobody knows what I might be telling that doctor. "You could tell him our mother had three heads, and he would have no way of discerning the truth!" Celia was right about that. I could say anything. And sometimes I did. Sometimes I told him about feeling so terribly left out, of being scored and ridiculed, of having no idea where my life took a hairpin turn. In ninth grade, I was happy. In tenth, I was miserable. Or so it seemed. I had difficulty, note the proper use of the term, in identifying the cause of my sudden demise.

Mostly, though, I talked about Jimbo and how happy we were together, and how our days were filled with love and joking, and how we'd managed to overcome all the pesky insults of living within the establishment, as coined by our hippy counterparts. We were hippies, I explained to Dr. Essent. I thought that was a good description.

I waited until Celia's Toyota chugged out of the circular drive before strolling to the water fountain opposite the entrance. She didn't need to see what I was doing. No one did. I leaned over and put my lips into the rainbow of water, swishing the clean coldness past my tongue, around my teeth. It was so cold! I held a mouthful of water still, warming it to the count of ten. Meanwhile, I extracted the plastic dosage bag prepared for me and unzipped the sealing ridge. There were four pills, two whites and two reds. Silently, and without hesitation, I added them to my already full mouth and swallowed like a pelican.

THIRTY-FIVE

Dr. Essent checked his calendar. "Do you know, we are nearly at the end of our sessions. Only one more week to go." His very dark eyes settled on my face and I had to look away, lest he see the utter relaxation displayed there. Twenty minutes had passed since Celia's departure. Twenty minutes of low metabolic activity.

"It's been fun," I started.

"Thank you for that," he said, smiling, "but there's really no reason for you to butter me up."

I liked him.

"Do you think you're feeling ready to resume your sessions with your regular therapist?"

"You're firing me?" I couldn't help it. I had to joke. I felt so good, so cheery.

Dr. Essent looked up as if surprised. "Well, you're in a good mood," he said. "Can you describe what has prompted this wave of good feeling? It might be good to identify the positive stressors, not just the negative. Can you trace your steps?"

"I can't explain it," I said, waggling my toes. Yes, it was still winter, and I should have worn boots. But I never liked to have my feet covered. My toes liked fresh air. "I just woke up feeling happy." That wasn't precisely true. I'd awakened at five to pee, and then I'd stubbed my toe on the way back to bed, catching the staple on an unpacked carton leftover from the new DVD player we'd ordered. It wasn't a big box, but the exposed industrial staple had slid under my toenail and wrenched a corner of it clean off. Jimbo had wrapped it in gauze, and even suggested I get a tetanus shot later, but I would not do that. Tetanus was not on my list of cares that day.

"That is very good to hear," he said, rubbing his pen under his bottom lip. If he was a poker player, that would be his tell. He slid the pen just under his lip and rubbed back and forth, like masturbation, coaxing the flesh where the lip meets the skin. His eyes assessed me. I'd have to be careful. "And are you taking your medication?"

The anti-depressant he'd prescribe for me was hardly effective. Compared to all the other meds, Lexapro was the least potent. It did give me a wicked case of diarrhea, though. And it was fun to say, "Go like a pro with Lexapro," Jimbo joked, doling out the pills.

"Yup." I forced myself not to smile. Dr. Essent had been astute back when I was too drugged to fake sobriety. He'd sent me back to the hospital twice in the last three years for drying out periods, something I abhorred and did not want to repeat. No, I would convince Dr. Essent that I was well balanced and able to maintain myself, outside of treatment.

"I really do feel good," I said. "This weekend I'm getting together with some old friends," I began, bolstered by the bravado of my own voice. "And also, I'm getting ready to think about planting my spring garden," I lied, "even though it's a little too early. The frost for our region lasts through the end of April." I would impress him, I was sure, with my vast knowledge of horticulture and weather patterns. "While I was sick, my family cleaned out my whole backyard," I said. "Did I tell you that? Of course, they had the help of the company my sister hired to do the work. But she was in charge. She told them where to clear and where to avoid ripping out the perennials."

He nodded, thinking. "Which friends are you going to see?" he asked.

I panicked, confused. Had I lost the thread of our discussion? What about the garden? I knew that returning to a favored hobby was a sign of good mental health, so why didn't he ask about that? "What do you mean?"

He shifted, getting comfortable. "You said you were going to get together with some old friends," he said. "Can we talk about that?"

I heard the clashing of little cymbals chiming between my ears, forcing my forehead to frown. Which friends? I could not remember what I'd conjured. Were they friends from school? I didn't have any friends from school. Not anymore. What have I told him? I scrambled for memories. What have I said?

I sucked on my bottom lip, wishing for my thumb. I loved sucking my thumb as a child and didn't see one good reason why it was considered unacceptable. Who did it hurt? To suck your thumb?

He made no effort to ease my discomfort. Rather, he just stared.

I heard a far-away purr, a low-frequency thrum that made it impossible to think. Who were these friends and where were we going to meet and what did I expect from this imaginary visit? I had no imaginary friends when I was a child. But I'd just gained a certain respect for them, for keeping track of the fabricated names and backstories. This was *not* easy.

"Charlotte?"

"What?" I sat my hands on the armrests, as if readying to leave. We both knew, Dr. Essent and I, that I would not leave before he released me.

"We were talking about the friends you were going to see."

Yes, that was it.

"Are these the friends you knew when you were with that boyfriend, Karl?"

Karl. He was never a boyfriend, not really. The one who killed himself. Oh sure, bring up Karl. God, he was handsome with all that long hair. He had no depth, as my mother would have said, no quality of character. So what if Karl wasn't the smartest guy. So what if he didn't have a job. Or a future. Or a driver's license. He liked me. We were part of something together, I thought. I was part of the group. My mistake was assuming that having sex meant something. I thought Karl really felt something for me.

I had told Dr. Essent about Karl's meanness, his degrading behavior, the way he charged up my credit card, my *father*'s credit card. "For emergencies," we'd agreed, father and daughter, both of us knowing I'd use the card for groceries and necessities like car repairs and wardrobe additions from Lane Bryant.

I told the doctor how Karl had cheated on me, how he had sex with another girl in *my* car while *I* was driving. I'd told him how I watched Karl crawl over the back seat of the car and lie on top of the girl back there, a girl he knew from 'way back,' a girl who needed a ride. I watched as his head lurched forward and back, forward and back, traversing the expanse of the rearview mirror from edge to edge. I didn't want to remember that. Why did he make me remember that?

"In my notes, the history on that event is not complete. Do you want to talk about that? To talk about how that relationship, and that death, affected you? Once you've exposed the poison…"

"I know. I know. It loses all its toxicity," I finished the quip for him. I knew the phrase from his all-too-familiar chant at inpatient group therapy. I knew it the way I knew the national anthem. Maybe better.

"When we first met, you said you wished you'd died with Karl." He had done his homework; he didn't even need to glance down at his notes. "You said, everyone would have been so much happier if I'd just died with Karl."

I nodded, remembering. I did say that. And it was true. I wished I'd died, many times in fact. "But that was before I'd met Jimbo. Things change, isn't that what you always tell me?"

I'd worked so hard for stability. And now, finally, I was gimbaled, rolling with the waves, maintaining my position. I did not want to think about Karl or anyone else for that matter.

I don't remember how we passed the last minute of the session. A debilitating thirst hamstrung my words. I should have stepped out for a moment to get water from the dispenser in the wall, but I didn't want him to see me walk. Not yet. I could not take the chance that I'd wobble or pitch. Despite my insistence on harmonic balance and calm horizons, I was beginning to feel anxious. My palms were wet, my lips were rubber. The sound of my own circulatory system deafened with thunderous silence.

Celia was waiting out front. I threw myself into her car. "Go," I commanded, staring straight ahead.

She obeyed, like I knew she would. "What's happening?" she asked after we'd passed the first set of intersections. "You look like you're going to throw up."

I washed a hand over my face and let the window open a crack. "It's nothing," I said. "You know I have a delicate system. I must have eaten something that disagrees with me."

"Bad clams?" she joked, driving on. I am sure, in retrospect, that she knew, somewhere inside, that I was failing. She was like that. We were like that. Thankfully, or perhaps fatefully, she said nothing more. Only, "See ya," when she dropped me off at the curb in front of my house.

THIRTY-SIX

My house had become a stranger to me. Boxes were cleared away; the table was wiped clean. How strange! I tried to remember the last time I'd seen the entire surface of my kitchen table at one time, but I failed to conjure a single image. Where was all the clutter?

I wandered from the foyer to the kitchen, hardly acknowledging the people standing around the perimeter. Everyone was looking at me, I could tell. But I was not about to interact. I first needed to acclimate, to adjust. What had happened here? The boxes that previously formed a moat around the kitchen table were in absentia. Where were all my things? I was a clutter bug, I left things out. That was how I liked things: Out.

My father was in front of the refrigerator. I watched him open the door and bend forward, moving things around on the wire shelves.

Finally, I spoke, "Where is Jimbo?" but no sound came out.

"Henry," my mother's voice was sharp. "You forgot to unload the produce." A brown bag of groceries waited near his knee. I watched him place a handful of kale into the lower drawer, or maybe it was arugula. I couldn't tell from here. Everything was so odd. I felt like I was standing in a movie scene. I recognized all the players, but the action was weird.

The refrigerator light was too bright. Was this even my refrigerator? I saw the little tattoo I'd scratched into the high right corner. My initials and Jimbo's initials, encircled by a heart.

Celia emerged from the hallway and wrapped her arm through mine. She pulled me close. I felt her ribs, the metal wire of her bra. "Feel good to be home?" she asked softly.

I wanted to respond; I really did. I should have marveled at the sparkling cleanliness of my kitchen and the obvious repairs completed in my absence. The hole in the floor just below the sink was filled in, the missing backsplash tiles replaced. The light fixture, a hand-me-down from Sylvia, glittered with new bulbs. It was bright. I liked it the way it was before, with only two or three little candelabra bulbs that flickered off and on, reacting to every footstep, every small human motion.

"Where is my husband?" I asked, turning toward the living room. "Where is everything?" Was that my sofa? The broken footrest that caught me on the shin, bruising my skin to purple so many times.

My father moved until he was next to me. "Surprise!" he said. He lifted a knee to the armrest, resting it on the black burn mark where I'd balanced a pot of Kraft Macaroni and Cheese years ago, melting the fabric underneath.

He pointed to the sofa's fascia. "I fixed the footrest," he boasted.

He leaned back on the wall, waiting for me to approve. I saw his palms pressed flat to the paneling. I knew, when he moved his hands away, a print of sweat would remain. Both of us had sweaty palms, my father and I.

"Your mother thought it would be a nice surprise," he said, "if we had the cleaning lady come over and do a Mr. Clean job. Look," he bent to point at something on the television console," she even washed under the furniture. She found this." He held out an inch of metal, too small to see from so far away.

I leaned in. "What is it?"

"It's the charm that I bought you all those years ago. We thought you'd lost it. Remember?"

I didn't remember. And I didn't like the sound of their voices in my house. My father never made comments like that, like *Mr. Clean.* This was too weird.

"Where is Jimbo?" I asked, moving toward the bedroom. It was such a tiny house: ten steps in any direction covered the area wall to wall.

"Wait!" Celia's voice stopped me. "We wanted to show you something. Come on, Mike. Let's show her."

Mike? Mike was here? I hadn't seen him. He must have been lurking in a corner somewhere.

A heavy arm draped across my shoulders. Mike. He was a big guy, heavyset and solid as a bear. I liked him a lot, especially before he decided Jackson could no longer come over to my house unsupervised. In his defense, I didn't disagree with him. Jimbo and I did have a lot of medical preparations in the house. Syringes and morphine lollipops and bottles without caps. Neither one of us could manipulate those security caps that sealed every pharmaceutical container, so we left them all uncovered.

"We've missed you," Mike said. "And we wanted you to know how much we absolutely adore you, so Jackson and I came up with this idea." He pushed me gently, urging me to walk ahead of him, into the bedroom.

The windows were uncovered. My butterfly curtains were all that remained of window treatments. Jimbo and I spend so much time in bed, we'd covered the windows to better see the screens of the television and of Jimbo's computers. He liked to lie in bed in a sea of laptops. He had at least five. A modest guess at best. I'd employed my best engineering techniques and fashioned window covers, cut from cardboard and foamboard, painted them light blue, same as the walls. I'd nailed them into place, fitting them tightly into the inside frames of each of the two windows. I must say, I did a spectacular job. The boards were hardly noticeable, and the light from the outside had not even a smidgen of access to the room. Like a cozy cave, our bedroom was.

"Surprise!" At sixteen, Jackson was already as tall as Mike. A spark caught in my chest. I didn't know he was here.

"I took off the hideous window coverings," he pointed, unnecessarily, to the winter sunlight streaming a white bed cover. "And then I remembered how you said you liked a gross brown Sisal rug in that big store where we always bought the gardening supplies."

I remembered.

"And so we went back and bought it, and we did all this." He spanned an arm.

The 1950s orange shag carpet in my bedroom was bare in so many places, it looked as if it suffered from mange. Rug mange. For a long time, I'd talked about redecorating my bedroom with a new rug, new paint. I talked about it, but I never did it. And now here it was. Done. I let my chin fall, pretending to study the new Sisal, indeed, the very one I liked. It floated perfectly over the floor, ending just a few inches shy of the exact square footage. The wood floor peered out from the baseboard, as if trying to get a look at me.

My head swam. I sat on the bed, on the stiff white cover that was entirely unfamiliar to me. My mother joined us wearing an apron of red plaid. Like Betty Crocker. "Isn't it stunning?" she said. I just stared. I had no words.

"Are you hungry? I made a fresh beef stew. Just the way you like it. No peas. Extra potatoes."

I swiveled my head side to side. Was I dreaming? Was I in a movie that recreated my life, my home, and my family, only with nicer linens and a new rug?

Mike stood like a clothing model, one hand resting on the door frame. "You know, you're really lucky," he said. "If I had a health crisis, my brothers wouldn't even send a card!" The air thinned, tensed. "Oh, sorry, didn't mean to sound callous. But it's true. This here," he drew a big circle in the air, encircling all of us inside, "this is such a great family. The best. We all pull together and help each other out."

Celia moved closer to her husband as if reeled in by fishing line. "You're a good guy," she said, caressing him with her eyes. "Did I ever tell you that? You're a good man."

"Not often enough, you don't," he joked.

Jackson opened the accordion door to my closet and then closed it again, as if testing its function. Where did they find such perfect replacement doors? "Do you want to see the garden?"

I nodded but didn't follow him out of the room.

Where was Jimbo?

"Jimbo is visiting his mother," my father said. Mind-reader. "He'll be back in a while."

"I made enough beef stew for ten people," my mother laughed.

"Are you coming?" Jackson yelled from the back door.

"Give us a minute," Celia called to her son. "Give Aunt Charlotte a minute to breathe." She shooed her hand, disappearing all of our family. She sat on the bed next to me.

"Overwhelmed much?" She picked my hand up and began to stretch my fingers one by one. An old game. "Seriously. How do you feel? Is it weird to be home?"

I shrugged, still not sure how to metabolize all this prepared, redressed energy. I was heavy in my skin, I felt my hips against the mattress, spread wide, secure. This was my room. This was my bed. But it all felt so strange.

Celia leaned into me, pressing our shoulders tight. "I have to tell you," she confided. "I was the one to come in here and clear out all the paraphernalia. I didn't want Mom to see it. I put all the meds in your closet, in a Tupperware thing. If I'd had any backbone at the time, I'd have thrown it all away."

My eyes connected with hers. "I didn't," she said, quickly. "I saved everything. But Charlotte," she said, her voice low, "there were so many pills. Loose pills, bottles of pills that had no labels. Where are you getting all this medicine? How do you know what you're taking?"

I stood up and reached for the closet. The door swung too fast, and I nearly pitched backward. There it was, right where Celia had promised. I saw the large storage bin alone on the floor.

"You never liked him," I said, turning toward my sister. Her face was tilted up at me, just like when we were girls and our heights were more staggered. Until we were teens, I was taller by a head. "You thought he was a low life, without a job or a career or an ambition. You never liked him."

She did not blink. And she did not argue. "I don't care at all, about any of that. I like him because he makes you happy. And that is all I really care about. That you are happy."

I believed her. I knew her, I knew her as well as I knew my own self. She wanted for me what I wanted for her. Completeness. Contentedness. A full life.

She had a full life. A husband and a child and a career and a house where everyone wanted to go for holidays. She took vacations and had sex, we talked about that. She possessed the strength to say no to her husband when she disagreed with him, and the confidence to know that he'd love her *regardless* of her stubbornness and her pain-in-the-ass characteristics. His love was real. For real.

I looked into the frying pan of her face and tried to imagined her freckles were little bits of sizzling garlic. Anything to change the subject.

"You have a long black hair hanging out of your nose," I said.

"Thank you." She smiled.

I smiled.

Voices permeated the walls. The house was made of spit and paste, Jimbo used to say he could hear me blink from two rooms away. My father's voice. Jackson's voice.

"Jackson is so grown up," I said.

"Not really," Celia answered. "He refers to himself as a 'grown ass man.'" She let out a singular breath. "He cried all the way over here today."

A pinch on the heart muscle, and I flinched. "He didn't want to come?"

"He misses you, that's all. We all do."

"How can you miss a person who's sitting right here?" I asked, clearer now. The sunshine in my bedroom was perky, I had to admit. I liked how the rays carved a Mondrian pattern onto the bed cover. It was artistic. And optimistic.

Celia used a knuckle to touch her eye. Was she wearing eyeliner? Once, she encouraged me to line my eyelids with a colorful pencil so the greenish-tinted eye color that was my one good feature would stand out. I'd tried it once or twice, using the pencil she'd bought me at CVS, and it did look really good. Dramatic. But then, I still had my same old face and my same old hair. No one looked at me anyway. I never tried it again.

She checked her hand. Yes, a blue smear proved it. She was wearing makeup. How did she manage, after all these years, to keep decorating herself? She dyed the gray out of her hair, she bleached the moustache that accumulated over her upper lip every winter. I looked at her lip and saw the little hairs dotting the skin. Winter was almost over and she'd neglected to get waxed? That was not like Celia.

"So, what do you think?" she said, standing. "Do you think you can handle a family dinner tonight? That's what we're doing in case you hadn't noticed. But before we go out there, tell me. Are you sure you want to go back to your life the way it was? I know we've talked about marriage being difficult and requiring both people to adapt and change. Are you certain, Charlotte, that this is what you want?"

Her gaze slid directly into my brain and my neurons jolted as if electrified. Celia was in my head. I saw her as a baby, as a toddler, as a child, as a teen. I saw her at her wedding, I saw her minutes after Jackson took his very first breath. I saw her bending over my bed in the hospital, begging me not to leave her. I smiled, remembering.

"What?" Of course, she'd picked up on that smile.

"I was just thinking about that first time in the hospital, when I had that bronchitis and I accidentally overdosed on Tylenol," I recreated the scene like a TV drama in my mind: The mayhem. The confusion. The voices:

"Did you intend to kill yourself?"

"Do you have thoughts of suicide?"

No! No! "I just wanted to get rid of a headache!"

Celia had been on a boondoggle, an all-expense paid trip to an exclusive golf resort, somewhere glorious, Puerto Rico maybe. I'd called her from the ambulance. I need you, I'd said.

She came into the hospital room that night, swearing like a sailor. I loved it when she streamed profanity. It was a pleasant shock to trace the words back to her flawlessly freckled face.

She waited for me to lead her through the memory. "You looked so nice and friendly, and the doctors were all so relieved that you showed up to get me. You barged in through the curtain, and said, 'If you leave me, I will never speak to you again! I will hate you forever and I will pay extra to have ASSHOLE carved on your gravestone.'"

"That sounds like me," Celia said, lifting my arm, guiding me from the room as if I'd lost my sight rather than my sanity.

If I'd been paying attention, I might have sensed something. A thin wire of tension in their voices. A falseness in their voices. Instead, I sat there, in the dense miasma of my own head, oblivious.

THIRTY-SEVEN

"Knock, knock." Jimbo pushed open the front door. "Where's the party?" His pink head crowned just above the doorknob. A diluted bleat of hellos rose from our seated powwow.

Mike stood. "Hey, I just realized. I think I parked in your spot. Do you want me to move the car?"

"Too late," Jimbo merged completely into the room and shed his coat. "I parked on the grass. It's so dark out there, I missed the driveway completely." His gaze moved from face to face, pausing nowhere.

"Hello husband," I said, luring him to me.

"Hello wife." He slid his hands into his front pockets; he'd already walked out of his clogs. Returning to normal. Now that Jimbo was here, the house warmed to familiar.

My mother vacated her seat. "Sit here," she said to Jimbo. "We've been waiting for you."

We had not been waiting. In fact, my mother had insisted we start eating immediately, as if we were racing against time. What was the hurry to start dinner? It wasn't even five o'clock.

"How was your mother? Is she feeling better?" My mother scurried, assembling a plate and utensils for Jimbo. She put a clean napkin over his lap. "She looked so tired."

Jimbo removed the napkin and held it to his nose. He blew, a wet and messy sound. "She's allowed to be tired," he said. "She's almost eighty."

"Let her know, would you, how grateful we are that she stayed for a while to help with our Charlotte," my mother mewed. "We know she really wanted to get home. But it meant a lot. That she stayed."

"Maybe we'll write her a note," my father said.

"Good." My mother stepped back, away from the table. She looked at me for a long time, as if studying a map. What did she see on my face? Evidence of weakness, I supposed. She was always trying to make me strong, to hammer passivity out of me. As if that were possible.

I looked back at her, struggling for defiance. I wasn't sure what I felt or how I felt. Everything was so mixed up. My parents hadn't pampered me in a long time, and now that they were here, cleaning and cooking and serving me, I felt guilty that they had to be here, that they had to help me. I did need their help. I had no delusions of independence. But I assumed that being married would provide all the support I'd need, that Jimbo would somehow take the place of my parents, that he would take care of me. I looked at him across our own table as he assembled a cube of beef and potato onto his fork, pressing the knife to the tines of the fork, European style. He had good table manners; I'll give him that. "Delicious," he said after his mouth cleared.

My mother signaled to my father with a bob of her head.

Jimbo stood and carried his plate to the microwave. He set the dish inside.

My mother clawed his arm, nearly upturning the plate. "Wait!"

Her feet flew, in two strides she tackled Jimbo, wrapping both arms around his torso, trapping his hands.

Time stopped ticking. We were inert, suspended like puppets waiting for a string to tug. It felt like everyone was moving in slow motion. My father was half-standing with one arm extended, reaching for the bowl of green beans. Mike and Celia were quiet as mannequins, my sister's mouth was frozen open. My mother remained attached to Jimbo, her face taut with what looked like panic.

My mother released Jimbo with a small smile, an apology. "You can't turn on the microwave," she said. "Not when Henry is nearby."

Celia and Mike made understanding noises. I looked from face to face, seeking a clue. Any clue. Neither one of them was willing to look at me.

"Would someone please explain," I begged. "I feel like the only person in the fun house who doesn't know the score."

My mother patted herself down, flattening her sweater with both hands. "It's nothing, really," she said. "Your father has a pacemaker. That's all. What has it been, Henry, ten days?" She extracted Jimbo's plate and handed it to him. Sorry, she mouthed.

"I guess it's been about that," my father concurred. "Two weeks tomorrow."

I looked at Celia who was busy studying the side of the salad dressing bottle, hiding her eyes from me. "Why didn't anyone tell me?"

"It's not a big deal, Charlie." My father pushed his plate away. He was finished. "Don't overreact."

Overreact? My father had heart surgery and now he's telling me not to overreact?

"Jesus, Dad." I shoveled a mouthful of beef stew, clinking the fork on my eye tooth. The stew had gone cold.

My father reached out a hand and pressed my arm. A sturdy gesture. I had no idea what I would do if something happened to him. "I promise you," he said. "This is not worth a worry. I had some symptoms, and they were corrected quickly. I feel great," he said. "In fact, I feel better than ever."

My mother looked past me to my sister. "Let's not talk about that anymore," she said. "Okay? You can ask any questions you want, and your father will answer. But let's not do that tonight."

No one said anything else. Other than the sound of Jimbo swallowing, I heard only silence. What was going on?

Jackson was in our bedroom, playing video games. He'd once

promised to stay away from porn and Premium channels, but I was sure that was what he was doing in there. That's what I would have done at his age, after all. I'd have watched every prohibited program on that split-screen at once.

He lumbered into the room like an oversized pup, stumbling and knocking his loose limbs into walls.

"Did you tell her?" Jackson looked from face to face.

The air stilled. Tell her? Tell me what? What?

Jackson looked up at me. "Are you okay?"

"Oh, Jackson," Mike exhaled.

"Oh," my mother said, her hands soapy in the sink.

"Fuck," Celia said.

My mother dried her hands and dropped into the seat next to me. I scanned her face without a thought in my head. If the worst of all things had already happened, my cataclysmic medical emergency, my father's heart pacemaker, what were they all wilting over?

My father's voice. "We were hoping you'd have some time to recover before we told you."

I looked to my mother as a baby looks for a breast: Feed me, heal me. She'd been a beautiful woman, my mother. But what I saw now—her face was only a foot from mine—was in conflict with my memory. Her eggshell complexion no longer glowed with candle-light luster. Her eyes were dim. She'd become asymmetrical, one eye hung lower than the other. When had that happened? When had she become so… dour?

It was because of me. I knew it then. The knowledge of my complicity in the degradation, no, the ruination of my mother crashed into me like the anvil falls on Wile E. Coyote in *The Road Runner*. I had done this. I had hurt her past beauty, past symmetry. Her face was the evidence. It was the chalkboard statistics, the graph that plotted all the hurt I'd caused, the damage done. She had raised me the best she knew how. And she did a great job. But in her heart, I knew she felt she'd failed.

My insides liquefied and slurred through my intestines. This was my fault. My mother's face. My father's heart. This was all my fault.

"I'm sorry" I tried to apologize, but guilt strangled my words and I was momentarily unable to continue. I wanted to disappear. I'd forgotten everything I'd learned from Dr. Essent. I was responsible for ruining my mother, for breaking our family. We would never be the same. Because of me.

"Oh, Charlotte," my mother said, pulling my hand into her breast. "We wanted to wait until you were feeling stronger. Dr. Essent insisted we didn't tell you while you were in the hospital. He said you needed to be surrounded by your whole family, in the comfort of your own house. And we agreed with him. You were so fragile then."

My heart did not beat. I waited, unclear.

Jimbo's voice startled me into the present. "Your grandmother died. While you were in the hospital."

The air stilled.

"We wanted to wait for you," my mother said, pressing my hand to her chest. "We knew you'd want to be with us. But our first priority was your well-being. We wanted you to be strong enough. We didn't want to set you back."

My father interrupted. "Doesn't matter Charlotte. It does not matter a lick if you were there at the funeral or not. What matters is you had a wonderful and long relationship with your grandmother and she loved you very much. We all do."

She died? My grandmother died? I heard a ringing sound in my head, flooding the space between my mouth and the ball of my skull with heat. I felt hot, that was it. I was too hot. I was on fire. I was in hell.

THIRTY-EIGHT

I hated myself. Hated. Hated. Hated.

Why hadn't I invited my grandmother to come to dinner the night Jimbo's mother visited? How could I be so stupid, so self-centered to neglect to include my grandmother? She'd have wanted to come to dinner, I'm sure of it. She'd have wanted to meet Jimbo's mother and to make jokes about what a bad housekeeper I was or how I only knew how to cook for an army, never for one.

Reality scraped its way into my addled mind. My grandmother was gone and I'd never see her again.

It was too much.

Where was I?

My mouth was packed with sawdust.

The bed was soft underneath me. I let myself sink back into the oblivion of sleep. Only in sleep would I find any comfort. I slept. And slept.

My eyes stretched open, my mouth full of sawdust. Waking up was always hard for me, doubly hard after I've had a sleeping pill.

I stretched my leg until it stopped at a pillowy lump.

"You bumped?" Jimbo said, imitating a butler from an old black-and-white movie. He was always quoting characters in movies. He must have memorized a thousand scripts! I opened my eyes to his smiling eyes. "And how is my lady feeling?" he asked.

My shoulders pillowed into the mattress. I stretched my neck and then settled back onto my orthopedic neck log. "I feel with my hands," I took the bait. I felt good; I was momentarily surprised at that. I felt good.

Jimbo said. "You've been talking in your sleep."

Curious. I waited, thinking. I was eating beef stew. Everyone was laughing. A happy family picture.

And then, I remembered. A guttural wail lifted from my heart and floated above Jimbo and me, above our bed. It swelled in the clean new bedroom, then spread, fast, like freed mercury, claiming space as its territory. "Oh no," I wailed to the ceiling.

Jimbo slid closer, tucking himself into my side, nuzzling his head under my chin. I lay on my back then, one arm over my face to protect my eyes from the grenades of guilt and grief that pelted at me. I felt the sting of missing my grandmother's birthday and the phone calls I'd declined to answer because, well, what was I doing? Watching a good TV show? Sleeping away the day? What could I possibly have been doing that was more important than talking with my grandmother?

Jimbo stretched his arm across my chest, trapping me to the mattress. "I'm so sorry about your grandma," he said into my hair. Tears striped from my eyes to my hair, soaking in at the temples. "Yummy," he said, licking at the salt, tickling my ear.

"Don't lean on my bad leg," I warned. "It feels like the nerve is on fire."

He moved his hand over my breast, without really touching the breast. Not a sexual gesture. "I'll get you a Neurontin." He reached for the nightstand. "That cleaning lady moved everything. I don't know where anything is anymore!" he said.

I heard the hum of the dishwasher. My mother must have turned it on before she left. Jimbo still didn't know how to use the dishwasher. I'd been showing him the function buttons but he simply refused to learn. It was one of those flaws that Celia and I talked about. Some things you overlook. Some things you don't. I overlooked the dishwasher and just about everything else about the house. Jimbo's mother had done everything from the laundry to putting antifreeze in their cars. He had no real-life skills. Not really.

A clean house never thrilled me. I know Celia never went to bed without first cleaning her kitchen down to the floor. "I hate having breakfast in a dirty kitchen," she'd say. My mother was like that, too. I, conversely, didn't even see clutter, much less feel bothered by it. In fact, I liked the dirt. It made me feel…organic.

Our bedroom was too clean. I missed the box of Altoids I kept on my night table and the four remote controls that should have been on the windowsill. Where were my bed socks, the ones I pulled on during the night when my feet were freezing? They should be accessible, in that pocket where the sheet cascades over the edge of the mattress, reaching to be tucked. "It's too clean in here," I said.

"Agreed," Jimbo said.

"Where were you when they did all this?" I asked. "I mean, did they ask you if they could change everything?"

Jimbo snorted. "Are you kidding?"

"Well, did they just barrel in here and start painting around you? Or did they ask you in advance?"

"Ask me what?"

"If you wanted any of this." I said. "Did you even say anything?"

He didn't answer my question. Instead, he said, "I wasn't paying any attention. I was hibernating in the living room, watching hockey. I have a good team this season," he said, referring to his fantasy hockey league. Jimbo didn't only bet on the horses; he loved soccer, baseball, hockey, boxing, and polo. I'd thought that five televisions in one small house was too many, but I let Jimbo make that decision. One of the best parts of being married was letting someone else make decisions.

"It looks like a hotel room," I said.

Jimbo log-rolled away from me, reaching toward the floor. "I can fix that," he said. He returned, right-side up, holding a tube of cotton candy. "I got this at 7-Eleven on the way home from my Mom's," he said. "That's the first time I've been in there when Plots wasn't working." Plots. My old friend. I never went to 7-Eleven anymore. Not since Plots moved back to Bangaluru. The sound of his name pressed against my bruised heart. I didn't want to think about Plots. I didn't want to think about anything.

It's amazing how much medicine helps the time pass. Even a little bit of medicine makes the time seem smoother. "A crutch," Dr. Essent said. "You're using the drugs to avoid what is unpleasant in your life. You can't do that. You must face your demons. Everyone must. Eventually."

I was not terribly interested in facing my demons just yet. And he was talking about drug abuse, which didn't really pertain to me. Well, maybe it pertained to me a little. But I had some extenuating circumstances right now. In addition to my regular pain, I had lost my grandmother. And Plots. No, I could not do this. Not alone.

Jimbo handed me the cotton candy. I tore off a neon blue tuft and wound it into my mouth. Jimbo did the same. Then, he lifted the crisp white bed cover and kissed it, leaving a blue lipstick stain on the end panel. "Look," he said. "A cotton candy kiss!"

I thought, just then, about my mother and Celia racing around Bed Bath & Beyond, looking for the new sheets now stretched flat beneath me. Me and Jimbo. I pictured them deciding, together, what color to choose. Who decided on navy blue? Celia? It was probably Celia. She knew I loved blue. My stomach lurched, just a little bit. Was it guilt that heeled the contents of my stomach, was it grief? How do you tell the difference?

Jimbo knew what I needed; he lofted a hand over my mouth, thumb and forefinger delicately hovering. "Open," he said.

I opened.

He dropped two pills into my mouth. "This will cure what ails you," he said. Another great thing about being married. Jimbo took care of everything.

I plucked off another clump of cotton candy and swallowed the pills. "You take such good care of me, husband."

"That's my job," Jimbo said, and he clicked on the TV.

***

I couldn't sleep. I got out of bed, pulled on a jacket, and went outside. I lit a cigarette and sat on the stoop with my legs apart, letting the cold air caress my thighs. My bare toes were crusty with dirt. "Better put some Blue Star ointment on those feet," my grandmother once told me. Blue Star ointment! I thought she was so old fashioned, so lost in time. Epsom salts. Baking soda mouthwash. Later, when Jimbo would send me to the store to buy Blue Star ointment or Epsom salts, I'd call her on the phone to tell her she was right! Her remedies were back in style.

I could no longer call her on the phone. Her scratchy voice, her no-frills commentary. I would never hear her voice again. Never hear her say, "Listen to your old granny."

She'd died in her sleep. A good way to go. She would have approved of that, I thought, pulling the smoke in deep. My engagement ring, her engagement ring, captured a starburst from the half moon. A pain deep in my stomach signaled hunger or nausea. Maybe I was getting sick. Or was I having a heart attack? My father hadn't had a real heart attack; the pacemaker was implanted to ward off the possibility of a heart attack in the future. Heart trouble was hereditary, same as a hammer toe.

Everything was falling apart.

I went inside, into the kitchen. My stomach ached, empty. I pulled a mug from the cabinet and filled it halfway with potato flakes, poured from an already opened box. With one finger under the running faucet, I waited for the hot water. My grandmother believed in comfort foods.

She made baked macaroni with hearty cheeses, she bought whole milk and used regular sugar in all her baked goods. That's how I learned to bake. From her.

Once the water was hot, I let it fill the rest of the mug. The flakes began to melt. I took a dirty knife out of the sink and stirred the thick white mixture, watching as the liquid became a porridge. Perfect. I added a pat of butter and a dollop of salt and leaned back against the counter. The only sound came from my spoon scraping the sides of the mug. Peaceful.

The panorama from this position was not peaceful. Newspapers had consumed the kitchen table. They were mostly sports papers; Jimbo didn't read the regular news. And they were not to be discarded. Cartons of seltzer water occupied two of the four chairs. Jimbo was addicted to fizzy water. The empties would go out with the recycling. For now, they lay like slain soldiers, scattered on the table, on the counters, on the floor between the spindly table legs.

I would inherit my grandmother's dining set, I knew that. Long ago, she'd asked Celia and me what we wanted from her house after she was gone. "Something to remember me by," she'd said with a wink. Neither of us wanted to talk about that. But she'd insisted. Celia picked the piano, an ancient cast-iron instrument that would cost thousands to move. I'd said I'd take the dining set. I'd remember all the meals we'd shared at that table, the games of gin we'd played together. We'd puttered away at jigsaw puzzles there, folded promotional flyers for my grandmother's Sisterhood meetings.

I eyeballed the floor. Would her table fit in my pantry? Even without the leaves, and there were four of them, enlarging the oblong table to seat twelve, the table was likely too big for my house. It might be turned sideways, or maybe I'd remove one of the mounted shelf units. But then, what would I do with all the stuff inside? A sudden cramp seized my stomach, just under the lowest rib. I put my hand there and pressed, feeling nothing but the density of my own body. I stretched, pulling my chest northward, making more room for whatever gripped my diaphragm. This had happened to me before. A spasm in the diaphragm, that's what the gastroenterologist had said. I'd had a CT scan and then an MRI. Both showed nothing but a normal anatomy. But I was unconvinced, demanding more testing, more guessing. Finally, they gave up, dismissing my symptoms with a bounce of the shoulders and a shoddy diagnosis: *spasm.*

Jimbo had some stomach stuff in the kitchen cabinet. Donnatal, Zofran, Levsin. I took two of each, washing down with a gulp of whole milk, right from the container.

I wiped my lips and stared at the chaos on the kitchen table. I would not feel better, not ever. I knew that. My pain came from a deeper place, a harder to reach place. I would no longer find comfort in my grandmother's gaze, in her arms, in her home. She was gone. And I was, again, alone.

THIRTY-NINE

"Hello wife." Jimbo surprised me. He usually didn't wake until I woke him. He stood in the kitchen like an apparition: white pajamas, too long in the legs, the pants covered his bare feet. Without his glasses, his eyes were unfocused. "Why are you wearing a coat?"

"I got up during the night," I started to explain. "I went outside, you know how I sometimes do that."

He pushed aside an empty plastic bottle and sat at the table.

I held the dishtowel to my eyes and pressed. "I can't believe it. That's she's gone. That I wasn't there when she died. Or at her funeral."

"And I didn't go," Jimbo said, "because I was in the hospital looking after you!" He smiled, a soft little smile. "My wife," he said, and I felt myself melting toward him. With a toe, he pushed a chair, welcoming me to sit.

"I'll miss her so much," I started to cry again. I'd been crying for the better part of the morning. I didn't know what time it was, but my swollen eyes suggested I'd been sobbing for a while. "She was the only person who really understood me," I wailed anew. "She understood how hard everything was for me, my weight, my life. She knew how much I wanted."

Jimbo swayed. Either he was moving or I was. I set my feet flat on the floor, pressing into the worn tile. I felt something under my heel. I lifted my foot. "What's that?"

Jimbo leaned forward, and then reached his delicate fingers to my foot. "Ah," he said. "It's a cap. From the top of a needle." He showed me the little conical bit of plastic, holding it pinched in his fingers. Syringes and needles were packaged separately; there was always a lot of trash with Jimbo's preparations. "Good thing it's empty." He flicked it onto the table. I cried again, leaning toward my husband.

"Oh, my poor little wife." He patted me on the leg, smoothing the nylon of my nightshirt. "I hate to see you like this. Hurting and crying and so sad."

I lurched my chair, moving closer to him until my head reached his sloping shoulder. I nestled there, in the nape of his neck. The smell of his skin entered my nasal passages, opening them like mint, welcoming the air into my nose, my throat, my lungs. I closed my eyes and rested in his softness.

"Try and remember what's important," Jimbo said, holding my hand. "She didn't suffer. Thank the Lord for that." He pulled my knuckles to his lips and kissed the top one, rolling his eyes toward the ceiling as if in prayer.

Jimbo held my hand tight; our fingers were intertwined. I saw his blue veins traversing the back of his hand, bulging like worms through the tender skin. "I just wish she'd waited for me," I said. "I wish she'd waited until I could say goodbye."

Jimbo nodded. "No one had that chance," he said. "Everyone was busy visiting you and working to get the house ready here. Your mother was here nearly every day, stacking precooked foods in our freezer or bossing the cleaning people around. We were all so busy," he said. "No one even thought she was on the brink. Or, at least, no one said anything to me."

He'd been busy, too. At the beginning, he vowed to be with me every day by the time breakfast came, which turned out to be seven am. That, we agreed, was unreasonable. He needed a lot more time to get himself together in the mornings. But he did stay by my side, in my bed, for most of each day. He only left when the nursing staff came in to announce the end of visiting hours. While I was in the hospital, he picked up his own newspapers at the 7-Eleven and he even brought me coffee sometimes. He was a good husband.

"I don't think I can bear it," I said. "She was the only person who understood me." My throat was a slowly closing vise. I coughed, choking. "I hurt! I can't stand it." I pressed my palm to my breast. Sobs overwhelmed me, practically toppling me from my seat. "I miss her so much already. I wish it was me. I wish I died instead."

I cried and cried, the dishtowel began to saturate. I stood, reached for the paper towels on the countertop and then eeled back into Jimbo's lax body. I slid to the floor. Crying felt good. I let it carry me, I floated on the current of my despair, feeling acutely the rippled curves of love and sadness buoying my body, lifting me nearly out of my skin and then depositing me back where I was, heavy as a boulder at Jimbo's feet. He had a hand on my head, rubbing, snagging in my hair.

"That's it, Charlotte," he cooed. "Cry it out. Let it out."

I held on to the flimsy fabric of his night shirt and let all my sorrow spill out of me. I heard myself wailing, "What am I going to do?" The question did not seek an answer; it was just a question, a weed caught up in the eddy of emotion. "I can't stand it," I said repeatedly. "I can't stand it."

Jimbo rose, and I clung to his leg. "Don't leave me!" I cried out with real desperation. "Don't leave me."

Jimbo stepped carefully around my parts, avoiding my hands and feet splayed on the tile. "I'm not leaving. I'm just getting some help."

He disappeared. Reappeared.

"I can't stand to see you hurting like this," he said, curving around me on the floor.

"Make it stop," I begged him. "Make it stop!"

He burrowed into his kit. I saw the syringe, the alcohol pad. He reached for my leg and, with a single practiced jab, his needle entered my body.

The needle rested inside, and then the liquid. Pushing. Forcing. I felt pressure under the skin, but then the subcutaneous cells moved easily, making room, allowing for the invading substance to disburse and spread. And then, it was done.

"You'll feel better now," Jimbo said, tossing the syringe with its needle still intact onto the table. "Just rest your head on me." He pulled me close and wrapped his arm around my shoulders. "Open your mouth," he said.

I obeyed.

"Lift up your tongue."

I lifted my tongue and accepted the dry tablet he deposited there. I didn't think I had enough saliva in my mouth to dissolve anything, the crying had left me parched. Or maybe it was the anti-nausea medication I'd taken during the night. I rolled my tongue like an ocean wave, curling it and unfurling it, encouraging the salivary ducts to release their tincture, to bathe my mouth and throat with wetness. My body began to slow, my muscles slackened, drained of energy, my head was feathery. My eyelids gave way, lowering gently over tear-slashed eyes. I watched as Jimbo repeated the process of filling a syringe, wiping with the little white square of alcohol, and then jabbing the needle into the flesh. His flesh.

What a relief from the intense pressure that had accrued inside my head. Crying made my skull feel tight, as if my brain was squeezed in a fist. But no more. I felt no more pressure. No more tension between my skull and brain. My face went slack. A bit of drool escaped my lips.

***

I don't know how I got into my bed. I reached out my heels, elongating my quadriceps, feeling the mattress secure against my body, supporting my back, my ass, my legs. My head felt like a post-Halloween pumpkin, carved out and a little tired.

I remembered one long ago winter, we vacationed on an island in the Caribbean. I remember the color of the sea. A glassine green that amazed with its clarity, fish swam past my legs as if I were an apparatus in an aquarium. I remember floating on my back, a most exquisite sensation, with my face to the sun and my back cooled by the gently undulating sea. What a heavenly sensation, to be weightless in the amniotic ocean. That night at dinner, I told my family that I wanted to live in the ocean, to stay in that moment for the rest of my days. My father laughed, said I was a mermaid, and tugged my still wet hair. How adorable, my parents must have thought. What they didn't realize, however, was that I meant it. I wanted to remain in that state, in stasis, floating free. And I would spend the rest of my days struggling, scrambling, to return to that place, that state of passive bliss.

I conjured that moment, that moment when I floated without a pain in my body or a worry in my mind. God, it was glorious! My skin was pink with health. My belly swelled with a little-girl's paunch. My feet, my legs, my neck: I was, all of me, lovely. Comfortable in my bathing suit, without any body consciousness, I was an ideal. A suggestion of a person. I could become lithe and strong and determined. I could have honed my mind to be sharp and specific as a harpoon. This was the time when fate would intervene and determine my future. I believed in fate. I believed that I had no dominion over the trajectory of my voyage. Fate made the disappointments easier. Where there is no fault, there is no failure.

I lay in the dark in my house, without motion beyond the slight expansion and deflation of my exhausted lungs. When was the last time I felt this peaceful? Not since that day in the ocean, in the Caribbean when I dreamed of being a mermaid. I could almost taste the salt on my lips.

"Hello wife," I heard him coo. "Are you in there?" His finger poked my breast as a child touches an unknown.

I would not wake. I would remain in this cocoon. An executive decision. I was taking charge. My mother would have liked that.

FORTY

The shrill toll of the doorbell tore into the underwater quiet. I lolled my head toward the sound. My eyelids would not retract; my eyes hid deep in the cavern of my scull.

Then, knocking. Fast, frantic. Insistent as a woodpecker on a tree.

"Charlotte?" Celia's voice.

Bang. Bang.

"Charlotte! Can you hear me?"

Bang. Bang. Bang. Bang.

My sister was waiting out there.

I wanted to respond, react. But my voice would not come.

"Charlotte, Jimbo. Open this door. You're scaring me!"

I listened to the frantic pounding of her hand on the hollow door for a long time, hearing not her panic but the rhythmic rumble of steel drums vibrating with music. Reggae music. Music to be enjoyed on the beach, with a warm breeze wafting over sunburned shoulders. I slept deeply, peacefully, soothed by long riffs of drifting drumrolls.

***

I heard mumbling. Jimbo's words floated into to the filmy scrim of my consciousness. "She's fine," he said. He used a manufactured voice when talking with my mother. Not arrogant exactly. Firm.

He sounded as if he were in command, able and capable. I'd have believed him, too.

"She's resting. We are very cozy. She's not hungry but I ordered from the Thai place. No. You don't have to. I'm taking care of her. I'm watching her. She's fine."

I slept. And then I kept sleeping. When I roused, night hid behind the bedroom shades and my bladder ached. My mouth was pasty and sour. I went to the bathroom and sat without opening my eyes. I filled a Dixie cup with water. *Water in, water out.* One of Jimbo's ditties.

A little army of pills waited next to the soap dish. Jimbo's next dose. I didn't want to be awake. I scooped the pills into my palm, washed them down with a last gulp of water, and returned to the swaddled bliss of my blue bedding.

Jimbo crawled across the bed on all fours and lay down beside me. He nuzzled my neck like a dog sniffing for food. "You have drool on your face." He toyed with my lips, pressing them together. His fingers smelled like peanut butter. They were light on my mouth, a phantom's touch.

FORTY-ONE

"Yoo hoo," Jimbo's voice was very far away. "Yoo hoo, Wifey. Is Charlotte home? Are you in there, wife?" I was in a cradle, rocking side to side. Jimbo's hand was heavy and flat on my sternum. He was rocking me. "Wife-o-mine," he said. "I'm looking for you! Come out, come out, wherever you are."

I was suspended and weightless. The rocking of my body symbiotic with the swells of the sea.

A splash, a spray of something cold graced my face. Jimbo flicked water on my quiet eyes. "Celia's here. She wants to talk to you."

Celia. Her small body emerged before me as a hologram. Her bathing suit had a smiling Minnie Mouse face on the front. A little girl's bathing suit. She had white cream on her nose. Zinc oxide. I remembered buying that bathing suit—the three of us, Celia, my mother, and me. Celia had cried while we shopped for our vacation outfits. She wanted to wear big girl clothes, like me. I had graduated to the Young Miss department, she had not. She was stuck back in Girls. In the dressing room, Celia's face spread with envy and awe as I tried on a two-piece bathing suit with a padded bra top.

The image of Celia in her Little Mermaid bathing suit shimmered, became watery, as if it were projected onto a puddle of water then evaporated too quickly. I struggled to find it. The memory was elusive. I lost her.

***

"How long has she been sleeping?" Her voice bubbled as if traveling through water. Her lips touched my cheek. Cold fingers pressed my wrist. Then, my neck.

Jimbo sputtered. "I don't know."

"Did you try and wake her?"

"I did. But she didn't want to get up."

Celia jostled my shoulder with a warm hand.

"How did you *not* notice that she's unconscious?" She badgered my husband. There was nothing I could do. I was a mummy, tightly bound in my own half slumber.

Celia barked at him again. "I need my cell," she said. "It's in my purse near the door. Hurry!'

Jimbo sobbed, "I don't know what happened." The mattress sank on the edge.

"Don't just sit there!" Celia shrieked. "Get the phone! Quickly."

"I don't know where it is," Jimbo started in his high whine. He whined when he was overstressed, like a little boy. I liked to tease him. Like a little boy who needs a nap. Thoughts did not transmute to words. My speech center was off duty. I sent ESP messages to Jimbo: *Lie down next to me.*

"It's at the front door!" Celia didn't have to be nasty. I tried to raise my hand, to stop her. I did not want to participate in this altercation between them. I did not want to defend or explain. I was tired of balancing the anvils in my life. I wanted to just stay here and rest.

"I don't know what to do!" Jimbo had begun to cry. I lifted my arms and held them out, framing my body, reaching for him. Somehow, however, my arms did not move. They remained trapped at my sides, tucked tightly into the trap of my bedding.

"I'm afraid!" he cried. "She was fine. She was crying about your grandmother, and I made her laugh." He was right. We were laughing.

"And then we watched *Law & Order* and then I must have fallen asleep because I woke up during the night and I saw that the television was still on. She never left the television on. She couldn't sleep when the light was flickering. She said the flickering made her think she was in a carnival funhouse, and she didn't want to sleep in a funhouse all night long." I nodded inside myself. That was right. He was right.

"Okay, Jimbo. You stay here and watch her. Watch her, can you do that?"

I heard whimpering from Jimbo's side of the bed. I wished I could soothe him. I wished I could crawl over to him and wrap my arms around him, holding him to me. But I could not. I could not move.

I felt the heat of my breath course through my body, lifting my belly and letting it ebb. Floating on my back, feeling the warmth of the sun and the water.

"I called 911." Celia used her nursing voice. "And my parents."

"Okay," Jimbo said.

"They'll meet us at the hospital," she said, meaning my parents. It would be good to see everyone. I felt wonderful, illuminated, and unencumbered. My mouth was a little sticky but swallowing seemed beyond my capabilities.

Sparks ignited the base of my brain. The energy above me had shifted, weighted now with capsules that presaged a change of direction. Atoms and ions spun maniacally. My grandmother. Celia. My mother. My father.

I heard my father's voice coming from deep in my memory. He'd broken his leg one long ago winter. I saw him now, lying flat on his back on the cement sidewalk, like a felled tree. "Don't be afraid, Charlie girl," he'd turned his head toward me and grinned. "Don't be afraid."

And so I wasn't afraid.

And then, it all went black.

ACKNOWLEDGMENTS

This is a hard book, and I truly appreciate every reader who opens their heart and minds to Charlotte Lansing. In 2015, I lost my sister to drugs, and for years, I was tormented by the question: How could this possibly happen? This novel is a portrait, a singular fiction, and an answer to the unanswerable question.

This book would have never made it off my computer without generous guidance from BK Loren and Pam Houston who lauded the writing and insisted the story must be told. I have a special place in my heart for Daniel Jones, formerly of the *The New York Times*, who eased me into the wrenching reality of internet critics, and for Claire Keegan who shared her personal philosophy of the writing world. I am a better writer and a better teacher because of all of them.

I am so grateful to have literary agent Susan Schulman at the helm of my writing life, and Darcie Rowan at the bow to navigate all things publicity. Thank you to Andrew Gifford and Adam al-Sirgany who are tireless in their commitment to bringing great books into a complicated world. Thank you to everyone at Santa Fe Writers Project for working on *Hello Wife* and making me feel worthy of your considerable efforts.

Peggy Keegan, Laurie Ekstrom, and Julie Wakeman-Linn read everything I write and I am immeasurably grateful for their help and humor, for ignoring my problem with commas, and for reminding me why I do this in the first place. You are all very dear to me, and I thank you wholeheartedly.

My children, Nathan and Max, my intrepid readers, my staunchest supporters, and my very favorite people. To my husband Phil who believes in me beyond reason: This would not be nearly as fun without you.

ABOUT THE AUTHOR

Lisa K Friedman is an award-winning essayist, author and educator whose work appears in newspapers and magazines in print and online, including *The New York Times*, *Smithsonian*, and in *The Huffington Post* where she maintained a humor column for several years. She holds a MA degree in Fiction from the Johns Hopkins University and a BA in American Literature from George Washington University. She teaches creative writing at American University, and mentors professional and beginning writers in the art of fiction. Find her at lisakfriedman.com.